HEAR ME

DARK SIDES

LYNN CRANDALL

Hear Me
Dark Sides Book Two
Lynn Crandall

Cover design by *James, GoOnWrite.com*

ISBN 979-8-9989576-0-4

❀ Created with Vellum

DEDICATION

To Mike, my all, my everything, my light and love. Thank you for reading for me as my upaid editor and proofreader and for always encouraging me.

ACKNOWLEDGMENTS

From concept, editing, proofreading, and formatting, to setting and technical information and support, I drew from great sources in writing this book. I am so grateful to everyone who worked with me to create this book: Owner of Woods Bail Bonds James Wood, Office Manager Teresa Woods, Surety Agent Shantel Lee at Roach Bail Bonds, Editor Danielle Stockdale at Keen Eye Editing, Development Editor and Proofreader HiDee Ekstrom, Editor Roxana Coumans, designer James at GoOnWrite.com, Engineer Daniel Kurtz, and my husband Michael Crandall. Thank you for sharing your experiences and expertise.

CHAPTER 1

*A*insley Durham pushed a fast pace walking away from her antique shop, Fancy This, shivers running up and down her spine. Dusk settling in on the early autumn evening dimmed the path to her car, but the low light didn't prevent her senses from picking up the presence of Dark Aspects behind her. As one of six Aeons living in Auralia, keen awareness filled her that she was empowered with special abilities, as were they all, to guard against Dark Sides. She didn't want to engage with any DAs tonight. Why were they always lurking? Wasn't it enough that she'd been running from them since childhood? Besides, she had other plans, dammit. Keegan was hosting a meeting at his place of business.

Another one. The meetings had become necessarily more regular since the darkness in Auralia had grown denser every day in the last few weeks.

Steps from her truck, she unlocked it with the fob and slid behind the wheel. She pulled into the street with figures in dark clothing approaching in her peripheral vision. She ignored the jolt when one of them ran up and pounded on her window, and she gunned the accelerator.

Her gut clenched, remembering the days when she first moved to

Auralia as a young girl with her family. People back then said hi as they passed by. They mingled at regular community events being held in public and private places. But all that changed in the weeks since Diane Butler had become a prominent city employee. City Manager, of all things, right under Mayor Joel Farrod. How could that have happened?

She drove a different route toward Keegan's business, one that would lose any possible tails, just in case DAs were following her. She didn't want to bring them along with her to the meeting. Her thoughts grasped at the reason she was here in the city. The threat of Dark Sides taking over Auralia had drawn the Aeons to the city years ago. Of course, they didn't know that then. They were just youngsters. Though the circumstances that brought them together were different, their energies worked to attract them and their families to the same destination, to Auralia, for what they would come to learn was the Golden City, according to ancient lore they had learned from their special dreams.

Keeping an eye on the rear-view mirror told her she had dodged the DAs, once again. Her vigilance remained. This was her life. For years, officially, since high school, she'd been working with the others to prevent Dark Sides from prevailing. The town was built on a harmonic resonance geographic spot. It was important. It could not fall to darkness without dire ramifications.

It gave her a sense of hope to know that the Aeons had tools to use in their fight. They relied on their abilities of powerful physical strength, keen hearing and eyesight, and an evolved heart and soul. Their individual traits empowered them further. Hers, psychic visions.

Technically, Diane Butler also was an Aeon, but she'd made it clear four weeks ago, when she'd been thwarted in her endeavor to turn Auralia dark in one fell swoop, that she was more Dark Aspect than anything else. Chills ran down Ainsley's spine thinking about how Diane had almost killed Payson and turned Braden into her slave.

All of that had shoved Ainsley into memories she'd tried to forget. Memories of her family running to hide from organized crime after her father had witnessed a murder. The days, weeks, and years spent hiding out in various safe houses, and how they still kept one in semi-working order off the grid. She shivered, trying to repress those awful memories, as she drove. She'd been only a child when that happened, but even now the ordeal haunted her. Fear of the mob returning colored her days.

Finally she drove up to Keegan's business. Dusk was settling in but light from the sign above the door lit her way in and entering the building helped settle her nerves. She made her way past the front desk, the scent of coffee and food and voices from her fellow Aeons further calming her. This place was safe and so were the individuals waiting for her.

She walked through the meeting room doorway at the back to their greetings.

"Hey, Ainsley. It's about time you made it," Cooper teased. "I'm starving."

Keegan lifted his head from pouring himself coffee, a smile on his face. "Oh, yeah, Cooper. You just got here minutes before her."

"Let's not talk about that." Cooper chuckled.

Ainsley laughed. Their happy faces lit her up. "I know you wouldn't all start the meeting without me, but I'm sorry I'm late. I had some last-minute customers." She took a seat beside Payson and nodded to everyone. "What smells so good?"

"I brought a variety of salads and sandwiches from Coffee Is," Skye said. "Take your pick."

"We can always count on you to share some of your coffee shop's good eats and drinks, Skye. I hope you all weren't waiting to eat. Go," Ainsley gestured toward the nearby table loaded with food. "Eat."

Payson stood, her eyes sparkling, and raised her hands to stop them. "Wait. Before we tear into our food, I'd like to make sure you've all gotten the save-the-date from Braden and me. Our wedding is a ways off but I want to lock in on the date next spring."

"It's in my calendar," Skye confirmed.

Ainsley raised her hand. "I wouldn't miss it, guys."

"The question should be, is there anyone here who won't be there?" Cooper asked. "I will be."

Ainsley's heart smiled as all Aeons not going as bride and groom confirmed their attendance. Group support always warmed her heart.

"Thanks, all." Payson beamed at Braden.

"Yes, guys. You're the best," he echoed.

Braden shoved back his chair. "Let's eat, I say," he announced, and the others followed.

Ainsley held back. A sober vision played in her head, one in which she saw Diane searching through her computer at her office.

"It's time we put the next step in our plan into action." Mayor Farrod *swished the vodka in his glass.*

"Mayor Farrod, I understand your eagerness, but after reading the manifesto Diane has put together for us, I'm wondering if we need more time to get organized."

Diane swiveled in her chair toward the two men across from her desk. "Tim, Tim, Tim," she said to the city Economic Director, Tim Brody. "The plan is solid. But I'm questioning your reluctance to move ahead. Cold feet?"

Tim adjusted his tie. "No. No cold feet." He leaned across her desk. "I'm as ready as you, Diane. Schedule the demolition."

Brody's tone made Ainsley shudder, taking her out of the vision. She blinked her eyes and let go of a breath. The room was quiet and everyone was staring at her.

"What? I said don't wait for me."

"You were having a vision," Braden said, speaking softly. "Want to share?"

She pursed her lips, then relayed her vision.

Payson nodded her head. "It's as we thought. Diane is not lying low and hasn't missed a step since we last saw her on top of Sheppard Media Tower with Benjamin, who, by the way, is another Aeon. He needs our protection."

"Would that mean our efforts to suppress Dark Sides have been minimal if not ineffective?" Skye frowned.

Ainsley scanned the others, landing on Keegan. He rubbed his chin in thought, his eyes cast down. She chewed on her lower lip, frustration burning, and she looked away. Keegan's special ability was clairaudience. He could hear the emotional and psychic energy of another, whether they be thoughts or speech, at any distance. She wondered if he had heard something but wasn't in the mood to share.

"Skye and I have been working with Advocates for Community Empowerment to increase support for a referendum voting down the construction of the Stillwell project," she said, trying to steady her voice. "Mickey Lopez, the ACE director, has been helping us get signatures. We have almost all the signatures we need to submit our petition. It's not sexy but it could be a game-changer. If we take the wind out of their plans to rid the city of Old Town, it might slow down the proliferation of darkness in the city. Old Town is a place people shop at not just to purchase things, but to tap into the positive vibes it offers." She slammed down her fist on the table. "I can't believe our meditations and volunteering throughout the city to raise hope and light among the residents have been all for nothing."

Outside, a gust of wind blew across the parking lot, sending leaves rustling. Tree branches blew crazily, casting shadows. Shudders went through Ainsley at the dramatic weather, but it exhilarated her, too. Everyone sat still, taking in the implications of Ainsley's vision and her words.

Cooper rubbed his hand over his bald head and sighed. "It's our Aeon mission to save the people of Auralia from Dark Sides. That's huge. But in the context of right here, right now," he pointed to Ainsley and Skye, "you two have the most at stake because your businesses are threatened by Principle Industries' Stillwell Project. I understand your frustration, Ainsley."

"And I understand that there is more at stake than our businesses. The fate of the city hangs in the balance. If Dark Sides gets ahold of our city, it will grow in power and reach beyond Auralia," Ainsley said. "So I cannot just sit here and make nice. We have to figure out how to affect the balance of dark and light. We have to."

Keegan cleared his throat. "Yes, we most certainly do. I don't think any of us are under some delusion that Dark Sides are going to simply go away." His piercing blue eyes landed on her and stayed right there.

She met his gaze, determining he needed to be awakened. She had always appreciated his stoic nature, the way he could slice through issues with keen insight, the way he could add quirky humor to any situation. But he seemed distracted. Unaware of the urgency of their situation.

"I didn't mean to imply that anyone is slacking off, not doing their part to protect the people of our community. But the manifesto we all received copies informed us of Dark Sides' intentions of claiming the city, in violent and devastating ways. The plan doesn't stop there. It should not just scare us, it should motivate us to go all out." Ainsley tried to rein in her quick temper. Sometime her red hair and impatience got the best of her. "That's what we said when Braden first found the manifesto and we learned that city leaders are in cahoots with the Irish mob."

"And now we know even more. The thugs are getting deeper into their dark deeds." Keegan thrummed his fingers on the table. "We have a better idea who to focus on. Those at the top."

"Inevitably, we're going to have to face Diane. I mean, she's one of us," Cooper slanted his head. "But she's not anymore. She's using her abilities, which seem to be expanding, for Dark Sides. She didn't use to be able to blow things apart and put them back together. But she did that with Braden and with Benjamin. What's next?"

"She has learned nothing," Braden added, "even after our efforts to bring her back."

"It's possible the manifesto is a plan with roots in the cataclysm of Atlantis, not simply something Diane dreamed up by herself," Payson said, her eyes wide. "We know those who caused the destruction in the past sent some of their kind to another place. We know our dreams were activated when we were young for a reason; Dark Sides was evident at that time. Each one of us woke up to our mission then, knowing what we know."

"Those involved in Dark Sides probably are more determined than they were during the time of our ancestors, due to the importance they place on gaining power," Skye said.

"And so are we," Ainsley said, feeling her strength build. "I say we're ready. Bring it on." She snickered. "However, I say that with some trepidation. I had a run in with a couple DAs when I left my shop tonight. One of them ran up to my car, and banged on it, muttering some expletives. I didn't like that. It was scary, I'll admit. It was also very annoying. I'm sick of them."

Laughter filled the room, then turned into sighing and head-nodding. A flicker of appreciation went off in her heart.

"Me too," Cooper said, raising his fist high. "Let's go around the table and report what we know, as well as offer suggestions."

"Me first." Ainsley frowned. "I'm sorry I don't have much to report. I've been meditating every morning and night with the group energy. But my shop has kept me busy every day and after work I don't have a lot of get-up-and-go." She cast a glance at the others, feeling low.

"We understand," Skye said. "I've noticed more of my coffee shop customers are losing light. I read their auras and they don't look lively. They are looking defeated."

"That goes along with what I've been encountering." Braden shifted in his seat. "Crime continues to rise, even though the Auralia Police Department is doing a lot with community policing, which means walking the beat and interacting with the community in positive ways, even for me as a detective."

Payson's expression sobered. "To get back to reporting, I'm confident my work as a recovery agent is making a difference, but I am very busy. Keegan knows as well as Braden and I from first-hand knowledge that, as Braden said, crime is up."

"What I'm seeing is a shift in the types of individuals seeking services," Keegan added. "There is the usual group of people who are suffering from addictions and violence, etcetera, but I'm seeing more deliberate and violent offenders, as well as family altercations. I think those types of crimes speak to the overriding sense of daring and despair."

Cooper sighed heavily. "As a counselor and an empath, my area of expertise is emotions. I would insert that the crimes, the disruption in daily life, all of the influences of Dark Sides, all signify danger. That danger prevails throughout our city, lying profoundly on the hearts of people. I've seen it in my practice and in the streets."

A hush drifted through the group as they took in the gravity of the news. Ainsley's gut clenched.

"It's only been four weeks since we made our plan to do things that would enhance light in Auralia," Keegan said. "I believe we need to continue our efforts, but I also believe we should be monitoring more closely what dark deeds the thugs are going about doing. What I'm seeing is that those at the top of the crime organizations, those orchestrating malicious activities, fall into a dark triad: narcissism, psychopathy, and Machiavellianism. Or put simply, entitlement, callousness, and deceitful manipulation."

"I get that. These individuals have perverted their minds into convincing themselves they're entitled to build a world to their liking, no matter what it takes." Braden eyed Keegan. "Anything and everything is up for grabs in their pursuit of power."

"And they don't care about anyone else or that others might suffer from their actions." Skye took a slow sip of her drink.

Ainsley stared into space, processing what Keegan had introduced. "I want to add that those behaviors could be found in any human being. It's not just their existence, remember, it's the personal choices that are made."

* * *

THE ROOM GOT quiet again after Ainsley spoke, as though all those around Keegan at the table had taken a collective pause. He'd always admired her fire and considered her his friend. Of course he'd noticed she was strikingly beautiful, with long red hair and sea-green eyes that sparked with intelligence. But her intelligence wasn't simply brains, she had compassion and insight. Maybe those things were the qualities he appreciated most, but which also scared him. If he let her get close, would she decipher his interior life and the things that built his distance from the others? Would she barge in on his secret?

He'd never been willing to risk it.

No, that wasn't it exactly. His patterns, the ones he'd put in place long ago, prevented even the slightest possibility of giving it a try.

He brought his attention back to the group and the purpose of their meeting. "From what we've discussed tonight, I would say we should break into teams to address different aspects of our approach to Dark Sides and mobsters."

"Yes, that sounds good." Payson grabbed Braden's shirt sleeve. "I want to team up with this guy."

Braden hugged her. "I think that ring on your finger makes it official, honey."

"If I may be so bold, I think Skye and I would make good partners, considering her expertise in reading auras and mine in sensing emotions and their stimuli, that is if you're okay with that, Skye," Cooper cocked his head and lifted his eyebrows in questioning.

"Works for me," Skye said. "I know I'd like to get busy learning more about mobsters who are infiltrating Auralia."

"Done," Keegan said.

"Payson and I can use our abilities of psychometry and maleficence to learn about Dark Sides and its awakening in our city, although I think we already know a lot," Braden said. "My maleficence could be used to push DAs into submission."

Keegan nodded. "I don't know about that. It could be useful in a pinch, but it would eliminate their right to choose. It's making the choice that makes a difference," he pointed out. "But other than that, getting up close and personal would be great."

"I don't have to force anyone to my will, but I could still manipulate them in a positive way."

"Yes, you're right. That would be powerful."

Ainsley stared at Keegan, her expression indefinable.

"Well?" he asked, his gut tightening.

She nodded. "Sure, Keegan. I'm good with partnering with you. With my clairvoyance and your clairaudience, surreptitiously getting in closer to Diane and her activities would make a good fit. That should be interesting."

Keegan sighed inwardly, but kept his excitement close to the cuff.

"Okay, everyone. Thanks for coming out to yet another meeting. We've all got our assignments. It will be safer for all of us that we're not going to be working alone. And please, keep an eye on your surroundings."

As the group broke up, Keegan hung back, waiting to lock up his business. He watched near the door as their cars drove off into the night. He lingered, expecting the last vehicle, Ainsley's truck, to drive away. He scratched his head, trying to peer into her cab from the doorway.

"Looking for someone?"

"Oh, you startled me," he said, turning around to find Ainsley with her hands in her coat pockets.

She dipped her glance, then pinned him with her eyes. He swallowed hard.

"I wanted to talk a minute with you."

Is this how her intrusion into his life would start? "Shoot."

She slanted her head and long strands of her hair fell in place over one shoulder. "Tell me if I'm mistaken, but you seemed distracted tonight. Is something wrong?"

A tiny tremor wound through him. "What? No." Keegan's heart stuttered. Words froze in his throat. He really wanted to know exactly what she was thinking, but it was nearly impossible not to hear them.

Ainsley tossed the straying locks of her hair back over her shoulder, but kept her gaze on him. "Okay, I just wondered. Have a good night." She strolled to the door, turning once for a second glance. "I didn't mean to pry."

He managed to walk out behind her, his body still in freeze mode. He couldn't tell her that he was worried about his brother Jayce. Or that his father was, well, his father. He couldn't tell anyone, much less an Aeon.

She stopped in the parking lot, the light of his business sign shining down on her. Her eyes glistened, tempting him to let down his guard. "I, I," he stopped.

"You..."

He tipped his head toward the sky. There was no moon, but the night was clear, with stars above. "I thought the meeting gave the group tangible starting points."

Minutely, but perceptibly, Ainsley's shoulders drooped. She nodded. "Yes, I think it was a good meeting. See you later."

He watched her walking away for a couple seconds, then strode back inside, disappointment and frustration with himself rumbling inside him.

In his office, he slammed his fist down on his desk. How could he have done any differently? He wanted more, he wanted to feel better, but there was nothing he could do.

And how could he possibly love another, or hope to save the city, much less the world, if he couldn't contain his own pain?

CHAPTER 2

*I*n the darkness of early evening, Ainsley slipped into her bed and slowly drew the blankets up to her chin. She sighed, releasing tension. The sheets draped her in softness and she nestled into the dip in the mattress. This was heaven.

The angst of the meeting earlier and the disappointing interaction with Keegan slid away. Weariness weighed down every inch of her after a long, busy day at Fancy This. Old Town Auralia had hosted its annual autumn sale event, and customers had flowed through her shop's door all day and into the evening. A smile lifted the corners of her mouth. Sales were high and congeniality had streamed from heart to heart. She loved her work, and meeting new people and rubbing elbows with old friends was simply fun.

Suddenly she sat up straight in bed. "Keegan, watch out." In her mind's eye she saw him walking down the street toward his home. "DAs are going to intersect you. They are planning to beat you. They're nearby." Her clairvoyance alerted to the Dark Aspects waiting for Keegan, just as they had so many times before, trying to prevent her and her fellow Aeons from raising the vibration of others and save the world from darkness. That would be a bad thing. It was the Aeons' job, but more than that, it was a mission that permeated their cells. It was who all the Aeons were, supporters of light, love, and peace.

Keegan's clairaudience would catch her warning, but Ainsley quickly got out of bed and pulled on clothes and a fall jacket. She couldn't let her fellow Aeon get in a fight of one against six DAs. She headed outside and down the street.

The only thing she could think of was Keegan out there all alone. He was strong and he had his special Aeon abilities. Still, she couldn't ignore the threat to them all when one was in danger.

Her feet pounded on the concrete road. Stomp, stomp, stomp, stomp, as fast as she could go. Running toward Keegan's house a few blocks from hers, she was drawn by his Aeon heart. It was something they all had; a sense of each other's presence, like a bright light from a lighthouse.

I'm coming, she thought silently, to reassure him.

Images of fists slamming and grunts and groans sent her sailing as fast as her feet could carry her to the action down the street. Closer she came, and the DA's faces came into view. She shivered. So much agitation and chaotic energy filled the night.

Ainsley didn't hold back. She had the element of surprise when she grabbed hold of one of Keegan's assailants and pushed him to the ground. She shoved her foot onto his belly. "Don't get up," she hollered and gave him her best menacing scowl.

He tried to roll onto his side, but she kicked him in his groin. He howled and drew into the curled position of an infant.

"I told you to stay down!" Ainsley turned around just in time to dodge a fist coming toward her, and took the kicker's breath away with a round house strike.

Another DA jumped on her back and Keegan ripped him off, tossing him to the ground.

Ainsley looked around at the bodies lying on the ground. "One, two, three, four, five, six," she counted. "I wouldn't call that a fair fight." She breathed heavily. "Are you all right?" she asked Keegan. His face was puffy and a black eye was blooming. Blood trickled down his face from a nasty hit.

Her heart squeezed when he gave her a slanted smile and chuckled.

"Thanks for coming. I heard your message just before I felt their presence when they found me on the street."

He was standing near her under the glow of a streetlight. She swallowed hard. "I came as fast as I could." She pulled a small package of tissues from her pocket and reached up to his bloody face, patting it gently to wipe off the blood. Electricity sparked from the touch and ran down her arm. She grimaced. "You're going to need to ice that," she stuttered, ignoring the spark. They'd been friends for too long for her to imagine him as anything but just that. Not after spending so much of her life avoiding relationships as a matter of life and death. The idea of letting down her guard made her stomach sour. Besides, Keegan had always been independent, almost detached. "You should come to my house and I can put on some ointment. You don't want it to get infected."

He turned to look down the street. "I don't know. It's just a scratch."

Ainsley realized she was chewing on her bottom lip and stopped. When he faced her again, his pupils were large and dark. She shivered under his gaze.

She ducked her head and felt the pureness of his heart flow through her. It was beautiful. As was the light in all the Aeon souls. It was precious to her, like moonbeams on a dark night.

"What did you say?" he asked.

"Nothing." She could shield her thoughts from him, but she had to do it purposely, and she'd gotten carried away for a moment. "I was just thinking about the moon."

He eyed her. "I'm sorry. I didn't mean to invade your thoughts, they just came to me."

"I know." She did.

He glanced at the DAs on the ground and toed one of them "We better get going before these wake up."

"I'm with you." She glanced over each shoulder one at a time." I need just a moment." She closed her eyes and focused her mind on the center of her heart.

"Oh yeah. I almost forgot. Boy, my mind is all over the place." Keegan shook his head and closed his eyes as well.

Ainsley didn't need to see light beams emanating from his heart to the unconscious DAs. The light was just there. She focused her attention on good will and peace inside her and directed it toward the men on the ground. All remained unconscious, but a couple moved around just a bit getting uncomfortable with the energy. It was enough to assure her they were receiving the best she could do for them. Now it was up to them to allow her offering to touch their souls and let it influence their choices.

One of the DAs moaned lowly. Keegan nodded his head. "Yup, it's time to leave."

"I'd like you to come to my house and get some antibiotic ointment on your wounds," she repeated.

"Unnecessary." He tightened his lips. "You know as well as I do these wounds will go away on their own."

"Not true. They're less likely to heal at all because they were given to you by a DA. C'mon. My house is not far."

He squared her and smiled. It took her breath away.

"I'm fine. See you later," he said and took off marching in the direction of his condo.

With one last look at the DAs, she sped off to her house accepting that Keegan could manage without her help.

The air felt lighter than it had earlier. She strolled with confident steps, not sensing any dark energies, just fresh air and nature.

She yawned as moments later she walked through the door into her house and went directly to bed. When she crawled in, her mind spun with thoughts. Why were the DAs hunting Aeons tonight? Why had Keegan felt distant? Despite their friendship, she didn't know much about Keegan's past, but something made him keep to himself. What was going on with him?

She rolled to her side, trying to tune out the questions. She lay on that side for two minutes, then rolled to the other, then back again. Finally, she laid flat on her back, pulled in a deep breath and blew out slowly. With those breaths, her heart stopped pounding hard and her mind settled into the rhythm.

In, out. In, out. In, out.

Her lids closed and she continued to inhale and exhale. Peace flowed in and out. She sent harmony and appreciation to Keegan, knowing it would help him sleep better after all the ruckus.

* * *

KEEGAN STRIPPED naked and sat on the edge of his bed. He rubbed his forehead and let his emotions run free rein.

Sobs shook his shoulders. Everything ached. After-effects of the fight with the DAs, no doubt. The ache in his soul was something else entirely. He'd seen too much. Heard too much. And there was much more to deal with, he knew. The ache stretched back so far, but he never seemed to be able to take care of it.

He fisted his hands. He wouldn't betray his brother Jayce or deny his father's poor choices. He closed his eyes, pushing all the emotions away, refusing to go to those places.

He flopped back on his bed, rolling from side to side. The things that wrestled in his heart took precedence over all but his Aeon duties.

He laughed to himself. Who would guess he'd put his brother's secret and the truth about his father ahead of the fate of the world? Only his fellow Aeons would understand, but they would also be the first to encourage him to face the truth: All he really wanted was to be loved and accepted for who he really was. The truth that balled in his gut told him he was unlovable, odd, and weak, even dangerous. Not someone anyone could love after learning the truth about him.

Tears meandered down his cheeks. When Ainsley looked up into his eyes tonight, he heard her heart's desire, though it was just budding. But she was good and authentic. He would not take advantage of her. Not tonight and not ever.

Keegan dragged the blankets over his stiff and sore body, hopelessness hardening his thoughts. He closed his eyes, and pounded his fist against the mattress. In his mind he could see his father's grim face.

"Don't you dare tell your mother, Keegan. It would kill her to know what I've done. Do you want to kill your mother?"

"No sir," he'd said, wanting to hit his father in his lying mouth.

"You think you know what you saw, but you're wrong. That woman is just a coworker. She's nothing to me."

"Liar."

Slap!

Keegan jerked, the sting of his father's hand against his face scorching hot.

"Don't ever talk to me like that or I'll beat the crap out of you," his father threatened.

Keegan crumpled. "But Dad, she's Dark. She's not good for you."

His father's laughter burned inside him.

"She's Dark, and I suppose you're Light, is that it? Shut up!"

That night he'd witnessed his father's deceit. He hadn't bothered to tell him he'd not only seen but heard, and those words were without question whispers only lovers speak. No, his father had never accepted that his son was an Aeon with abilities that couldn't be ignored. And later, he heard his father's involvement with DAs in a business venture that made him a rich man.

Keegan had known with certainty when he'd had his dream of Atlantis at twelve that it was not simply a dream, it was information about his true identity. It was as much a part of him as his bones.

He laughed sharply. He could still see the alarmed look his parents had given him when he'd shared his dream, and how they'd kept him at arm's distance from that point on, choosing instead to focus primarily on their real estate empire and other businesses they owned.

He sat up in bed, leaning against the wall. Why was he having all these thoughts? He didn't need this torture.

Or did he? How many times had he and his fellow Aeons reminded each other that the only way through difficult things was through? He put his hand to his heart and let the warmth of light and love embrace him as he slid farther under the blankets. A different kind of tears filled his eyes and in his mind's eye he imagined Ainsley's face, framed by the light and love she'd sent his way.

CHAPTER 3

*A*insley hit the button to turn off her alarm, shook off sleep, and went straight to the kitchen. She started the coffee maker and stared out the kitchen window. The quiet hum in her gut reminded her of her connection with the other Aeons. It told her that all was well with them for the time being.

She stripped out of her pajamas, then stood under the water spray in the shower and sudsed her body, singing a familiar song. Why was she so blissful this morning, she wondered. Did she need a reason? Joy was a wonderful thing to feel.

She dried off and heard the coffee maker beep. In the kitchen she savored the scent of fresh coffee as she poured herself a cup. She took a seat at the breakfast bar and crunched on a bowl of cereal, keen awareness of the beat of life making everything seem up close and precious.

Her phone rang. She frowned. It was her mother. "Hi Mom." She loved her parents and her sister, but every time her mother called she complained.

"Hi," her mother said. "I'm in the office today adding up numbers and thought I'd give you a call."

Her mom's false cheerfulness set off warning bells in Ainsley. "Numbers remind you of me?"

Her mom chuckled. "No. I didn't mean that. My mind was wandering. How are you? I haven't seen you in a while."

There it was. Her parents lived in another town, Ronen, a couple hours from Auralia. "I'm running my shop almost every minute of the day."

"You work too hard, sweetie. Take some time off and come for dinner one evening. Your family misses you. Your sister wants to bring her new boyfriend to meet the family. Please, can't you come?"

"New boyfriend?" Chills ran up and down her spine. "I don't think that's a good idea, all things considered. We need to know more about him before, well, we can't trust just anybody. But anyway, I'm sorry I can't get away. Tell Jane no, for now." An image rose in her mind of her family sitting around the dining room table, quietly eating their spaghetti and salads. Her little sister Jane looking bored and distracted. That got to her. Her sister dutifully checked on their parents while finishing up her senior year of college. "You all could come here. I could make my specialty barbecue beef sandwiches and sweet potato fries."

Her mother sighed. "I wish you'd move here. We could see one another more often, be a family. It would be safer if we all stuck together." Her voice went low. "You know what I'm referring to."

She did. It was the thing that had defined her family early on. The crime. The aftermath of her father seeing it. The uprooting from her home town and leaving her identity and her friends, her life, behind. The constant threat on their lives. Over and over again, until she gave up having friends.

"Mom, I know that would make you happy. I would love for you to be happy." She bit her lower lip. Her mother didn't like to hear her talk about her mission. "I am doing good work here. I have to be in Auralia."

"If you say so."

"But I'll try to visit soon. I promise."

She hung up and tried to get back to her center. Closing her eyes, she breathed in and out slowly, and purposefully raising her energy to a higher plane.

But it wasn't easy. She knew it wasn't her job to take care of her parents, or even her sister. If she could without sacrificing her soul, she would. But she'd made the choice to follow her path and her mission. Everything else came after that.

Then everything shifted and she stared out the window, in the grip of a vision. She didn't see the trees outside in her yard or the flowers lining the walk up to her front door. No. The dream she'd had so long ago suddenly held her in its grasp. Without effort, the view opened to her.

Just like the dream she'd had when she was ten, she saw her mother and her father in tunics and robes hurrying to gather up belongings. Their dried mud and wood home was crumbling apart. She saw it as clearly as she had dreamed it so long ago.

The woman she knew as her mother tells her she needs to hurry to catch the sailing ship waiting at a nearby oceanside.

The ground shakes and they run outside as great chunks of their home fall to the ground. Her mother smiles a tight smile at her. "It's time to leave this place. We're going to a very nice place where there will be green grass and sunshine and new homes."

Fear tugs at Ainsley's heart as her parents hold her hands, pulling her along as they all run around boulders thundering down and wide cracks opening up the earth. Large buildings tremble and fall down in pieces. Dust is everywhere, and she coughs.

Suddenly her hands slip free of her parents' hands and she's alone. She runs in the same direction they'd been following, looking all around for her parents through the dust clouds hanging low in the air.

"Father! Mother!" she cries. Where could they have gone?

She reaches the beach and sees the ship, sails billowing. It was just as her mother had said. Many others run up a large ramp into the ship. Others on board beckon her to come to the ship. Hurry, hurry, they shout.

Hot steam streaming from the earth's cracks fills the air around her and she can't see what's going on. Is this ship meant to hold every inhabitant of Atlantis? That's impossible. She takes a few steps, scouring the people on board, but there are so many not on board yet.

Ainsley presses her hands against her ears, trying to block out the deafening sound of rocks smashing into the sea and people screaming.

"Come, come up the ramp. It's time to pull anchor and head out to sea," the captain hollers. "Time has come to head toward the new land," he shouts to the small crowd gathered.

Ainsley feels the pull of something very strong, but there's no one dragging her. She can't ignore the pull and walks up on deck.

The captain calls out a command and oarsmen below deck turn the ship away and out to sea. Away from her home.

Panic fires in her chest. She looks around for her parents and only sees strangers' faces.

"It's going to be all right," says a woman standing next to her in a long dress and sandals.

"I can't find my parents," Ainsley cries. "I lost them when we were running through the streets."

"I'm sorry. Many people have been lost. Only those who have a place in the new land are making the trip. I'm sure your parents knew of your mission and that it was not theire place to go with you. We are leaving because we have a mission. You are part of that mission, sweetheart," she murmurs and smooths Ainsley's hair.

She's not her mother but the woman has a kind face. Still, Ainsley cranks her neck to see better and looks for her parents' faces.

The ocean swells in huge waves, taking them up high and dropping them down in water trenches. She holds her clenched hands close to her face, and tries not to show her fear. But tears begin to fall, and she sobs, not knowing how she'll go on if she doesn't find her parents. It is obvious to her that what she has known for ten years as home is dropping toward the deep ocean floor.

The energy shifted again and Ainsley swiped at the real tears on her cheeks. It amazed her that at thirty years, some twenty years older than when she first had the dream, it was as clear as it had been back then. She'd told her parents about it and they had smiled knowingly, as if they had been expecting it, but probably they simply appeased her. Whenever she had a vision they dismissed it, and after her sister was born they created a new story: Ainsley had ADHD and got lost in thought.

The dream had forecasted the future and had given her a strong knowing in her gut that drove her to accept her special abilities and use them to help people. She knew that was a part of her mission.

She closed her eyes to the memory of her dream and hung her head in her hands. The memory was so fierce it made her heart pound. Her dad and mom, Theo and Asa Durham, the ones she knew in this lifetime, were her rock and her soft spot, but she'd never shared her true identity and abilities. Their reaction to her telling of the dream let her know it was best to keep a secret. She'd let them think the dream was just that.

She could only imagine how hard it had been on that little girl in her dream to lose all that she'd known, including parents who loved her. In the present reality, she didn't live it, but it happened to some part of her in the ancient past.

The dream at ten had given her information about who she really was: An Aeon, a direct descendent from the people of Atlantis. She carried the genes of her people and the mission to protect light in others and in doing so save the world from the darkness that destroyed the island and the advanced civilization that had lived there. Only a few had seen the disaster coming and had traveled to another place to prepare for the others. All but the few who took the ship to a faraway land had survived, as did the many people who had caused the catastrophic end of Atlantis. But they too made plans for survival and had relocated to another part of the world, she later learned as her fellow Aeons had shared their dreams. Those from the ship she'd taken had lived apart from those people.

Something inside her had answered her question from long ago: what had happened to her parents way back then? They never made it to the ship, and together they'd sunk into the deep waters along with many, many others. The woman who had been so kind to her had become her surrogate mother and kept her safe and loved. Now, in the present, Ainsley continued that mission to prevent cataclysmic events so that the people of earth could take the next step in expansion. But working in her shop, was she doing enough?

Maybe not. But for now, she sat crossed legged on a large, soft pillow and prepared to meditate.

CHAPTER 4

*A*t seven-thirty a.m., the sun was just lighting the sky as Keegan sliced through the water at Wherryite River in the early morning, reveling in every pull of his arms and the velvety feel of the brisk water flowing over his skin. He didn't have to think about anything, he just focused on his breathing and his strokes.

The sounds of nature around him kept him at ease. His connection to nature was different than what others experienced. When a chipmunk chirped, he heard more than sound, he heard the energy of the emotions the chipmunk felt. The little sounds carried on waves of aliveness gave him goosebumps. The interaction filled him with gratitude and knowledge that all of nature was sentient and evolving to greater awareness. It served as a sense of hope for him.

Stroke by stroke he slipped through the water. He wanted for everyone to have the kind of peace he had in the moment. It energized him, and joy sped up his strokes.

He doubled over in the water and rolled, changing his direction. Time flowed slowly as he centered on his swim and nature's support. His thoughts stilled, and the only thing he was aware of was the present moment. The only sound in his head was that of his small splashes as he cut through the river.

Popping up for another deep breath, Keegan finally headed back, knowing work waited and that it was past time to join the daily group meditation of the Aeons. He dipped low in the water, savoring his last strokes.

Focusing on what he was doing, pain shot up his arms, but that was good soreness. It was the workout he'd wanted. He ignored the discomfort and swam in the direction of the bridge where he'd started. He gritted his teeth and streamed through the river water so fast he left a wake behind him he hoped no one saw.

When he reached the bridge, he pulled out of the water and walked into the locker room inside the boathouse. A quick glance at the clock on the wall told him it was eight-fifteen, and his body tensed, as his psychic hearing picked up Diane Butler, the prodigal Aeon, chiding Ainsley at Fancy This.

"I needed you and you were always preoccupied," he heard Diane say.

Startled to learn Diane had resurfaced, his heart sank. He knew Ainsley could take care of herself, but he wanted to help her. He was the only Aeon who could, because others wouldn't hear what she was facing with Diane. He'd never known another person who did what he did, always walking a fine line between meddling and supporting when the things he could hear beckoned his heart to get involved.

But this was different. Diane's darkness was thick, devastating, dangerous. It could overwhelm an Aeon if they got swept up in it. The group had nearly lost Braden and Payson not long ago, when Diane had targeted them. His heart clenched with memories of Diane trying to deconstruct them both on top of the Sheppard Media Tower in downtown Auralia, using her telekinesis ability.

Knowing the conversation he'd heard hadn't necessarily occurred in real time, he grabbed a towel and clothes from his gym bag and toweled dry, then dressed, eager to get to Ainsley's shop but aware of his surroundings. The last thing he wanted to see was a Dark Aspect to slow him down. Sometimes it seemed as though they were always around. His best defense was avoidance when he was alone, he thought, rubbing the bruised shoulder he got in last night's fight.

Keegan strode outside and headed in the direction of Fancy This. Just then the air cracked with energy. Dark energy. His feet got heavier and heavier as he ran, until he had to stop. He bent over from the waist to catch his breath. Cramps in his legs turned into spasms that hurt like hell. Like nothing he'd ever had before. It had to be related to approaching DAs. They didn't have special abilities like the Aeons, but simply their presence could drain anyone, making them vulnerable to painful and consuming darkness. And they could detect the light in them as something to eradicate.

Keegan's knees buckled and he had to hang onto a tree trunk to keep from falling. His brain was mush. He put his hand to his head, trying to focus. Determined to retain his senses, he gathered his strength into a solid, invisible beam and directed it to where he heard DAs talking about him.

"He won't escape this time," he heard one say, and with that threat he felt strength return, wrapped in his determination.

"No, he doesn't know we're right on top of him," another one said, and both laughed menacingly.

Keegan stood straight and filled himself with light and love. The DAs would not take him over, he vowed, and beamed friendship and good cheer to them, hard and unrelenting.

"No, no," one cried. "This is too much. I can't withstand this energy."

"Why are we trying to kill this guy? He's not so bad," said the other. "Wait, what am I saying? He's an abomination. I can feel his good intentions and positivity. It's hurting my head. Let's get out of here while we can."

Keegan heard their footsteps running away from him, and sighed, hoping his stream of light did more for them than simply bring up fear. As beings, they each deserved so much more than the junk Diane dumped on them: greed, death, destruction. While DAs saw something to destroy all around them in the world, he saw Aeons filled with joy and love and a world of opportunity. Accepting his goodwill was a simple choice that could change everything for them and the residents of Auralia.

* * *

AINSLEY PAUSED outside the back door to her shop, stopped in place by the knowledge that Keegan was being trailed by DAs. Where were all the other Aeons? It was only eight-fifteen in the morning but she couldn't help but wonder what they all were they doing? Why weren't they contacting her and coming to Keegan's side?

She shook her head. They didn't have her psychic ability, so of course they wouldn't know he was in trouble.

I can be there with you in minutes. Do you need help? Call me.

Waiting for a response from Keegan to her energetic message, she entered her antique shop from the alley door and dropped her purse, laptop, and keys on a counter in the back room. Concern for Keegan knitted her brow, but if he didn't call she would believe the best, that he was safe. She walked directly to the front door and flipped the Closed sign in the window to Open and unlocked the front door, ready to start her day even though her shop opened at nine.

She surveyed the merchandise on the shelves surrounding her, eager to unpack the many beautiful things she'd picked up early in the morning at the Antique Market just outside of Auralia. She knew that dark aspects were pulling the city apart. Crime was up. Civility was down. Danger perched at every corner. Just this morning another murder had happened, the twentieth this year in Auralia. But her shop let her express her values of respecting the past and ties that bind through time. It was her way of anchoring the city's inhabitants to light.

Suddenly she stilled, as a vision gripped her. She turned her head to look out the window, but she didn't see the buildings across the street. With her clairvoyance, she clearly saw Diane Butler fuming at a meeting in a conference room somewhere. Several men sat with her around an oval wooden table, arguing.

"Principle Group is investing a pretty penny as well as talented personnel, Diane." The man at the table gave Diane a sour look and kept blinking. *"I don't care about any EIA. Take care of it. The casino and development*

project continue. The casino opens in eight weeks. Do you understand me?"
the man shouted.

So Diane was back. There'd been no sign of her for four weeks following her dramatic moments on top of Sheppard Media Tower when she'd tried to kill Payson and generally caused chaos. Ainsley's pulse rose and she focused harder on the scene before her.

Diane's face was a rock. Ainsley couldn't detect any emotion.

"Of course, Mr. Russell. I'll get right on the Environmental Impact Assessment in any way necessary to get the casino opened."

"See that you do." Barry Russell, CEO of Principle Group, marched out of the room.

Diane's had been tight and her eyes stern. Ainsley's fingers curled into fists and her nails cut into the palms of her hands. She shook her head and walked to her desk at the back of the room and sat down to try to process the vision. She didn't have any emotions for Diane. She was creating her life with her choices. Diane had the right to live her life the way she chose. But Ainsley wanted no part of the life Diane led, seeking power and wealth above all else. There was nothing fundamentally wrong with those endeavors, but when they're out of balance, with no regard for the rights of others.

She opened her inventory list on her laptop and began scrolling, but another vision opened, grabbing her mind.

The vision hit hard, and the scene shifted to Old Town Auralia.

Diane walked across the street toward Fancy This and stood outside the door. She looked up and down the street and hesitated. She chewed on her manicured fingernails. Her eyes flamed.

Ainsley concentrated on the vision, though Diane's chaos burned in her gut. *One more time Diane looked through the window and Ainsley saw the determination in Diane's dark eyes.*

The expression on Diane's face was dark and disdainful. Ainsley shivered. She hardly recognized Diane. She'd gone DA a long time ago. In the vision, she looked angrier than Ainsley had seen before. She emanated a fiery energy that consumed light. It seared Ainsley's skin, but she continued sending light to her. There was always hope that Diane would allow the higher vibration to fill her.

She gripped a candlestick holder with both hands, grateful she could experience the vision as though she were looking through a two-way mirror, before the scene actually happened. She had a unique opportunity to stare into the darkness that drove Diane to make the choice to go deeper and deeper into Dark Sides, desiring to reap the 'benefits' of it. On the surface, it was giving her all she'd ever wanted: power, wealth, and status. She mattered, in those states. She no longer cared about the side effects. The pain and suffering she wielded laid havoc on the population as she influenced others in the city to blindly create a life of crime just to attain Diane's goals.

At the same time that Diane turned away, the vision closed. Ainsley now knew why she'd had the vision. Diane would come to Fancy This, and bring her anger and frustration along. Driven by jealousy and pain, she'd been on a crusade to ruin Payson and Braden's relationship and she'd come close to succeeding. Now, her vision warned Ainsley to be prepared.

She realized she'd been holding her breath, and exhaled. Looking around her shop showroom she remembered she stood knee deep in boxes of new merchandise. At the antique market, she'd found a goldmine of antiques. The thought soothed her heart, as she refocused, thinking about all the history she'd purchased to sell in her shop. She strode out to the showroom and pulled an item from a box. Carefully unwrapping it, she admired the iridescent bowl. It gave her happy sparks. Its shiny finish shone in the sunlight slanting in from a window.

Slowly, carefully she set the objects around on a table in the center of the shop. Pleasure in the objects' appearance made her smile, and calmed her apprehension from the visions.

"What are you so happy about?"

So immersed in her new merchandise, Ainsley hadn't noticed the door opening or the little bell ringing. "Oh, Diane, I didn't hear you come inside," she said, sitting up straight and consciously filling with love. How could she have missed her approach?

Diane scanned the room, frowning. "Humph. You should probably keep a better eye on things. Someone could slip in here and steal some of this stuff." Diane's face puckered. "Though why anyone would want any of it I don't know." She flipped a lock of her dark brown hair away from her face.

"You know what they say. One person's junk is another person's treasure. I guess it's all in the eye of the beholder." Ainsley squared her shoulders and walked to her front counter, protection for her merchandise running through her blood vessel under Diane's harsh assessment of her shop and its wares. Diane's darkness pricked at Ainsley's skin and her breath caught in her chest. She wanted to run, but of course she stood her ground.

"Besides, you should have seen me coming with your clairvoyance," Diane added, picking up one of the new blue dishes and examining briefly before setting it back down. "Why would anyone want this in their house? It is quite gaudy." She continued to wander around the showroom, picking up pieces and putting them back in place while sharing her assessments.

"What do you want, Diane?" Ainsley's patience waned quickly. Diane's energy attempted to invade hers, searching for something. She drew in a deep breath and sent Diane a dose of peace and joy, crossing her fingers behind her back that Diane would accept it.

Diane spun around to face her. "Stop it. I'm not one bit interested in allowing your light to contaminate my energy field. I'm doing great without it."

Ainsley continued sending it. "I asked you a question. Answer me. Why are you here? You don't seem to like anything in my shop."

A brief look of sorrow flashed over Diane's face. It cut into Ainsley's gut. Diane looked at her and their gazes held for a split second that felt like a stop in time. She put her hand on Diane's shoulder. Instantly the moment stopped.

"Don't touch me," Diane shrieked.

Ainsley stepped back, but Diane lifted her hand to slap her. Ainsley grabbed her arm mid-air. "Relax. I didn't mean anything by touching you other than to be supportive."

Diane dropped her gaze to the floor. "I can't trust you or anyone like you. Don't you understand?" she asked.

Ainsley steepled her fingers. "I'm sorry. I do understand. I have trust issues too." Memories of her troubled past were never far away.

Diane pulled herself together. "Don't psychoanalyze me."

Ainsley sighed. "Do you want, anything?" She raised her hands and looked around the shop. She suspected Diane was on a scouting mission, solely interested in gathering information.

Diane squinted her eyes. "Because I was bored."

Ainsley wasn't about to push her out the door. Diane was such a conundrum. One minute she was all dark and scary and the next moment she was vulnerable and sad.

She stared at her. Waiting for her to talk.

Diane twisted a lock of her hair and shifted on her feet. "If you're waiting for me to break the silence, you can kiss my ass."

"Do you want to purchase something? If not, go. I don't allow loitering."

Diane pursed her lips. "I do want something for my office. Some-thing blue." She slanted a grin.

Ainsley shook her head. "Here you go." She handed her one of the bowls Diane had already criticized. "That will be fifty dollars, plus tax."

Diane walked to the check-out with Ainsley and paid for the bowl. "Next time I visit you in your quaint little shop I hope you'll be more hospitable. I had a really frustrating morning and I came here for a change of pace. I really wanted to talk about Braden. Every one of you Aeons gave me a hard time when I wanted him to work for me. You never heard my side of things. You didn't give me a chance." Her lips quivered.

And Fancy This is the only place you had to go? "That's not true, and you know it. You were very angry the last time I saw you. You wouldn't listen to us." She eyed Diane. How could she help? Ainsley sighed. "So you wanted to come here and pick out something pretty to help lift your spirits. I'm sorry you've been having a bad day. There are plenty of pretty things here. Walk around and see what appeals to you." She smiled at Diane

"Thanks. I will take another peek around." Diane remained stiff and aloof.

Ainsley dove back into her project of removing merchandise she'd bought from the boxes, all the while keeping an eye on Diane strolling through her shop, expecting nothing. She moved smoothly from box to box, placing each object in just the right spot. A few customers came in and she talked with them, then went back to work, emptying the boxes. Diane was taking her time.

Her back aching from bending over, she stood and stretched. The sunshine outdoors beckoned. Her heart skipped a beat. Keegan strode past the window and strolled inside.

"Hey, what are you doing here?" Ainsley asked, running her hands through her long, red hair.

"I came here to check on you." He gave her smile and scanned the shop, his eyes intense.

She shrugged her shoulders and directed her gaze toward Diane.

"Oh. I see." Keegan eyed her. "You okay?"

Diane's cologne wafted around the entire shop. "Of course she's all right. She's been helping me find something." Diane's lips tightened and she stood rooted to the floor. "Don't you have somewhere else to be?"

"No." Keegan smiled and shook his head.

Ainsley chewed on the inside of her cheek. She shouldn't be so negative about Diane. Being positive was a lot harder to carry off when she was around, but Keegan was managing to do it, brandishing that smile.

He threaded through the aisles, seemingly unaware of Diane's presence. Ainsley continued to spread light energy around her and toward Keegan, hoping to influence the atmosphere.

"Geez, this is awesome. I haven't been here in a while." Keegan held up a large, pottery, hand-made sink basin. "Talk about a great find. I could install this in my bathroom at home. I've been looking for something distinctive to put in there."

"You've come to the right place." Gratitude streamed through Ainsley and she beamed at Keegan.

Diane's lip curled. "Oh, that old thing? Why would you want that?"

"It's the right style for my house. I like old things that have endured through time. They carry a lot of presence, and that appeals to me." He continued to gaze around the shop, seemingly unaffected by Diane's attitude. "You don't have to like it, Diane, but I do." He gave her another grin.

"I don't. I would never put something like that in my house. But I have good taste." She frowned and turned away.

"This coat tree would be great in my foyer. With its old hooks it makes an attractive way to hand up hats and coats. Or I could put it in my bedroom to hang up worn clothes that aren't yet dirty enough to launder."

"Eww," Diane said.

Keegan's enthusiasm spilled into the room. "Hey, Diane, would this vase look good on your desk in your office at city hall? It's a beautiful antique."

Diane suddenly flashed a smile at Keegan, and fluttered her eyelashes. "It's got class. I'm surprised there is anything in here suitable for my tastes. But I like this," she said, holding it up to the light and watching the various colors of glass dance in the sunlight. "I'm going to buy this."

Ainsley was as surprised as Diane that she liked the vase. Keegan had made a real smooth move in getting Diane's attention and turning her mood from bitter to sweet.

"I'm going to look around a little more," Diane said, and threw a wink over her shoulder at him.

Keegan seemed to freeze. Mechanically, he placed the sink on the floor and set down the hat tree. "What do I owe you?"

She rang up his purchases, eyeing him. "Are you all right?"

He brought up his wallet on his watch and paid, his eyes blinking deliberately. "I'm fine. Just realized that, umm, could I leave these things here? I could pick them up later. Sorry. No vehicle."

"Of course. You look a bit, squeamish." She put her hand on his arm across the counter.

He lifted his gaze to her. "I am a bit. Sorry."

"No, that's okay. Just be careful walking home." Ainsley dropped her voice. "I know you had DAs following you earlier. Call if you need me. Promise?" She gave him a smile, directing kindness at him.

"Promise. Hey," he glanced around the shop and saw Diane leaving. "I guess she didn't find anything else she wanted." He let out a long sigh. "Want me to come over tonight to keep you company?" Keegan put his hand on her shoulder and gave her a slanted smile. "I'd like to be sure you're safe."

Relief flittered over her at seeing him relax again. "I'll be fine. I can handle her," she said, clearing her throat. It didn't matter if she wanted to accept his invitation. What mattered was protecting herself and her family. Gears inside her went into action automatically, warning her to keep him at a distance.

His gaze dropped. "Just holler if you change your mind." He pulled back his hand and stared deeply into her eyes. "We're working together, remember."

CHAPTER 5

Fortunately for him, Keegan was a swimmer. That meant he had good lungs and endurance. He needed to be in good shape to run as far and as fast as he could as he sprinted away from Fancy This. Sure, Diane had left. But his one goal was to get as far from her as he could, as quickly as possible. So when he reached Best Bond Company, he shoved open the door and locked it behind him. He didn't mind helping out Ainsley, even liked it. But he'd felt Diane's attempts to take him over. He'd never forget how she'd appropriated Braden and made him a different man. No way. He liked his life the way it was.

He strode to the back of his business to the break room and made coffee. Without wasting a moment, he walked to his office and soundly shut the door. He sunk into his chair behind his desk and caught his breath. He was safe in his workspace. Maybe it wasn't the best hiding place, but he'd had to think fast.

He checked his watch. It was almost ten o'clock. Client files waited, so he started going through documents submitted by two clients, his heart slowing to a normal, steady pace. He slanted his head, curious at the large physical reaction he'd had to Diane, shame creeping up.

The reaction he'd had was like a reflex, and now that he thought about it, he wished he'd stuck around Fancy This a bit longer. Since he went there to protect Ainsley, it made no sense to leave her so quickly. Diane's reputation for hurting others was enough to make anybody run away. Her mesmerizing skills and dark heart made for a dangerous combination. Still, he was no coward. Damn it.

He ventured out to the coffeemaker and poured a cup, then sauntered back to his office and settled into his chair. He tuned his ears to the voices in his head, his eyes closed as he focused on the solitary essence that had struck a chord with his clairaudience. His inner hearing caught psychic energy. What he heard made his skin prickle.

"Your orders for the day, Dawson, are to keep watch on the owner of Fancy This. You'll know her when you see her. She has long red hair, she's slender, and dresses kind of flaky. Just hang close to Fancy This and you'll see her coming and going."

"I don't want to get caught for stalking. I'm on parole, remember?"

Keegan dropped his head in his hands and focused harder. He didn't know the voice of the man talking with Diane. But he definitely felt the heavy energy of a DA.

"Stop worrying about that. I've told you I can keep you safe." Diane's voice had turned sweet and sickly. "You're doing important work, Dawson."

Keegan clenched his teeth and fisted his fingers. Everything in him wanted to protect Ainsley. But how could he? He had no idea who Diane was talking to and it seemed impossible that he could watch her twenty-four seven.

He stood and started pacing. Obviously, she was talking to a man, a DA, one who worked for her. A DA who will be stalking Ainsley. Hmm, maybe he could do this. He didn't usually work in the field, not since he bought the bonds business, but he still had the instincts of a bounty hunter.

His phone buzzed in his pocket and he pulled it out. It was Braden.

"Hey," he said into the phone. "What's up Braden?"

"How busy are you today? Would you be able to meet at Skye's place today? I'm going to let everybody know."

By everybody Keegan knew Braden referred to the rest of the Aeons. "Are you going to invite Diane?" The thought of seeing her twice in one day didn't set well with him, but the thought needled his brain.

"Hmm. She probably wouldn't show up, but she is one of us."

"Not really. She's not acting like one of us. I'm not sure she's safe to be around. I ran into her at Ainsley's shop. She made me squirm. Is there any point to asking her?" Keegan's mind searched for the right answer.

"You brought her up. But I get it. I'm thinking as darkness is rising we have to hope she'll break away from Dark Sides and help us."

Keegan blew out a short breath. "I think that's a stretch. But there may be some logic to keeping her close so we can keep tabs on her. Okay. What time?"

"Would six work for you?"

"I'll be there."

"Listen, did something happen at Fancy This between you and Diane?"

Keegan could picture Braden's concerned expression. He chewed on his thumbnail and mulled over the question. "Like I said, she made me squirm. It reminded me of how she treated you. I think it's curious that she hasn't been around in a while and all of sudden she pops up. I have a lot of questions."

"I understand and I'll be sure to keep track of her if she comes to the meeting." Braden sighed. "We all face the challenge of Diane's choices."

"Right. Honestly, I overheard a conversation she had with one of her DAs and it wasn't nice, to put it mildly. I'm afraid for Ainsley because of that conversation. I don't know why Diane would be targeting her. I know Diane has done terrible things to you and Payson, but if she's reachable, I'd like to try to connect with her." Sunlight gleamed through a window, boosting hope in Keegan. Was Ainsley's safety the reason he had suggested Diane be invited to the meeting?

"I think we all probably have reservations. For me, she's fatal. I'm not even talking about what she did to me. It's only been a few weeks since I witnessed her try to kill Payson on top of Sheppard Media Tower. And what happened to Benjamin? There's just too much crazy with her."

"I'm probably burned by what happened to you. But what she's done and what she's doing could be all the more reason to try again to help her come back to the light with us." Keegan twirled a pen.

"You're right, you're right. We should talk about it before we make a gesture toward her return."

"That's the only thing I'm saying. I'll see you later." Keegan shoved his phone back in his pocket and walked out to unlock his front door. He couldn't let Diane's darkness get him down. That would make him more vulnerable to her powers. He shook his head, marveling at her turn toward darkness. But one thing he knew, he couldn't run like a scared rabbit again. That was stupid. No, maybe it was a reaction from a young part of him. He couldn't let that happen again.

Resting his feet on his desk, he leaned back in his chair. Thoughts circled in his head. He couldn't erase his childhood. His parents were too busy with their lives and didn't truly understand him. When he'd had his Aeon dream at twelve, his parents wanted to fix him. They thought he had a problem and needed psychiatric help. Rounds of medications put him through a very rough patch.

He shook his head, remembering. He hadn't needed drugs, he'd needed understanding and support. Keegan knew what the dream was about because of the dream. It was still vivid in his brain and it reminded him that he had a purpose: to use his skills to work with his fellow Aeons to help humanity make the world a better place. Being a former bounty hunter had put him right smack in the middle of those who lived, to at least some extent, on the edges of darkness. But he'd chosen that profession because he could help people in trouble. Maybe even turn them away from darkness and give them another chance. Personal choice was what it was all about, but sometimes it needed support and guidance.

Memories rose of Diane from when he'd initially first connected with the group. He closed his eyes and let the memories take him back.

Images flashed of Diane when he'd first met her in high school. Payson had introduced him to her. He'd been so captivated by her brown eyes. They snapped with what he'd interpreted as zest for living. He'd warmed up to her immediately, but he soon learned to understand the snap in her eyes was rage. A defense. A reaction to so much sorrow. After her parents were killed in a car accident, she had been placed in her grandmother's custody. Her life got unnavigable.

Keegan moaned just under his breath. The theme of loss continued with Diane's grandmother. Of course, she'd lost her daughter and son-in-law, leaving a big hole in her heart.

He dissolved onto his desk, rocking with the memories of such great loss and how the Aeons as teens had tried to contain Diane's pain. But Diane had already learned from her grandmother that love was conditional and there was none for her. Not from her grandmother, who drifted into alcoholism.

As young Aeons, the group tried to accept her as is but she didn't let them close. He knew she equated love with pain and exhibited maladaptive tendencies. That's what the Aeons' counselor, Claire Eve, had told them. He'd tried to reach Diane despite those ways of coping, but she simply wasn't there, and she'd already decided her only way out of her pain was to be with Braden, Payson's Braden.

He couldn't fault them, though, for wanting space. They'd done their best to include her in Aeon social activities, but it wasn't enough for Diane. Rapidly, she'd turned dark, trying to find a way to live with the pain inflicted by her grandmother, and use her inner turmoil. He'd watched her turn to silence among the Aeons, and darkness, angrily seeking power in dark ways. She aligned with bullies and others who felt cast aside.

Love would never give up on anyone, not even DAs. His gut clenched, realizing the same principle applied to Diane. And it was about time he applied it to her.

A glance at the clock surprised him. He'd let an hour go by

working and reflecting. He couldn't let another moment pass. He pounded out a text to Braden.

I know we agreed to wait to invite Diane back, but maybe we should just go with our guts. I'll do it. I'll do it. You don't need to be involved.

He took a sip of his coffee and turned back to his computer. Minutes later his phone alerted him he had a text.

Sure, Keegan, you can let Diane know about our meeting. I guess you have your reasons. I need to caution you, though, not to lead her on. I know you wouldn't but she is so vulnerable she may misinterpret your kindness.

Right. I appreciate the warning, Keegan responded. He paused, feeling something else churn his thoughts. Braden, I'm so glad you're back. I bet when Diane mesmerized you it was hard for you. But it was hard for me, too. I hated that she took away your life and replaced it with a different one. Just saying I'm happy you broke from her grip.

Keegan pressed send and felt a special kind of peace fill him.

Thanks. I'm glad too. See you at the meeting.

Keegan breathed in deeply and slowly let it out. He centered himself and filled with light and love. He needed to be solidly in his body when he called Diane. Quickly, he made the call.

He steadied himself, listening to the phone ring. Once, twice, then she answered the phone. "Hello, Keegan." Her voice was uncharacteristically soft. "What do you want, dear?"

Oh damn. Why did she use an endearment? "The Aeons are meeting at six this evening at Coffee Is," he said, ignoring her sweet talk. "We'd like you to join us. Can you make it?" He could hear her breathing on the other end. It rattled his nerves while he waited for her response.

"How sweet, my lovely, for letting me know. Who will be there?"

"The rest of the Aeons," he said, trying to cover his irritation at her question when he'd already told her. He fidgeted with a paperclip. Maybe this wasn't such a good idea after all. Diane might use information from the meeting to squash their undertakings.

"I'm checking my calendar. It looks like I can be there. Yes, my answer is yes."

"Great," Keegan's voice was flat. "Really great." Now that he'd talked with Diane he questioned the wisdom of his actions. There was no backing out now. He tried to add more enthusiasm to his second response. "I'll see you tonight."

"I'll be counting on sitting beside you. There are things you and I could discuss."

Keegan's throat got dry. "I'll see you there." His voice came out scratchy.

He disconnected and placed his phone on the desk, his thoughts distant. Fear rocketed his pulse. He didn't want to subject the Aeons to another episode of Diane's craziness. He closed his eyes and focused on steady breathing. If there ever were a time he needed peace and high energy thinking it was now.

He tuned to his deep hearing, hoping to pick up her conversation and find her location. It was kind of like eaves dropping in on her, only it was psychic energy he heard, intentions, and plans, sometimes before they materialized. At least that's how he thought of it. Immediately he picked up a conversation between Diane with one of her DAs.

"That was fast. What do you have for me, Dawson?"

Her slithery voice prickled Keegan's skin.

"It's only been a short time," the man said. "I watched Ainsley in her shop but she's not doing anything you'd be interested in."

Keegan overheard what sounded like a slap.

"Ow. What was that for?"

"I expect more from you than that. She'll be working in her shop all day. Go back and stay on her. And don't presume to claim you know what would interest me."

Chills ran through Keegan. He swallowed hard, as fears for Ainsley tightened his muscles. "It's all right," he said out loud to himself. "It's good information for keeping Ainsley safe. It doesn't mean it's happening now."

He didn't rush his breathing. It was important to give his gut enough time to relax into his own thinking, not what he'd already heard and done. He tuned his hearing to the sounds of life outside his window. Horns honking soothed him into a smile at people going through life at different tempos. Children laughing brightened his perceptions of the world around him. He smiled. Sometimes he bemoaned his Aeon abilities. Sensitive hearing meant regular over- whelm. But it also led him to appreciate the variety of expression of life. Sure it kept him on his toes, but he'd learned to handle it and tried to focus on the benefits.

He opened his eyes, refreshed, grounded.

"It's past time to get to work," he chided himself, and clicked on the file for requests for bonds from people in trouble with the law. That's what he needed to focus on right now. His job of helping people, espe- cially those at a crossroad, like his clientele. Best Bond Company was open twenty-four hours to meet the needs of people seeking a bail bond. That was his priority, right up there with the Aeon work. For him, serving justice and helping others find their way was his Aeon work.

Diligently, he inspected applications for details of their financials and specifics of their crime or crimes. His heart stilled for a nanosec- ond. The name on an application jumped out at him, and his shoul- ders drooped.

Benjamin. Clover. The missing barista at Coffee Is. The young man Diane had mesmerized, directed to walk off the top of Sheppard Media Tower, brought back up and led away. A little more than four weeks ago.

Keegan shook off the shock resounding in his body. In some ways this application was good. It proved Benjamin was alive.

But not doing well. According to the warrant, he'd stolen an automobile and ended up in a car crash. No one had been injured, but he'd been arrested for driving under the influence because of erratic behavior, though he'd passed the breathalyzer test.

Keegan groaned inside, certain Benjamin was still under the influence, just not that of any substance. He presently was in jail and a court date had been set for tomorrow morning. Typically, those arrested for DUI were left in jail to dry out for eight hours, so that timetable squared, but not the rest of the report. Benjamin was a good guy.

Keegan pounded his desk. It was Diane's work. What was she up to?

Benjamin was an Aeon. He would not be left on his own to deal with whatever Diane had planned.

CHAPTER 6

*a*insley checked her watch. Her stomach growled. It wasn't noon yet, but her breakfast was gone. A hot cup of coffee and a blueberry scone would fit the bill, but she couldn't abandon her shop.

A shiver ran down her spine as she heard the back door open and close. The sound of her employee, Iris Sams, coming in shouldn't be something that set her nerves on edge. It wasn't a normal reaction, but would she ever be normal?

Iris walked onto the shop retail floor. "Good morning, Ainsley.

Her voice was cheery to Ainsley's ears. "Hi, Iris. I'm glad you're here. I would love to make a snack run. Are you okay with it? I'll be quick."

"Take your time." Iris smiled brightly. "Everything here will be fine."

"Would you like something? I'm going to run to the bakery down the street."

"Thanks, but no. I had a big breakfast." She rubbed her stomach.

Ainsley laughed. "You're the best." She shrugged on her coat and walked briskly out the front door, heading down the sidewalk toward the bakery a couple blocks down. It specialized in traditional English pastries and tea varieties. She was a bona-fide coffee drinker, but lucky for her, the coffee also was good.

As she walked, she admired the old growth Oak trees that peppered Old Town. It was early autumn and there hadn't been a freeze, so the Oaks still clung to their leaves. Other trees had turned golden early, and were now shedding leaves. Everything about Old Town was slower and more deliberate than other parts of Auralia. Shoppers here came to browse, not simply to run in, get what they came for, and leave quickly. There were more casual conversations and shop owners got to know their customers. Ambiance prevailed.

Her gut clenched, thinking of this place being bulldozed and replaced with sleek Big-Box retail. Determination was a rock in her gut. She and Skye had to double-down their efforts to collect signatures for their referendum and prevent that from happening.

The scent of cinnamon and spice filled the air as she walked up to the bakery door. Inside, she waved at the staff behind the counter.

"Hi, Ainsley," said one. "What can I get you today?"

"I came for a blueberry scone. Do you still have some?"

The woman waiting on her perused the bakery case. "Yes, we have a couple left. How many do you want?"

"Just one. And a black, dark roast coffee, large."

On her way back to her shop, she got a pleasant whiff of the nearby Wherryite River. The moist scent wafted in the air, filling it with freshness. She couldn't lose all of this.

Back inside her store, she set down her food and beverage at her desk and checked for emails and orders via her website. Conversation between Iris and a customer made her smile. The customer was telling Iris that she appreciated the shop for its quaint appearance and comforting merchandise. While Iris rang up the bill, Ainsley strode over to chat with the shopper.

"That's a good choice. I admire that teapot and teacups," she said. "I love the dainty flowers on them."

"Me, too. They have such character. I can't wait to use them for my book club." She stared into space, silently for a few seconds. "They remind me of my aunt and how she hosted tea parties. Women gathered at her house, sharing with one another what was going on in their daily lives. It didn't seem important to me when I was young and sitting on the edges of those parties. But looking back, I see that it made a difference to those women. I'd like to create something similar with my book club."

"Oh, that sounds like fun." Ainsley smiled. "I never had that kind of thing in my life. It sounds amazing."

"Come back again," Iris called.

The shopper was carrying her package out the door. "I certainly will."

Ainsley walked back to her desk, took a bite of her scone, and sipped her coffee, nonchalantly, savoring every bit. Sounds of Iris checking out other customers drifted back to her, but it was all just background noise to her bookkeeping. After a bit, she lifted her eyes away from her work, noticing the rush had died down. She walked out to the main floor. "Thanks for relieving me, Iris. I appreciate it. Boy, you should go get a scone. They're delicious. And the aroma in the bakery was to die for."

"Maybe I'll do that right now while there is a lull."

"Go," Ainsley urged.

As Iris walked out the door and down the sidewalk, Ainsley's skin dimpled, trepidation thudding inside her. Sending a gaze around the surroundings outside the window, her senses picked up the presence of a DA nearby. She sped outside and strode up and down the sidewalk until she was confident whoever it had been had left.

Back in her store, she focused on grounding herself in her self-confidence and power. It wasn't going to be easy for Dark Sides to take her out.

...

KEEGAN PUSHED AWAY from his computer and hollered out to his office manager slash surety agent. He rubbed his eyes. "Ricki, I need to talk to you." He'd vaguely heard her arrive earlier, but was too deep in his work for it to register.

"Sure, be right there," she called back. "Yeah, boss?" Ricki marched in, ready for business.

"What does your schedule look like today? I need you to draw up a bail contract for a Benjamin Clover. He was arrested for reckless driving."

"Sure, I can do that."

"The client has disappeared, somehow," He knew it sounded crazy to Ricki, but not to him.

Ricki's big, blue eyes widened. "You mean he has skipped, right?"

"Umm, this one's a bit tricky. The perp was arrested, but I've learned he disappeared from his cell."

"What? Did he somehow escape to another part of the jail? Did a guard let him out?"

"It appears he simply disappeared. Poof."

"Poof?"

"Exactly."

"Like I always, say, there's never a dull moment in this business." She stepped close and peered at the details of Benjamin's contact info from the city. "Who is this Diane Butler? An aunt or sister? His girlfriend?"

"You might say that. She's the one who submitted the application. He was driving her car when he hit another. Here's her last known address and phone number." Keegan handed some paperwork to Ricki.

"Can we sign a contract with someone who is missing? Ricki raised her eyebrows.

"I'm confident we'll have him soon. I'll get a bail bonds agent to find the guy. Keep me posted."

"Okay. On it, boss."

Keegan perused his file of contract bounty hunters, ignoring his growling stomach. Lunch time was long gone.

Contractors updated their schedules on the company's website, so checking it was the first step in the process. He chewed his thumbnail, a little concerned by the whole deal of Benjamin's accident and Diane seeking help from him. His eyes stopped near the top of the list of available recovery agents. Payson Silver. This was his lucky day. She was a popular agent, renowned for finding the most difficult skips. Her schedule was always full, but it looked like she was open.

He quickly punched in her number on his phone and tapped his fingers on his desk. His call went to voicemail. "Hey Payson, it's Keegan. I have an unusual skip I could use your help with. The job needs a quick turnaround. Call me."

He twirled his chair for one full revolution, then pushed to his feet and wandered out to the next room, where he stared out the window. A college student, Benjamin was a new Aeon, one Skye had taken under her wing. That was before Diane mesmerized him. Time to bring him back from Dark Sides was limited, and every minute counted.

Keegan ran ideas through his brain, possible places where Benjamin could be: the Second Street gym; his apartment; Coffee Is. None of them were likely. He'd been missing in action for days, which meant he hadn't been to work at Coffee Is lately or Skye would have told the group. He hadn't seen him at the gym, either, and he had kept his eye out for him there. Braden had reported there was no evidence of Benjamin at his apartment, either. As far as he knew, that left only one place to look for Benjamin, and that was Diane's house. When she'd taken over Braden she'd moved him there and tried to supplant his own place with hers. If Benjamin was living with Diane, it would be challenging to bring him back to the group. They had to locate him quickly.

"Hello, Keegan." Ricki waved her hand in front of his face. "Lots to think about?" She slanted her head and smiled.

He chuckled. "I guess I went AWOL for a minute and a half, huh? Yes, things are on my mind." Ricki was not an Aeon, but she was very much the perfect office manager and had a sweet soul. Like most of the world around him, she knew nothing about the Aeons and their mission. She was blissfully ignorant of Dark Sides and how it exerted an impact on the city. He laid a finger along his nose and refocused his gaze on her. "Umm, I'm doing it again. Sorry."

"That's fine, boss. Business is busy, which is good. But I understand it means you have a lot to do. I wanted to tell you I reached out to Diane Butler. Boy, she's a piece of work."

"Yeah, she is. How did it go?"

"She was very uncooperative. Claimed she hasn't seen Benjamin in days. But she signed the contract and emailed it back. I'll take care of the paperwork."

"Well, I'm trying to reach Payson right now." He glanced around. "I've forgotten why I came out here."

"I know." She didn't stop typing and didn't turn to look at him. "You had to wander. It helps you think."

Delight flitted through him, releasing another chuckle. "You are good," he said, and pivoted to walk back to his office.

Ricki was right, but he didn't know he was predictable. He dropped into his office chair and grabbed his cell. Still no response from Payson. It was hard to wait.

Impatient, he punched her number again, tapping a pen against his desktop while her phone rang in his ear. On the fourth ring, she picked up.

"Hi, Keegan. What's up?" Her silky voice soothed him. Payson was the best bond agent he knew. Not only was she uncanny at locating skips, she always treated clients with respect, unless they showed her they didn't deserve it.

"I just discovered Benjamin was arrested for reckless driving. I have a contract with Diane, his apparent representative for bond. Are you interested in finding him for me?"

"He's not in jail?" Suspicion laced Payson's voice.

"Right. The story is he was, but he has disappeared. With Diane involved, I wouldn't put it past her to make him literally disappear."

"So how did it happen that Diane is responsible for his bail?"

"I don't know. I'm hoping once we find Benjamin he can tell us what happened, including an explanation for why he was driving hazardously and where he's been."

"My god, he's lucky to be alive. Did anyone get hurt?" Payson exclaimed.

"No one. He was lucky."

"That's something. I guess not only has he been missing, he's gotten himself in deep trouble. I can't help but think Diane is behind this."

"Yeah. I hope he can fill us in on what happened to him. But the police consider him a skip." Keegan stopped tapping his pen. "You can take care of it?"

"Yes. I'll get started on it right away. I'll let you know as soon as I have something to report."

"Thanks, Payson. Be careful."

Keegan struggled to settle his mind. This business with Benjamin was tricky. Everything about it could be a trap, and he had just sent Payson into it.

He turned back to the bond applications. Distracting himself with work was the only thing he could do. It would be helpful if he could sit here in peace. But with his senses constantly vigilant to catch conversations and all that was afoot, he was hard-pressed to find it.

Instead, he listened hard for anything he could detect with Payson that would be dangerous. He stilled his mind as best he could. He should have gone with her.

He scoffed. Yeah, she would have liked that. Payson resisted even Braden, her fiancé's, interference in her cases.

This silence was strange. He closed his eyes and tried to relax. He started belly breathing to a count of four as he breathed in, and four as he breathed out, long and slow. His mind followed the well-known path of breaths and higher energy in his brain. Stillness settled over him except for soft voices. One he didn't recognize. The other was Payson's.

"I mean you no harm. I'm interested in the reason you're following me." It was Payson.

"Following you? I'm not following you."

"I know you have been, and lying will only guarantee my anger."

A heavy pause hung between Payson and the DA, and Keegan counted the passing seconds. He didn't know Payson's location. However, he knew Payson could handle herself. He pursed his lips and tightened his focus on the exchange.

Silence pervaded. Payson's voice was calm, solid. The other voice dripped with deceit. Keegan's teeth clenched.

Reluctantly, he dropped out of the connection. He suspected, but didn't know, that Diane had dispatched the DA to prevent Payson from finding Benjamin. Keegan had to resign himself to letting it go. He had to accept that other Aeons in the group could take care of themselves, and that trying to help them could cause more harm than help. Arguably, the female Aeons were strong enough to take out any DA. But he didn't like the odds, nonetheless. He just couldn't trust that all would be okay without his intervention.

He shrugged. It didn't take a psychiatrist to understand where his vigilance came from to protect others. Fear for his mother's well-being had resided just under his skin during his childhood after he'd seen his father kissing another woman. His father had used Keegan's sensitivity to keep him quiet. From that moment on, he'd put his heart and soul into protecting his mother from his father's betrayal.

Feelings of guilt and shame released a memory in his mind.

"Keegan, pass the potatoes to your father." His mother's voice was patient, gentle.

Without looking at his father next to him sitting at the end of the dinner table, Keegan handed him the dish. But his dad wouldn't take it.

"Look at me, boy," his father insisted.

His breath froze in his chest. Fear of losing his family, their love, the life he knew, constricted his breathing further. His gaze took in his younger brother, carefree from the knowledge Keegan carried. He looked into his mother's face. He heard her voice, gently wishing he would obey his father. She didn't know that his father threatened their family. Tears filled his eyes, and he slowly looked at Sully, hating him, but obliging his mother, protecting her from the pain of the truth lodged in his belly.

This couldn't go on. The burden of taking care of his mother and his brother weighed him down. How long could he continue? He couldn't take care of Payson and Skye, and as much as it pained him, he couldn't protect Ainsley from every dark threat.

His cellphone rang, startling him out of his reflection. How ironic. It was Sully. Sully Barnes. "Hi, Dad." He didn't try to mask his lack of enthusiasm.

"Hi, son, I need a favor."

Keegan chortled. "A favor? You mean like cover for you while you sneak out tonight after Mom goes to bed? Or help one of your crook cohorts get out of jail?"

"Now, hold on. You can't talk to me like that. You don't know what you're talking about. Besides, I'm a legitimate businessman with a reputable company. There's no call for that kind of disrespect."

Keegan fisted his free hand. "Excuse me? I must have a bad connection. Legitimate, reputable? Tell your story somewhere else."

"Who do you think you are? You think you're better than me?"

His dad's voice gravely and harsh and all high-and-mighty gave Keegan a sour stomach. "No, I do not. But I'm no crook and I've never cheated on a woman. Can you say that with a straight face?"

"Look, son. I didn't call to get you all riled up. We haven't talked in a while. You don't know everything about me. And just maybe you could give your father a break."

It wasn't like his father to admit his wrong-doing, ever, and Keegan didn't expect that from him. But it really burned his blood to protect his secret, to say nothing about the pattern of illegal behavior he'd followed throughout his lifetime.

But, he should at least hear him out. "Go ahead. What do you want?"

"I have a job for which I need a guy who can drive a semi. It would be a regular job, driving products to Chicago and working in my warehouse loading trucks."

Doubt and mistrust rose in his gut. "What's the product?"

"Umm, you know I distribute a range of products. What does it matter what the products are?"

So his dad hedged, rather than giving a straight answer. Keegan's skin itched. "Why would I know someone who could drive for you? I don't understand why you're asking me for a name."

"Look, this isn't a big deal. Don't make it one, son. I know you work with people who have served in prison. I just thought maybe one of them could use a job."

Keegan sat silent. Little hairs on his neck stood erect. There was more to his father's story than he was admitting. He closed his eyes and grounded himself, opening to a sense of what the truth could be. He knew in his heart that his dad was moving closer to going dark. He didn't have much time if he were going to save him. He wanted that. But it might just be out of his hands.

CHAPTER 7

*A*insley checked her watch again and pressed her foot harder on the accelerator. Time for the Aeon meeting had crept up on her and she'd forgotten to close Fancy This early.

Chills ran down her spine as she wondered if something bad was up for discussion. Urgency seemed to be on the agenda at every meeting.

Finally, she pulled into street parking not far from Coffee Is and glanced around. Nothing in the near vicinity set off her alarm bells. As she climbed out of her truck her senses let her know the others were close. She smiled to herself and closed the vehicle door.

The autumn air was still warm, but she was eager for crisp, fall days. She closed her eyes and listened to the sounds of dried leaves racing across the ground in a gusty breeze and smelled the pumpkin muffins baking inside Coffee Is. This is what life could be like. Just peaceful, if it weren't for the heavy burden she bore to save the city from darkness.

"Welcome, Ainsley." Skye stood behind the counter, where she was filling a cup with coffee.

"Hi. It smells wonderful in here. Seasonal."

Skye walked to the end of the counter and smiled at her. "It is. You can take a seat in the conference room at the back. Keegan, Cooper, and Braden are already there. Payson called and said she'd be late. I'll be there in just a few."

"Okay. Can I order an Asian Chicken Wrap and a medium dark roast?"

"Of course. I'll bring it out to your table. I like it that you try different things on the menu." Skye twinkled as she rang up the bill while another person filled a cup and handed it to Ainsley.

"I like your variety." Ainsley paid and walked to the back room, absorbing the eclectic vibes. The coffee shop's décor was interesting and diverse with work from local artists, but Skye always added a few pieces that reflected seasons. For autumn, she'd placed small wreaths of bittersweet branches on the tables and hung straw brooms on the walls.

Cooper and Braden were laughing, talking about Cooper's nephew playing T-Ball over the summer, as she walked up. With his bald head and muscled body, Cooper could easily be mistaken for a bounty hunter himself. But he wasn't. He was actually Dr. Cooper Munson, a licensed mental health therapist. She pulled out a chair next to him and sipped her coffee. Keegan remained quiet, drinking his coffee and eying the others. He gave her a slanted grin that made her smile. His face was still tanned from summer, reminding her he was an avid swimmer.

He got up and walked around the table to take a seat beside her. She didn't know if it was because he wanted to be near her or had something he needed to tell her about their work together.

"Hey." His voice was breezy, like a fall wind.

"Long time no see," she joked. "How has your day been going?" Small talk was not her strength, but it seemed like the only right thing to do.

"It's been, umm, interesting." He shook his head. "Unsettling things are happening. I worry." His brow creased. "How about you?"

"Yeah, it was an interesting early morning. You okay?"

"Sure," he said.

"Thanks again for showing up today at my shop."

"No problem. Always ready to stand with a fellow Aeon." He dropped his gaze. "I apologize for leaving you so quickly. To be honest, Diane had me spooked. But it won't happen again. Also, I wanted to thank you for coming to my rescue on the street." He pinned her with his blue eyes and her heart skipped faster.

"No problem. I didn't want you to face the DAs alone." They'd been through a fiery situation together and here they were chatting, just as though they were ordinary people passing the time.

"Yeah, that's weird, isn't it?"

Ainsley laughed. "You're listening to my thoughts. Should you be doing that?"

"Sorry." He cleared his throat. "Uh, we've been working together for years, and yet a little dust up has us feeling weird."

"You don't have to apologize every time you hear my thoughts. It's kind of like shorthand. I like it." She cracked a grin his way.

He smiled warmly and nodded. "Sometimes I can't hear, and I don't know why that happens. I keep trying to get more control."

"I know." The soft blue of his eyes sent shivers through her. To her, they were coworkers, and coworkers didn't get into romantic relationships. Except Braden and Payson had, but they'd been together for a long time. They made sense.

"I agree," Keegan said, blushing through a smile.

Ainsley lowered her eyes. "There's that smile again." She lowered her eyes and looked at him through her lashes. She shouldn't be encouraging him. Shouldn't let him know she was attracted to him. She'd never had a long-term relationship, not with all the hiding in plain sight and moving around with her parents. With Keegan, it somehow felt right, but she wouldn't impose on his space.

Keegan raised his eyebrows at her. "I have something to tell you."

"Go ahead, spill." Goosebumps popped up on her arms.

"I should tell everyone." He rapped on the table. "I need to let you all know that Diane is coming tonight. Braden and I talked and decided including her could help our mission."

"Just how would that help?" Skye asked, her eyes wide.

"Well, it might help *her*, drawing her back in to our fold. If that were to happen, we'd have her on our side, rather than against us. I wonder if our efforts to suppress Dark Sides aren't strong, because our team isn't whole. She was meant to fight with us. We were meant to fight together." Keegan sighed heavily and leaned back in his chair. "Look, I understand it's a risk."

"I'll say," Cooper added. "You two really feel she could come back to us, reject Dark Sides? If you think so, we should give her a chance."

Ainsley shook her head. "It is a huge risk, all things considered. But how can we not?"

CHAPTER 8

"Well, Keegan, thanks for the head's up." Skye nodded. "If she shows up it's going to be, umm, interesting."

"Yes, but I think we can handle it," Braden said. "What's the worst that could happen?"

Ainsley chuckled. "Don't ask."

"Don't mind me, I'm going to skip out and get our food." Skye slipped through a kitchen door.

Ainsley noticed Keegan sitting up straighter in his chair, and she felt the razor edge that always sounded in her gut.

"Diane is here," Keegan announced quietly.

"Hi all." Diane walked in. "So nice to see all your lovely faces. Where are Payson, and Skye?"

Ainsley felt a group hard swallow. With Diane's attempt to kill Payson not too far in the past, her mention of her now jarred her senses.

"Skye went to get our food, and Payson is working. She'll be here when she can," Braden offered. "It's been a long time since you've been with us for a meeting, Diane."

Diane lifted her nose and plopped down on the other side of Keegan. "I've been busy." She gave Keegan a coquettish smile. "When

Keegan let me know you were having a meeting I decided I should catch up."

Goosebumps prickled on Ainsley's skin. Why was Diane bearing down on Keegan?

Just then Skye walked back in and set food in front of everyone around the table. Conversation stopped.

"Here you go, Braden, Cooper, Ainsley, Keegan. Diane, I hope you like what I made for you." She stood and surveyed the table, then took an open chair beside Diane.

"Thanks, Skye. I for one am very hungry and this sandwich looks great." Braden took a bite of his food and eyed everyone.

"Thanks, Braden." Skye stared at her own plate.

Ainsley felt what she suspected everyone was feeling—awkward. She admired the others for inviting Diane, and making an effort to include her would be an important conversation among the Aeons. But she couldn't help but wonder if the chill in the air was due to the weather outside or Diane's dark energy projecting out.

Silence pervaded as each one ate their meal. It was as though Diane's presence sucked their thoughts out of their brains.

"Why are you all so quiet? I've—"

"Diane, what have—" Cooper interrupted Diane, his voice nervous.

It was fine with Ainsley that he interrupted her. The silence pressed down on her as she weighed her questions. "Go ahead, Cooper."

He cleared his throat, and ran his hand over the top of his head. "We were talking about my nephew. He's five and is playing T-Ball. It's hilarious to watch. He can hit the ball off the tee but running around the bases is a bit of a challenge for him and most of the kids on the team."

"I'm sure they're all a bunch of cuties, though, right?" Skye's smile was contagious, and the energy lifted.

"I got to say, they are that. Of course I'm partial to my nephew. He's my brother's son."

"That's fun," Keegan grinned. "My brother is younger than me, and

I have enjoyed watching his games over the years. He was a pitcher on a college team. He had a good arm."

Diane shifted in her seat. "You have a brother in college? I didn't know that, Keegan."

"He graduated. There are probably a lot of things you don't know about me, Diane."

"Like what?" She scooched closer to him.

"Here comes Payson now." Braden motioned her to the seat beside him.

"Hi guys." Payson shrugged off her jacket and took the seat beside Braden. The intimate smile that slipped between them told a story of a lifelong friendship and love that Ainsley admired. "I had a skip to gather and get his bail settled." Payson sipped her coffee. "Mmm. I love the fall coffees, Skye."

"So your skip is out on bail? Huh." Diane gave Payson a pointed look. "You always get your man?" Diane's lip curled.

"Pretty much. This guy had a strange story. One minute he was behind bars in jail and the next he was sitting on a park bench in the downtown plaza. At least that's his story." Payson's eyes held Diane's.

Ainsley quivered inside. Everyone, including Diane, knew Benjamin was the skip. Payson was putting herself in Diane's sight, and that hadn't gone well for her in the past.

"What a joke. He must be lying." Diane turned around to face Braden. "What is this meeting for? I've got things to do."

Braden pinned her with a straight-forward look, no malice, no expectations, just something to let her know he knew her involvement with Benjamin. "The Aeons have been taking deliberate actions to raise light in Auralia and to counteract the forces of darkness."

Diane scoffed.

"Something you want to say, Diane?" Braden asked.

"No, I just had to clear my voice. Is that all right with you?"

Braden ignored her and continued. "Let's update Diane on our efforts."

The conversation got lively as each Aeon relayed the specifics of their efforts. Diane quietly listened and Ainsley noticed a rise in light and love amidst the group. All but with Diane. Thinly veiled contempt filled her face.

"I don't understand what you all think you're going to accomplish with those activities. They sound plenty lame to me." Diane rolled her eyes. "Why don't you drop pails of honey over the city and turn everyone into a goody-two-shoes?"

Silence.

Payson cleared her throat. "You can't be serious, Diane. Why would you mock us?"

Diane crunched on a pickle, her gaze roving around the group. "You haven't included me in any discussions about the state of Auralia. How do you think that makes me feel?"

Ainsley sighed and dug in. That kind of thinking, that the world revolved around her, was what needed to be healed and lifted. She couldn't make Diane choose to heal and put in the work, but she could hope. "Diane, you were invited tonight, specifically, because we all wanted to make sure you know you're welcome. I'm glad you're here, but things in Auralia have needed our attention. What have you been doing? Why haven't you kept in touch? We could use your light to help raise the energy in town." She felt all eyes on her, but she couldn't ignore the obvious. Diane wasn't here to help. Unless things had changed with her, which it didn't appear they had, she had other intentions.

"Since being made city manager, I've been busy with my work. It's important. It is going to create jobs for residents and draw tourists. All good things for Auralia." Diane held up her hand and examined her maroon-painted nails.

"Wonderful. I'm glad you're on board with our mission," Ainsley added.

"I have a question," Keegan said.

"Wait, wait just one minute," Diane said, her voice menacing. "I didn't come to this meeting to defend myself. Why am I under the spotlight?"

Braden sighed heavily. "I think we all have questions, mainly because you haven't been working with us. But we have seen you around, spreading darkness, and we don't know why. That's all. I'm sorry you feel attacked."

"I don't have to take this interrogation. I have questions, too, you know." Her chest rose and fell rapidly.

"First, answer my question," Keegan said. "Where have you been keeping Benjamin? I'm concerned about him, especially because he was arrested for committing a crime. He is legally out on bail now, but where has he been? He's been missing since you lead him out of Sheppard Media Tower."

Diane waved her hand. "Crime, smime. He's fine. He's been living at my house. He had to have somewhere to go after you all abandoned him. He is safe and cared for in the best way possible."

"I saw him today, you all know." Payson eyed Diane. "Diane, he was not himself. What happened to him? Why was he sitting alone and confused? And while I was conducting a search for him, one of your minions targeted me."

"Minions? I don't know what you're talking about."

Nerves rattled through Ainsley's body. She had all she could do to remain seated. Diane was turning everything upside down. Watching the others remain composed, she calmed her breathing. Diane had dodged the questions, typical Diane behavior.

"I don't feel like that, Diane. I don't feel committing a crime is nothing to be concerned about for Benjamin," Keegan said, twisting to face her. "You know as well as anyone that Benjamin was arrested. I know you're trying to influence him into criminal ways. But Benjamin deserves to live a life of his own making, not something you've impressed on him." He leaned closer to her. "I'm going to do everything I can to free him. If you're going to be a part of this group, you'll need to release his mind."

She narrowed her eyes and pouted her lips. She stared at each one individually for minutes, and they remained still. "This is why I stay away. You all pick on me. It hurts my feelings. Why can't you accept who I am and show me some kindness?"

Keegan gazed warmly at Ainsley, and her heart did flip-flops. What was that for? Was he trying to reassure her all would be well?

She wasn't convinced. Or since she came to his aid during the fight, was he trying to pay her back? Confusion rattled her brain.

He turned back to Diane, giving her a questioning look. "Do you understand what that would look like, Diane? We've never rejected you." He spread his hands on the table. "We do accept you unconditionally. Based on your behavior and words, we know you. We don't live like you do, taking over another person's life, for example. Accepting you doesn't mean we simply step aside and let you spread darkness. Your choices take you away from our paths." He shook his head and sighed.

Diane sent her gaze around the table again. "Not one of you understands. You've never had to live through what I've experienced." She frowned.

"Your experience in your younger life was terrible. You're right, no one has been in your shoes. But it doesn't matter, because everyone has a burden to bear. We've all experienced hardship," Skye said. "Your particular path is about you and how you decide to deal with your life circumstances. We're here to support you."

AINSLEY SLIPPED her hand over Keegan's and opened her heart to send light and affection to him. A wave of warmth washed over her, a sign that he'd done the same. Light radiated out to the others, as well.

Diane noted her hand on Keegan's, then glared at her, and she responded with directing wishes of the best for her.

"Let's start over." Ainsley gathered her thoughts. "We touched base with you today because we want you to participate in our mission to save Auralia from darkness. You're welcomed with open arms. I'm sorry if you feel we've been disrespectful of you and what you've endured." She paused to weigh her words carefully. The last thing they all wanted was to give Diane fuel for her dark undertakings. "But you have to understand that you've instigated activities that were the exact opposite of our Aeon mission. We have been doing volunteer work, meditating together, helping people. We accept you, but we cannot support your harmful endeavors, whatever your reason for following a dark path. It's a choice."

Immense warmth filled her, confirming that her fellow Aeons were directing love toward her and Diane.

In her mind's eye, she saw Diane struggle with the effects of that love. She was an Aeon at odds with her mission. So inured with darkness, she struggled to see a different life for herself.

Tears ran down Diane's cheeks. Her lips twisted, and finally a decision registered in her expression.

She shoved back from the table and stood in front of them, her eyes almost black. "You all seem to think I need your acceptance. I, in fact, am doing very well without you. I have a great life. I hardly feel the need to thank you for the invitation. It has been a farce." She turned toward Keegan and flashed a beautifully wicked smile. "I appreciate your thought. It meant something to me. Let's talk soon." She spoke softly, intimately to him and stared unblinking into his eyes.

Ainsley swallowed hard, and shook Keegan's arm. He turned to her and smiled. Her heartbeat slowed, recognizing that he'd just turned down Diane's invitation to stand beside her. Such a stand endeared him to her and built trust she sorely needed.

Keegan pushed back from the table and rose to his feet. "Diane, please let Benjamin go unharmed. He has a destiny with us," he said firmly, his eyes looking deep into Diane's. "Don't interfere."

Diane slowly blinked, then let out a long sigh. "Do you think I would harm him? He's a wonderful boy. I can care for him better than any of you," she proclaimed, her gaze swiftly sweeping the group. She pivoted and strode briskly out of the shop.

"Well, that didn't go so well," Braden said. "I guess we should have expected Diane would respond with hostility. It was a nice try, Keegan."

"Phew," Keegan exclaimed. "She shot me a blast of powerful dark energy. It was chilling."

"I know that feeling." Braden shook his head. "I'm glad you knew what she was doing. I wish I had had the wherewithal to remain myself when she mesmerized me."

"We all know better now," Payson said, rubbing Braden's arm.

"From what each of you shared about your work on raising the energy level in Auralia, I would have to say we're doing a lot to at least keep darkness at bay. For now. But I fear a reckoning is coming, soon." Keegan rubbed his forehead slowly.

"I have seen a glimpse of that reckoning in my visions," Ainsley said. She sighed heavily. "I fear it will come when we least expect it and it will be hard."

CHAPTER 9

*K*eegan eyed Ainsley as she walked toward the door along with the group of the others. He couldn't help but take in the contours of her body as he walked behind her. His heartbeat sped up. He caught up to her stride with little effort and paced beside her. Her faint scent of something fresh, like rain, wafted around his head. "That was some meeting, huh?"

She sighed and grimaced. "I'll say."

He pushed out the doorway into the brisk evening air. "Do you think I was too hard on Diane?"

"No," she said, shaking her head emphatically. "If we want to entertain the idea of supporting her return to the group she needs to know how we feel about her darkness. She can't be an effective light healer if she's more DA than Aeon."

"I know. I just felt like inviting her and giving her a second chance—"

Payson held up three fingers. "Third chance. We've gone through this before, remember?"

"Right," Keegan said. "There was the time when we were kids that we implored her to stick with us and step away from darkness. Then we tried again a few months ago."

Braden shook his head. "It's hard to believe, but the last time someone, you, Payson, begged her to walk away from darkness was on top of the Sheppard Media Tower and she left you in her dust."

"I wasn't there, but I'll never forget that she tried to kill you, and almost succeeded." Keegan shuddered.

"Well, I'm counting on things not getting that bad again," Ainsley said. "Good night all."

Payson and the others walked to their vehicles, waving goodbye.

Ainsley stopped beside her truck and leaned back against it. Imagining her relaxed and cuddled up in a soft fleece throw, her hair fanning out above her head fueled Keegan's desires.

But he knew better. He'd been friends with her for years. He didn't want to assume something he had no right to. He had no right to sensual thoughts.

"Are you okay?" he asked, watching wisps of her long red hair lift hypnotically in the breeze.

"I am. Just worn out from all the drama at the meeting. And I'm afraid."

"Afraid of what?"

"Well, of what Diane may do next."

He didn't miss her eyes dragging up and down his body, and swallowed hard. "She's just a distraction from our mission. She'll get bored with harassing us eventually. But we're strong."

"I know. I know. I hate thinking like this about her. But we should never underestimate her and the lengths she'll go to get what she wants."

His skin tingled under her gaze. "I won't."

"She seemed to settle her intentions on you now at least twice. I'm worried."

He nodded. "It was eerie." He wanted to lean his arm near her and get close. "Nothing is going to happen to me."

"Promise?" Ainsley asked.

"Promise. Their gazes held for a long couple of seconds and his insights danced, releasing feelings he hadn't felt before. "Good night, Ainsley. See you later." He walked to his Jeep and climbed inside. He sat there in the dark and watched her drive away. He turned out of the parking lot in the opposite direction toward Best Bond Company.

With daydreams of Ainsley's smile still on his mind after his drive back downtown, Keegan walked into his business.

"Hey, you're back," Ricki said as he passed by her desk.

"I am. You're staying late."

"I wanted to finish up. I have loaded Benjamin's bail documents," she said.

"Thanks. Have I ever told you you're a godsend?"

She turned around and chuckled. "A couple of times. I'm taking off soon."

"Have good evening." He went to his office.

Keegan hadn't had a private moment at the meeting to get an update from Payson on the disposition of Benjamin, but knew she'd be in touch soon. So much talk, talk, talk at the meeting. He was ready for some solitary, nature time to sooth his nerves, but that would have to wait until he tied up some loose ends at his desk.

Just then he heard someone walk in.

"Hi, Ricki."

He knew that voice well. He grabbed her a cup of coffee and walked out to greet Payson. "Hi, there. You got info for me?" He handed her the coffee.

"Sure," she said, reaching for the mug. She sipped a bit, then smiled. "You guys make good coffee. It hits the spot."

"You've got to thank Ricki for that."

Payson nodded to her.

"Come on back," he said, motioning to his office.

She followed him and pulled out a chair from the table in his office.

"Well, I have good news. It took a bit of doing but with Benjamin's bail paid, I got permission from the judge to take him to my house. His court date isn't for a month. Meantime, he has to wear an ankle bracelet, but he deserves it."

"He does?" Keegan raised his eyebrows. "I don't know if someone who is mesmerized by a DA is in control of anything, including his driving."

"That's fair. I'll check with his public defender. Maybe we can get that bracelet taken off."

"Yeah, that seems fair. What shape was he in when you got to him?"

"When he was booked he passed the breathalyzer and urine tests, so he's being charged with reckless driving, not a charge for intoxicated while driving. He was in a daze when I found him. He still was when I left him at my house. I saw to him lying down in my extra bedroom. I'm giving him space to rest first, then we'll have to help him come out of Diane's entrancement."

"Yeah, I remember Braden came out of it after associating you with familiar things, things that were good. Things that didn't pressure him but gave him positive power."

"Yes. That's what we'll do." She smacked her hands against her legs. "Well, I should get back to him."

"Honestly, I don't feel good about him staying with you. You and Braden have already been through a lot. Diane is going to try to find him, and it won't be hard for her to deduce where he is. Then she's going to come after you both. I want to take him to my house."

"No. Diane has already made moves on you. I saw them tonight."

"I'm aware, but I'm not going to hide. I'm going to help Benjamin." He couldn't let Payson take any chances. Payson's keen senses and her strong light were important to the Aeon cause, and the same with Braden. He wouldn't put them at risk when he could take the heat of them.

She saluted him. "I didn't know it was up to you." She slanted him a grin.

"You're not going to win this one, Payson."

"You could do a lot by sending positive energy to us all, including Benjamin. You don't need to take him under your roof."

"It's already decided. I'm sorry for being such a pest, but I strongly feel it's what should happen."

"Okay. We can go right now."

"Sure. The sooner the better." He slipped back into his jacket and grabbed the keys to his Jeep. "Lock up, okay, Ricki?"

"Sure. I'll be out of here in a few minutes."

He walked out with Payson and kept his eye trained on her as she climbed behind the wheel.

"I hope this pick-up is uneventful," she said through the open window and turned her car toward her house.

"Me too." Keegan knew the way but he would just as soon keep Payson in his sights. Parts of his brain went back to his thoughts. He wanted to tune into Diane, but his brain was too tired. He needed that nature fix, but this drive would be the closest he'd get to nature today. He couldn't complain. Payson had done her job swiftly and it was his idea to move Benjamin.

He followed her out to her secluded, rural home and Payson drove up to her gated property and punched in her code. The gate opened and she pulled up to her garage, motioning him to pull in the driveway. He took satisfaction in knowing Payson was safe out here, safer since he and Cooper had installed a higher grade of security when Diane came after her.

He strolled up the drive, taking note of the fall yellow and orange chrysanthemums, purple coneflowers, and pink dahlias that security lighting lit up along the front sidewalk. He paused and breathed in a deep breath and let it out. The tiny bit of nature relaxed his brain enough to ease the overwhelm rattling in his head.

"Come on in," Payson called, and he walked the rest of the way inside.

"I love it out here," he said. "It's a really nice spot."

"Thank you," she said, and closed the door behind him. "I love the nature that surrounds me here."

Gratitude for little things like purple flowers flowed through him. He tossed his jacket over the arm of the couch. "Where is he?"

"Upstairs." Payson led him up to the extra bedroom and they peeked in.

"He's still out of it," she whispered.

"All the same, I'm taking him."

Keegan strode over to the bed and gently shook Benjamin. It took a few shakes but finally Benjamin woke up and looked at Keegan with bleary eyes. "Hey, buddy. Sorry to wake you but I need you to get up. I'm taking you to my house." Keegan's gut squeezed at the blank look on Benjamin's face. "C'mon. Everything's going to be all right. Just lean on me."

"It's like he's been drugged. He's worse than when I brought him here, but he was a handful." Payson took hold of Benjamin's other arm and helped Keegan walk him down the stairs to the living room."

"This is good. We can let him sit here," Keegan said.

"Here you are, Benjamin." It was Diane, standing just inside the living room door. She turned her fierce intentions on Payson. "You're meddling again, I see, Payson. Get out of my way. I paid his bail, he is under my care. How did you find him, anyway?"

"Never mind that, how did you get in here, Diane?" Keegan bristled.

"I have my ways. You should know that by now."

Payson and Keegan resumed walking Benjamin to Keegan's vehicle.

"Not according to the judge. I returned him to jail, where he was relinquished to me," Payson said.

A strong energy reverberated through Keegan's body, shaking him so hard he could hardly hold onto Benjamin. "Back off, Diane," he ordered. "You have no right to take him."

"Let's just see about that," Diane threatened. "Benjamin, come to me. I'll take care of you, honey, just as I have been."

Benjamin lifted his head, his eyes dark and dull. "Okay," he mumbled. He tried to get loose from Keegan and Payson's grip, but the effort was too much. He sank back into their arms.

Diane growled and sent a harsh burst of dark energy in their direction.

Trembling like a leaf, Payson hollered. "Ah, this is not right, Diane. You can't overcome us." She held tight to Benjamin.

"You bitch," Diane uttered. "When will I learn I'm not a part of your little Aeon group? I'm a leader of my Dark Aspects. We're more powerful than you ever could become. You both are on the wrong side." She let loose a cackle and Benjamin's knees buckled. Keegan caught him just before he dropped to the pavement. He shoved him into the back seat before Diane could snatch him.

"Diane, get out of here." Keegan grabbed her arm and started escorting her to her car down the driveway.

She pulled away from his grasp and slapped him. "You haven't won him over. I'll be back for him."

Keegan rubbed his face, as she climbed into her car, while he stood beside the busted gate, hanging by its hinges. She gave him her middle finger and smiled, as though she'd gotten her way and drove off.

"Whew! What a fury Diane is. I'm just glad she's gone." He closed the back door of his Jeep and looked down at Payson. "Are you all right?"

"I am. Diane is so strong, but light and love are stronger. I know she isn't responsible for the actions of all DAs, but after that little show of her power, I can see why average humans succumb to it. It's ferocious," Payson shook her head. "How are you? It looks like she hit you hard. You've got a red mark."

"Honestly, I'm shaken, too. But I'm fine. I'm going to get out of here. Benjamin is in bad shape." He stared wryly at the gate. "Cooper and I can work on that."

She shrugged. "Don't worry about it. Braden can see to it. Aren't we all used to taking care of Diane's destruction?" She looked away. "I'll let the others know what happened here. You take care." Payson patted his shoulder. "Stay in touch."

"I will." He slid behind the steering wheel, shut the car door, and pulled into the street, then took off toward his house. He glanced over his shoulder, checking Benjamin again. He was still. Without thought, he streamed light and peace toward him and Payson, wishing things would get better but suspecting they truly were getting worse.

CHAPTER 10

*A*insley loaded her breakfast dishes in the dishwasher, distracted. She knew Keegan was occupied working taking care of Benjamin. She knew that, but she didn't like it. Diane had proven over and over she couldn't be trusted. And Diane's interest in Keegan didn't get past her at the dinner meeting. Geez. Diane wasn't even changing her MO.

Frustration burned in her stomach. Diane was trying to get her hooks deep into another Aeon, and this time it was Keegan, even if he didn't want anything to do with her.

Ainsley closed her eyes and breathed out a slow breath, attempting to refocus. Keegan could take care of himself, she had to remember that.

One by one, she gathered some of her house plants from around her house and put them in a box. She could use some good vibes at her store. She loaded them into her car and headed out, setting her intentions on positive. Guilt pressed on her mind. Being an Aeon, she was supposed to be able to spread light, love, peace, harmony, but with her background, she wasn't always in an upbeat frame of mind. She had come to admit that where most people saw benign she saw danger.

Traffic was heavy on her way to Old Town, so she was forced to keep her focus on driving all the way until she pulled into her parking space behind her store. She bent over the back seat where the plants were sitting and lifted the box. Breezily, she carried them to her shop, pausing to enjoy the brief moments of sunshine and cool air outside. Inside, she set the box on a worktable in the private space at the back of her shop. She shrugged off her jacket and picked up one plant. She knew just where she wanted to put it. She stepped into her showroom with her key to unlock the front door and held the violet above a shelf just inside her shop, shifting other objects around.

Suddenly, she sucked in a sharp breath and dropped the plant. All she could see was a room at Keegan's house and Diane trying to mesmerize him.

"Keegan, you're the perfect person to liaison between me and the professionals I work with, like Mayor Farrod, Barry Russell, and Principle Group CEO Tim Brody. They respect you. They'll listen to you about the benefits of the Principle Group development projects here in Auralia."

"I don't know, Diane. I have my own business to run." Keegan's eyes were wide and dark. His voice was soft, low, as though he were transfixed.

Diane rubbed his upper arm. "Just listen to me. I know what's best for you. Trust me. I'm going to go upstairs and get Benjamin, while you rest right here on the sofa."

Ainsley doubled over. The vision made her sick. She looked at the mess on the floor where she'd dropped the potted plant and tried to shake the effects of the vision.

She bent to the floor and picked up the pottery pieces from the flowerpot and tossed them in the garbage, then mechanically swept the dirt into a dustpan and dumped it in the trash.

The memory of the vision stirred her anger. Ainsley knew Diane would not get away with her plans to take over Keegan. He had a right to live his own life.

Just then, she heard the backdoor open and close. She pulled herself together as best she could, as Iris walked in.

"Good morning." Iris beamed. She eyed the plant in Ainsley's hand, roots exposed. "What happened?"

"I got careless and knocked off this plant. The pot broke, so I was just about to look around for another one." Ainsley's nerves rumbled. She didn't have time for small talk, but she couldn't just run out on Iris. That would raise suspicion that she didn't want to address.

"Would you like me to help you look?" Iris scratched her head, training her gaze around the room.

"That would be so helpful." She tried for casual, nonchalance.

"Sure. I could replant this for you," she offered, opening her hand for the plant. "I have a green thumb, so this guy would be in good hands."

"Okay, thank you." Ainsley went to her desk and tried to focus on ordering antiques for the shop. Her mind clouded with fearful thoughts. Restless, she started pacing across the retail floor.

"Ainsley, is something wrong?" Iris asked from the back room. She walked up to Ainsley, stopping her in her tracks.

"Yes. There is a problem I feel I need to address. I'm afraid I'm going to have to leave you to mind the shop again."

"Don't worry about a thing. I'm happy to take care of things. I'm sorry something is bothering you." Iris gave her a frown. "Whatever it is, I hope it's not serious."

"Thank you, Iris. I'll be back as soon as I can."

Ainsley pulled on her jacket and walked out the back door, anxiety pushing her to hurry.

Inside her car, she sped out of the parking lot on her way to Keegan's house. Her gut twisted, hoping it wasn't too late and not knowing what to expect at his house. If her vision were off, he might be miffed that she was interfering.

She thought of his smile and his gentleness with her concerns. She shook her head. No, he wouldn't get angry with her. He would understand.

His house was not far, and a few minutes later she pulled into his driveway. Her pulse raced. She didn't know what she would find. She should have prepared what to say, but she didn't hesitate to run up the sidewalk and knock on his front door.

She caught herself holding her breath, and let it out quickly.

The door opened and Keegan gave her his friendly smile. "Hey, come on in. What's up?"

She walked by him and noted confusion in his eyes. Her heart squeezed. "Are you busy?"

He gestured to the couch. "No, I was just chilling." He looked around the room, and started tidying up.

She eased into the couch. "Are we alone? Is Benjamin here?"

"Umm…" He glanced upstairs, and lowered himself into an upholstered chair across from her. "Last I looked he was sleeping. He's been very tired since he got away from Diane. I think the fall from the tower a few weeks ago and the mesmerizing has sapped all his strength." Keegan rubbed his chin. "Yeah, we're alone. Are you okay," he asked, leaning closer.

"Honestly, I'm on edge. I had a vision that troubled me." She smoothed her pants, gathering her thoughts.

"Tell me about it," Keegan said, knitting his brow.

"I saw Diane here with you and Benjamin."

"What?" His eye widened.

"Like I said, I saw her here with you and Benjamin. She was talking low to you, as though trying to convince you to do something for her. Then she went upstairs to get Benjamin."

Keegan blinked, blinked, then tilted his head at her. "What was she saying? I don't have any memory of her being her or talking to me. I didn't hear anything either."

"In the vision, you looked like you were in a trance."

His hands flew to his face. "Oh my God! This is not good." He dropped his head in his hands. "I've been so concerned something like that might happen, what with all the attention Diane has been forcing on me. It's why I left your shop so suddenly yesterday."

Ainsley placed her hand on his knee. Even through his jeans he was warm. "It could have been a vision of what could happen, but hasn't happened yet."

"I know, I know." He looked deep into her eyes, searching. "Thank you so much for telling me. I know I've been dismissive of your concerns about Diane and me. I'm sorry for that."

"You don't need to apologize, but I appreciate it. I am only apprehensive. I'm not trying to interfere in your life." Warmth spread in her heart at his understanding. "Are you sure Benjamin is upstairs?"

He jumped up and ran upstairs two at a time. "Benjamin, are you sleeping?"

The door creaked as he opened it and Ainsley waited. She heard the door close quietly, her eyes directed upstairs.

Keegan slowly walked downstairs. He slid back into the chair in front of her and smiled. "He's there. Still asleep. I guess it was a false alarm, but thank you for the alert. I have to stay vigilant." He eyed her. "Do you think it's suspicious that Benjamin is always so tired?"

"Maybe," she said. "He's been through a lot, though. I mean, what has been the effect on his body of Diane using telekinesis to disappear him, twice? We should keep a close eye on him."

"Yeah, I should. He's been waking periodically. We've talked. He told me he has nightmares and phantom pains. He needs a lot of support, so I've been streaming light to him."

"That's excellent. I should do more of that. In fact, we could ask all the Aeons to do that as a matter of course." A clean, mild fragrance of outdoors emanated from Keegan, coaxing her to lean closer, but she didn't. A little giggle tickled her insides at the thought and the corners of her lips lifted.

"What's that smile about," he asked, shifting in the chair.

It wasn't that she was afraid of being too forward. For heaven's sake, no. But she wanted to respect his privacy, and she'd already talked to him several times about things happening in his life. She wanted to walk the line, not jump in with two feet.

"I'm just happy you allow me to give you information from my visions. It means a lot to me."

He frowned. "I don't want Diane to come here and mesmerize me. I don't want her to mesmerize me over or Benjamin. He's just barely gotten away from her. He needs time to gain back his independence."

Ainsley leaned forward and met him eye to eye. "I wish I could tell you why Diane is focusing on you. But it doesn't have to make sense. What I do know is that you're strong, Keegan. You can resist Diane. As long as you remain aware that the vision is informing you of what could happen, you'll be able to detect if she tries. All of us Aeons need to take steps to prevent that vision from coming true."

Keegan nodded, and let out a long sigh.

She didn't blame him for questioning his strength. The job of protecting the city and its residents had been long and intense, with no sign of letting up.

"You're right. Of course, you're right." He unleashed a smile that lit up her soul. "Enough about me. We have work to do. It's still pretty early. Would you like some coffee or something, and we can talk about how we're going to learn more about Principle Industries' plans?"

"We do need to get to work on that, but I left my employee in charge of the shop. I have to get back." She ran her fingers through her hair, thinking.

"Of course. And I should get back to work as well. Boy, this Diane thing really did a number on me. I'm going to stay here to be available for Benjamin." He glanced around the room as though preparing for battle. "Yes, let's break for now and talk later. How about tonight? We could meet at your place, for a change. But you're welcome here."

"It's probably best if I come here. That way we can keep an eye on Benjamin. Tonight works, say, six-thirty?"

He slapped his palm against his forehead. "Yes, Benjamin needs watching. Six-thirty is a good time."

He walked her to the front door, and she caught the scent of his warm skin and spicy fragrance again. It tickled her senses nicely.

"See you later," she called as she walked out to her truck. As she backed into the road, reluctance skipped in her heart. Should she stay to monitor Keegan? The vision had been so vivid, so scary. If only she could do more than simply see things and not know if or when they would occur.

CHAPTER 11

*K*eegan swallowed the water he's sipped and answered his phone, curious what Payson wanted.

"Keegan, I have good news," she said. "Benjamin's attorney submitted a request to the judge for expedient removal of his ankle monitor. As soon as there is word, there should be a call coming his way."

"Thanks for following through. Do you think he has a chance?"

"The lawyer thought so. Benjamin has never been in trouble before and the charges were minor, though I wouldn't mention that to Benjamin."

"Got it."

He sat down at his desk in his home office right off his living room and opened his lap top. He started up his payroll program and began the process of paying Ricki and his freelance bounty hunters. It was work he could practically do on autopilot, which was perfect. His mind was running fast with distractions: when would Benjamin stop sleeping so much; what were possible deeper truths behind the problems in Auralia; what could he do to bring Diane back?

He shook his head, taming his thoughts and concentrating on his payroll and budget. He'd purchased his company from the previous owner after he'd worked in the field for a while. It was satisfying to serve justice, but he was more interested in management of good people, people who had been with the company since before him. As owner, he prided himself in giving individuals income and in always stressing respect for others.

Footsteps overhead alerted him that Benjamin was out of bed. He checked the clock on the wall and saw he'd been working for more than an hour as morning turned to early afternoon. Pushing away from his desk, he walked into the living room just as Benjamin came down the stairs. His hair stuck up all over his head and he had red creases stretching across his face from lying down on the pillow.

Benjamin stopped mid-step. "How did I get this thing," he asked, pointing to his ankle bracelet.

"Oh, that. Want to take a seat and wake up for a few minutes?" Keegan gestured to the couch and dropped into the upholstered chair nearby. "You look like you slept hard."

Benjamin eased into the couch and leaned his head back against the cushion. "Boy, I did sleep hard, you're right. I feel like I've been hit by a Mack truck. You can imagine my surprise when I woke up to find this." He propped up his foot on the couch.

Keegan twirled his thumbs, watching him closely. "You were in a car accident. Do you remember that?"

Benjamin closed his eyes and sat quietly for a few minutes. "Nope. How long have I been here?" he asked, opening his eyes and looking around. "I know I slept here last night. That's about as far as I recall." He rubbed his eyes. "I don't remember anything, and particularly, not this thing." He shook his leg.

"You don't remember the police taking you to jail?"

His eyes widened. "Jail? What did I do?"

Keegan leaned his arms on his knees, peering watchfully. "You hit a car."

"What?" He bolted up. "When did I do that? How? I don't remember that. Did I hurt anyone? Wait a minute. That can't be good." He plopped down again and scrubbed the top of his head.

"No, it's not. The good news is you're charged with reckless driving."

"That's the good news?"

"You didn't have any substance in your system to give you a DUI, so that is good."

"Geez, reckless driving. I'm not a reckless driver. Did I hurt anyone?" he repeated, staring at Keegan, eyes scared.

"You did not. But—"

"There's a but?" Benjamin interrupted. "Could this get any worse?"

"You disappeared from your jail cell. No sign of you anywhere in the facility. Payson found you downtown sitting on a bench. You were pretty dazed. She took you to her house after bailing you out of jail. We both brought you here. We thought this would be the best place for you to serve house arrest until your court date."

He dropped his head in his hands and moaned. "I don't understand, I don't understand."

Keegan's heart went out to him. "Of course you don't. So much has happened to you. Luckily, I can explain some of it."

Benjamin sat up and squared his shoulders. "Please do."

First, Keegan explained what had happened to Braden weeks ago, and how Payson couldn't allow Diane to take over his life.

"Braden broke free from her hold on him, but because Payson fought her and almost died." Gently, Keegan revealed the hard truth about Diane, knowing Benjamin might resist it. "Payson was terrified for him. Diane blew up his life and in doing so, erased his love for Payson. It was devastating for us all."

"I hardly know Diane. You're telling me about something she did months ago and to someone else. Are you leading up to what happened to me, 'cause I feel I've been somehow taken over myself. I don't know. It's like I kind of remember some weird places and weird stuff, but it's all very hazy." Benjamin shook his head back and forth, as though trying to take in something unbelievable. "And just who are you referring to when you say 'us all'?"

"I'm talking about a group of my friends, who are also your friends. You've seen us together at Coffee Is."

"Okay, that answers that question. I do remember those people. Faintly. They're nice." He shook his head vigorously again. "What is wrong with me? Why can't I remember anything but Diane taking care of me, helping me out, for some reason I can't explain. Why did I need help?"

Glad Benjamin was associating the Aeons with familiarity, Keegan pulled in a deep breath. "This isn't going to be easy to hear," he started. He continued, describing how Diane had prodded him to walk off the top of Sheppard Media Tower to get back at Payson and her friends."

"What?" He jumped to his feet, almost losing his balance. "You're telling me I jumped off that building. How did I survive? This can't be true."

"Sit down. It is. You did survive. Diane, well," he struggled for words. He started pacing, wondering how in hell he could tell Benjamin what really happened. "Let's go back a bit. If we do that, what I'm about to tell you will be more comprehensible." He sat back down and leaned in. "Tell me about your family, school, and friends. Back when you were just a kid."

"Oh my God, what are you doing to me? My brain is mush, and you're asking me to think back."

"I know it seems crazy, but humor me."

Benjamin sat quietly for so long, Keegan began to worry he'd gone too far. He could try to listen in on his thoughts, but he'd made that vow and he didn't want to break it. He just had to wait and see what would happen. But he could direct love and compassion toward him, supporting him in the difficult time.

"I always thought my parents were great. They came to my baseball games, my basketball games, my track and cross country meets, and always cheered me on. Funny, he said, staring out at nothing, "the one time I really needed their support, they let me down."

"What happened?"

"You're not going to believe this. When I was thirteen, I had the weirdest nightmare." Benjamin stared at Keegan, his eyes misting.

"Try me."

"Well, in my dream, I was alone in the dark, and some strangers were coaxing me to come with them to a ship off the shore of an island. I didn't want to go, but these people told me I had to. I can't explain it, but after I woke up from that nightmare, I had such peace. I knew everything was going to be all right. I knew I had a purpose in being alive. I was supposed to do something important, and I knew in my heart, that it was real, not just a nightmare."

"That's some dream." Keegan had to pace himself. He couldn't just spill all his knowledge about Atlantis and the Aeon's mission. Benjamin would never believe him. "Is there more?"

"Yeah, there's plenty more. I told my parents about the dream. They laughed it off, made fun of me for taking it seriously." He stared upward at the ceiling, as though searching. "But I never forgot how I felt that night. And I've never felt that peaceful and knowing again. I moved on with my life, not knowing what to do about my knowledge. I still don't know." He turned back to face Keegan.

"So the dream and what you learned about yourself stayed with you."

"Yes. I've kept trying to figure out what I need to do, who I am, what is so important that I have to do. But heck, I'm probably nuts." He let go and leaned back against the couch. "I don't know why I spilled all that to you." He rubbed his temples, his eyes dazed.

Keegan touched Benjamin's knee lightly, trying to keep him focused. "No, you're not nuts. I can assure you. I understand you feeling that way, more than you know. But sometimes, really hard things can lead to something good."

"Yeah, yeah, yeah, I know. What doesn't kill you makes you stronger." Benjamin frowned and heaved a long sigh.

"It's not just a cliché." Keegan put his feet up on the ottoman. What he was going to say would startle Benjamin, but that might be just what he needed. "I had my dream at about the same age you did. And like your parents, mine struggled with accepting it as real, to say nothing of what the implications were on my life. But in my heart, I knew the dream was more than a dream, it was the truth about who I was and what I was to do with my life."

His attention rapt, Benjamin peered at Keegan. "Really? You had a weird dream, too?"

"I did. When my parents couldn't accept what I told them as important, I kept insisting. They had me psychoanalyzed, which took me in a terrible direction, denying who I was. Loneliness and despair took me over. I tried to deny the truth myself, but it wouldn't be ignored. I grew up in Auralia, just down the street from Payson. It turned out that she was just like me. We took solace in our sameness."

"I find that hard to believe. You lived near each other and just naturally gravitated toward each other?" He grimaced, trying to process what Keegan was telling him.

"It's the way of things for us, and by us I mean our group. We are called the Aeons, and we use our special abilities to fight darkness and raise the vibration in our community. It's our way of helping the world evolve."

"Oh, that's all. I mean, sure, you're an Aeon, a special being. An alien from outer space."

Keegan shifted in his seat. "You can make light of it, you can try to walk away. Heck, you can go back to Diane and she'll captivate you with her darkness." He dropped his feet to the floor and focused on Benjamin. "But the truth is, you're an Aeon. You're one of us. You belong here in Auralia and we can use your help in saving the city."

Benjamin pursed his lips. He blinked, twice. He leaned his head against the back of the couch and said nothing. The clock on the wall counted out the seconds gliding by, and Keegan watched Benjamin, letting the words sink in for him, expecting him to be able to handle his new reality.

Suddenly, Benjamin burst out laughing. Keegan smiled, rubbing his chin, amused at his reaction.

"So, you're suggesting that a bunch of people, the Aeons, are super-heroes running around the city, fighting crime. And I'm one of them. Do I get a cape or a Spidey outfit?"

"No, we are not superheroes. But you are one of us."

"How do you know this stuff? What makes me one of you?" His face serious, Benjamin gritted his teeth.

"You know it, too. Center yourself and dig down into your gut, where your dream lies. Do that right now, then tell me I'm wrong." Keegan kicked back again, watching Benjamin quite naturally shift his intention internally, closing his eyes and breathing deeply. His face contorted slightly, then relaxed. He started breathing hard and chewed on his lower lip.

Outdoors, clouds blocked the sunshine and tree limbs swayed. Keegan wanted to be present for Benjamin, but distractions cropped up: is a storm coming; I'm thirsty; what is Ainsley doing while I'm sitting here; do I dare listen for Dark Sides activity; is a DA approaching?

No. He stopped himself from wandering and attended to Benjamin.

Finally, he opened his eyes, sober, wide-eyed. "I'm speechless. What can I say? I mean, you were right, I do know I'm an Aeon. No, I didn't have the terminology, but everything, I mean everything was right there inside me. The dream finally made sense. I'm related to an ancient line of people. People who were good and wanted the world to evolve. I'm a part of that. My God, this is immense."

It was Keegan's turn to laugh. "And now you know."

Benjamin jumped up and walked back and forth, gesturing. "There is so much I can do. What I'm learning in school, my eventual degree in psychology, my personal values, it all lines up." He ran his hand over his mouth, aghast. "When do I start?"

"Good question. In many ways, you already have started. You said it yourself, everything lines up. But the next step is for you to understand what has happened to you and to recover. Remember? That's what led to this conversation."

"Oh, yeah. Diane did something." He sat back down. "What did she do?"

"It was important for you to recognize your identity before I told you. Also remember, what happened to you has brought forward your knowledge and your mission."

"Mission, huh. That makes sense."

"That's what we Aeons have been calling the work we do behind the scenes in the city. Our special abilities help us take care of business. Mine is clairaudience. I have psychic hearing. Payson's is psychometry. She can gather information through touch. We all have keen hearing and vision. We're fast. We can send light and love to others with our minds. Each of us can detect what we refer to as Dark Aspects, and we can sense another Aeon."

"Now that you mention it, I know I have abilities, I just never gave them much thought."

"Do you know what your special ability is?"

He shook his head. "I don't know. I might not have one. Could you be wrong about me?" Benjamin got flustered and his eyes widened.

"No, I'm not wrong. I can feel your identity. I could before we had this talk. All the Aeons have known about you. In fact, Skye hired you to keep an eye on you, believing that at some point, you would join us."

"No way! Why didn't any of you tell me?"

"It wasn't the right time."

"Now is the right time?" His gaze downcast, Benjamin got thoughtful. He dragged one foot in front of him across the carpeting.

Sounds exploded in Keegan's head, and he knew they came from Benjamin's mind, trying to grasp all that he was learning. He centered himself, grounding to the earth, and breathing deeply.

"Tell me what happened to me." Benjamin's voice was quiet.

"Diane is a Dark Aspect, or what we call DA. She is actually an Aeon gone dark. She can deconstruct objects and change the weather. She can deconstruct whatever and whoever she wants, as well as mesmerize them. That is what she did to you. She kept you in that state, substituting your life for the one she wanted you to have, under her control."

"Why would she do that? That's just wrong."

"You're very right. It was wrong. You had to be rescued and brought back. That is why you're here now. I'm protecting you from Diane and supporting you while you recover from the block she put on you. I can only imagine that she wants to use your abilities for her own pet projects, which are unhealthy for Auralia."

Just then the doorbell rang, and Keegan startled at the same time Benjamin flinched.

"It's okay. I'll get that." The vision Ainsley had warned him of popped up in his mind. A deep vibration rumbled in him. He couldn't take any chances. "You go into my office and close the door. Keep quiet. I'll tell you when it's safe to come out. No matter what happens, stay in that room."

Benjamin turned a confused expression on Keegan. "Do you really think that's necessary?"

"No time to discuss it. Trust me," he said, ushering Benjamin into his office and closing the door.

The doorbell rang again, and again. The doorknob twisted back and forth, fighting the lock. Tension tightened his shoulders, and dread weighed him down. He peered through the peephole in his door, suspecting Diane standing on the other side. He couldn't risk her blowing up his home. He squared his shoulders and opened the door.

"Finally!" she spouted. "I've been ringing the bell for a long time." She pushed past Keegan into the living room.

"C'mon in," he said, sarcasm dripping. "What do you want?" He left the door standing open and fortified his boundaries.

"Where is Benjamin?" She whirled around. "I demand to know where he is."

Tension pounded through him along with her demands. She wasn't going to get the best of him. Not now, not ever. "I am not obligated to tell you anything, Diane. I don't understand why you've marched into my house and made such a commotion." He gestured to the door.

"I'm not leaving until you tell me where Benjamin is." She crossed her arms over her body, standing resolute and tapping her foot.

"I can't do that." Keegan crossed his arms over his chest and stuck out his chin. "Why do you need him? I told you at the meeting, you have no right to mesmerize him and run his life."

Diane's expression softened, and she placed her hand on his arm. "Keegan, c'mon. You know me." Her gaze intensified on his. "I'm sorry

I burst in like that. Actually, I wanted to talk to you. You're the perfect person to liaison between me and the professionals I work with, like Mayor Farrod, Barry Russell, and Principle Industries CEO Tom Brody. They—"

Her hand on his arm warmed his skin. Thoughts formed in his brain. What would be wrong with considering what Diane was proposing? A change might do him good. She was still talking. But the words were fuzzy. He shook his head, then brushed off her hand. Ainsley had foreseen this intrusion on his life. Words formed with a struggle in his brain, but he sent a message to Ainsley: I need support.

"Stop. You already asked me. I don't need to hear any more. I'm not interested in working for you. I have my own work."

Diane pressed her lips together tightly. She lifted her arms and made circles in the air. He knew what she was up to, and it would take all his strength to rebuff her intentions. The vision Ainsley had seen was transpiring in real time right before him. His pulse raced and urgency slammed through him. He had to stop her.

The throw draped on the back of the couch lifted toward the ceiling and swirled around eerily, as the walls began trembling. Pictures on the bookcase shelves slammed to the floor, and turbulence filled the room.

Keegan hardened his body, pressing his feet to the floor, and straining his mind to push Diane to leave. Unsure his new ability would be strong enough to force her to his will, he pounded his fists against his leg and hollered, "Stop, Diane. Enough of this."

She turned fiery dark eyes on him, and fear pummeled his body. Again, he hardened himself to the falsehoods she hammered against him.

"You're such a fraud, Keegan. You can't even stand up for yourself, you're so weak. Your silly beliefs won't stop me."

Calmly, he sent light, peace, and friendship vibes to her, without hesitation or trepidation. "Watch me. My beliefs are strong, life-giving, important. You will not prevail."

Strength filled him, over and over again. He knew it meant Aeons were supporting him. Psychically, he heard Ainsley's words. "Diane is not stronger than you, Keegan. All the Aeons' powers are with you."

He smiled to himself, sensing the power of his fellow light workers. This was one battle Dark Sides would lose.

"Wipe that smile off your face," Diane yelled. "I won't forget this, Keegan. I will have Benjamin."

Keegan watched as her arms fell to her sides and her shoulders caved inward. The blanket dropped and the room quieted. He wanted to shove her outside, but sorrow stopped him. She had only darkness around her.

"Go, Diane. Leave now," he said.

She coughed sharply, straightened, and stared him down. "There are others who will want to help me in my work. I'll find Benjamin and he will be mine. You will pay. This isn't the end of it."

CHAPTER 12

*D*iane marched out and Keegan shut the door solidly behind her, sighing with relief as he locked the door. He sprinted to his office and tore open the door. The room looked empty. "Benjamin, where are you?"

"I'm here," came a quiet response. Benjamin crawled out of the back of the walk-in closet, his face ashen. "Is Diane gone?"

"You can come out. She's gone. You're safe."

"For now." Benjamin followed him out to the living room and dropped into a chair. "I could hear her yelling and the room was shaking. Man, that stuff was spooky. She can do all that?"

"She's very powerful, but not as powerful as all the Aeons together." Keegan grabbed two bottles of water from the fridge and joined him. "Here, drink this. All that chaos can be draining. Water will help."

"I have to thank you, Keegan. You saved me. Thank you."

"You don't have to thank me. I'm just glad you're on the team now. Together, we'll all work hard to fight Dark Sides and make the city a better place to live. Its influence on Dark Sides will reach beyond the city into the world, helping all beings."

"I never realized there was a problem with darkness in Auralia. Is there a portal to hell here or something?" He shifted his feet, back and forth.

"No, but Auralia is located on a special location that is geographically significant. It has geological resonance, which enhances vibrations." He held his tongue on expounding. Benjamin's eyes kept flicking around the room, as though he was already on overload. "Maybe you should go lie down. You look tired."

Benjamin's focus centered on Keegan. "I don't know if I can ever relax again." His voice drifted off.

"Yes, you will. You've got a lot to process. Give yourself a break and go take a nap. I'll be here with you to make sure nothing severe happens." He slapped Benjamin's knee. "Let's go, upstairs, one foot in front of the other."

Without a word, Benjamin walked upstairs, into the guest bedroom, and closed the door, shutting out the world.

Keegan's heart went out to him. He'd gotten a hard glimpse at a reality he'd not known existed, something many, many people never confronted. They remained well within their belief systems, going through life as though the beliefs were the truth, unwilling to challenge them because of implications. If they faced the truth, they'd face considering making changes.

Aeons knew everyone had a right to believe whatever they chose. But they also knew that being truly alive required conscious choices. Diane thought she was running her life, but was she? Or was she running on autopilot rooted in her childhood trauma?

He sighed, and began picking up his living room. He shoved his books back on his shelves and put fallen knick knacks back on his living room tables. Mindboggling what chaos a taste of Dark Sides could do.

He walked into his office and sat down in front of his computer to do a search. Plans filled his mind for working with Ainsley. He'd much rather think about her—her face, her soft hair, her eyes alive with vitality—than do research. But he had to prepare. He punched in a search for Irish Mob, knowing the beauty of access to anything he wanted on the Internet, just hoping he didn't get caught by the mob's security.

His search brought up pages and pages of information about the mob: it's formation in the early days, members that had been put in prison, members in prison who were still active, industries, and reach.

He sat up and ran his fingers through his hair. So much to process and digest, it all made his head spin. One thing that was clear to him, the mob loved to infiltrate smaller metro areas, which would explain why it was staking out its place in Auralia. Locating in mid-size cities helped them run under the radar of law and get their fingers into privately-owned small businesses they could use for money laundering.

His attention strayed as he stared out the window. Leaves dropping from a tree in his backyard scattered across the lawn. The colors reminded him of Ainsley's vibrant-colored hair. What would she think of his father?

It was useless. Thoughts of his father intruded, and his gut clenched. What was his dad up to that he wanted to hire ex-cons? He didn't know how much more patience he could sustain for his father's felonious ways, but how they might affect Jayce made him sick inside.

* * *

AINSLEY KNOCKED on Keegan's door, and sent her gaze darting around the exterior of his home. His place was situated on a spacious lot that gave him separation and privacy, things she knew he valued. Trees surrounding the yard were lit by a nearby streetlight, casting shadows across the lawn.

The door opened. "Hey, Ainsley." Keegan stepped outside and looked up and down the street.

"Are you okay?" she asked, following his line of sight.

"Yeah, just being careful." He closed the door and led her into the living room. "Want something to drink? I have juice, water, coffee, tea. You name it."

"It's too late for coffee for me. I'll take water."

He left for the kitchen, leaving her to take in the room. She settled into the couch, noticing the overstuffed softness of the cushions. "I didn't notice earlier that you've bought new furniture," she called out to him, trying for light-hearted to start off, but fully knowing what all the Aeons had sensed: Keegan and Benjamin had been assaulted by dark energy.

"I was overdue."

She eyed the décor, appreciating the cool blues on the wall that carried throughout the room in window treatments and upholstered couch and chairs. An abstract painting hung on the wall, echoing the warm colors with accents of greens and golds.

"Here you go," he said, walking in and handing her a full glass of water. "It's filtered."

"Of course, it is." She gave him a smile. "Did you decorate yourself?"

"Hell no. I consulted with an expert, my mom."

"Nice. My sister is good at that kind of thing, too. She's busy with college." She set her glass on a coaster on a soft brown, wooden antique side table. He'd purchased it at her shop months ago.

"I remember those days," he said, chuckling. "I'm glad they're over." He eased into a comfy chair opposite her and put up his feet on a stool. He fixed his gaze on her.

She wriggled on the couch, feeling his focus. "Well, shall we begin our project?"

He rolled his neck and closed his eyes, before refocusing on her again. "I've been thinking this afternoon about how we could proceed." He looked upstairs.

She followed his eyes. "Is Benjamin sleeping again?"

"Last I checked. He's been up there for a while. Our visitor this afternoon stressed him out. Turns out, your vision was mostly correct. Thank God you warned me." He scratched his head with both hands.

"What happened?"

"It was just like you said. Diane created quite a scene, but I was able to repel her efforts and keep Benjamin safe. What an ordeal."

'I'm sorry that happened. I'm sure she'll try again."

"I'm grateful you alerted the group and that all of them sent us positive energy. It helped. I've got to get stronger." He rubbed his chin and went thoughtful. "I don't want to hate Diane or any of the DAs. They have their reasons for following Dark Sides."

"That's true. But those reasons are what they need to work on, not project their hatred and pain out into the world." She sipped her water and went deeper with her thoughts. "No one can do their inner work for them. But when we offer them our natural essence of love, we support them in healing."

"I know." Keegan sighed heavily. "I'm going to be fine. I just need to process some heavy stuff. But we can get to work." He rolled his neck and lowered his gaze.

Ainsley closed her eyes and opened her senses. Instantly a vision popped up. "I see," she paused, "um, Barry Russell walking, now scrolling through plans on his computer screen." She got quiet, waiting for the vision to play out. "Russell is peering at a schedule. I'm seeing what he is seeing and feeling what he is feeling. He's intense. The Stillwell development isn't moving ahead as he planned. He marches out to his secretary. He's yelling at her, saying, 'Get me the mayor.'" Shocked, she came out of the vision, gasping.

Keegan stared at her. "Mayor Farrod is involved? I didn't hear anything, but I was paying attention to you."

"Oh, sorry. I didn't mean to distract you." She chucked lightly, then sobered. "We have to remember that my visions are not set in time. For my visions, time is fluid. And I didn't get anything about what Russell wanted with the mayor. Maybe you can?"

"I'll try."

He closed his eyes again, and Ainsley could sense him grounding himself to the earth. The room was still and she didn't hear anything from upstairs, but she wondered how Benjamin was doing. Her thoughts strayed while she waited for Keegan. She heard a low hum as the furnace came on, its heated air sending a whiff of his scent wafting in her head. It warmed her, like sunshine. It was his smell, clean and honest, not overwhelming or phony.

"I got something."

She opened her eyes and waited again for him to reveal what he'd captured with his clairaudience.

"I have the same caveat to what I hear psychically that you do with your visions." He squeezed his eyelids shut, as though trying to tune in again to what he'd picked up. "The mayor was talking to the economic director, or rather, Tim Brody was talking to the mayor, sharply. As you said, the development schedule has lagged behind the scheduled plan. He kept alluding to 'the Big Boss,' not being happy and that heads would roll. Brody pressed Farrod into promising he'd get around the 'legal mumbo jumbo' and speed up demolition and construction, in that order." Keegan opened his eyes.

"That's interesting." Ainsley chewed on her thumbnail, pondering what Keegan had learned. The word 'demolition' stuck in her throat, knowing that would mean she would lose her shop in Old Town.

"He also said he has doubts about Diane's dedication to the project, and mentioned he's not the only one, again, alluding to the Big Boss." He drummed his fingers on the table beside his chair. "It gives me the willies, just listening in on these guys. There's no doubt they're DAs, but not just the run-of-the-mill DAs, they have a much denser, more sinister energy. They've been at this Dark Sides business for a while."

"We have to dig deeper, and learn the identity of the Big Boss. We already suspect, or I should say, know the Irish Mob has come to Auralia. What if the BB is the head of the mob? BB." Ainsley shivered. "We have to find out."

"I can do that. I'm a bounty hunter. I find things."

"But you haven't actually done that for a few years. You've been a desk-jockey."

"Business owner," He corrected, slanting a grin. "And two years, exactly. It'll be just like getting back on a bike. Now, how about I make dinner? I make a mean pizza, fresh from the freezer," he joked. "I can just pop it in the oven."

Ainsley couldn't help but chuckle. It shortened the space between where he stood in time and where she stood, though neither of them had moved closer physically. "How could I refuse?"

He jumped up and strode to the kitchen.

"Need help," she asked, trailing behind him.

"You're kidding, right?" He opened the freezer and unearthed a pizza, slapped it down on the counter and ripped open the box. "It's cinchy. But if you want to add any toppings to this cheese pizza, I have options." He turned on the oven to preheat.

"Do you have mushrooms, peppers, or olives?"

Keegan grabbed a bottle of green olives in one hand and handed her a pepper and container of mushrooms with the other. "Here you go. I'll turn on suitable music."

"Don't wake up Benjamin." She pulled open drawers in search of a knife and cutting board, then began slicing the vegetables.

Stanzas of smooth jazz quietly filled the house, and she swayed to the beat. Keegan jumped into a pose, pretending to play an alto saxophone to the melody. His expression softened, and it did things to her body: her pulse raced, her breaths deepened, and heat spread through her. She put down the knife and sank into the moment.

Keegan opened his eyes and stilled, his gaze pinning hers. His lips parted slightly, then swiftly and without hesitation, he stood in front of her, with no space between them. He gently took her face in his warm hands, leaning so close she felt his breath on her cheeks. His eyes drew up to hers and paused.

She tilted her head, never looking away, as he brushed her lips with his. His presence, so profound and direct, swept her away to a place she'd never been before. It was heady, and all-consuming. Her eyes closed, she leaned into him.

Suddenly she wanted more. Much more.

Keegan touched his forehead to hers and stepped back.

His hands still rested on her shoulders, and she looked up into his clear blue eyes, desire crumbling away.

"I'm sorry," he said, "I was out of line."

Ainsley pressed her lips together tightly, crushed. She turned away and grappled to rein in her tumbling emotions.

Just then, an upstairs door opened and Benjamin walked downstairs and into the living room. "Hey," he called. "Is anybody home."

Keegan rushed over to meet him. "Yeah, right here. Glad to see you're up. Feeling better?"

Ainsley sucked in a breath, wondering if their little incident would come up for discussion any time soon, then shook off the thought and joined them. "There you are. Hey, Benjamin."

"Hey, Ainsley. I didn't know you were here. I wasn't sure even Keegan was." He rubbed sleep from his eyes and shifted his gaze around the room. "What are you two doing?"

CHAPTER 13

For someone who could beam light and love to others, Ainsley sure was inept at knowing when to open to the promise of love and when to protect herself from getting her hopes smashed.

Tears streamed down her cheeks, and she angrily whisked them away. She'd managed to hold herself together as she excused herself from the pizza dinner Keegan had planned and on her drive home.

Now inside her home, she sought the comfort of her bedroom and slumped into a ball under her blankets in bed, still dressed.

She pounded her fist against her pillow. Why oh why had she let down her guard enough to let feelings for Keegan run amuck? Hadn't she vowed to keep her Aeon relationships strictly business? Hadn't she steered clear of any romantic relationships?

He'd been right to back off. She rolled onto her back and stared up at the ceiling in the low light from the streetlamps.

Friendship with Keegan was all she'd ever had, and that should have been enough, she knew. But loneliness welled inside her, and she'd had enough of it. For too long, it had laid heavily, a constant voice warning her it was all she could have, keeping her safe behind walls.

Confusion about what lay ahead and what she could have pommeled her brain, and she pulled up the covers to her chin, willing her mind to clear.

The sound of her cell ringing sent her farther under the covers. Talking to anyone was not on her to-do list at the moment.

It rang again, and she burrowed deeper under her pillow. When she heard someone leaving a voicemail, she ignored it.

It rang again, and again and again. She bolted upright in bed. "Jeez, can't a person just hibernate?" she huffed, exasperated.

She grabbed it and listened to the first of three messages.

"I need to talk with you, Ainsley. I'm thinking of dropping out of college. Please call me, sis."

The pinch in Jane's voice sunk Ainsley's heart. She'd been so neglectful of her, busy with her own life.

Quickly she tapped on the next message. It was Iris. "A man stopped in today, asking for you, Ainsley. He wouldn't give me his name. He said he'd be back. But…he scared me."

Ainsley lay back in bed, fear gripping her heart. What was going on?

Hard knocking on her front door startled her. Who could that be? Her pulse raced with fear that she'd been remiss in ignoring her phone. What else could be happening?

She ran downstairs and through the front room, the knocking incessant. When she peered through the peek hole she shivered. The man standing on the other side of the door was holding a gun. His dark energy burned through her. She chewed on her lower lip, weighing her options.

Where were the visions when she truly needed a head's up?

The man knocked hard again, then looked over his shoulder, motioning another man to go around the house.

Trapped. That's all she could think about. Just like when she was very young. She grabbed her head. Think, think. She took another peek, and saw the man was holding Jane by the arm. Dark vibrations scrambled through her, and the man stared at the door.

"Why didn't you call your sister?" he hollered. "If you don't open this door right now, you'll never see her again."

She yanked open the door. "Let go of her," she demanded. She marched out to the porch and kicked the man with the gun between his legs. She knew she had to create chaos and fast, before the second man came back. Jane ran to her, nearly tripping over the man on the ground.

"Come on, get inside," Ainsley yelled, stomping on the man rolling in pain. She pulled hard on the gun he was still holding and tore it away.

Inside, she locked the door, pulled a side-table in front of the door, and shoved Jane onto the floor behind the sofa. Without hesitation, she ran to the back door and bolted it locked, then shoved a chair up against it under the doorknob.

While heading toward the stairs for her phone, she double-checked Jane. "Are you all right, honey?"

"Yes," she said barely loud enough to hear. Tears wetted her face. "They want to know where Dad and Mom are. I wouldn't tell them."

"Oh, Jane." But Ainsley couldn't stop. She punched in 911, and waited, while in the back of her brain signaling the Aeons for help. She paused for a nano-second, then couldn't help herself. "Keegan, I'm in trouble." There was no question in her mind. Diane had sent these DAs to threaten her. And she'd upped the ante by targeting her sister. She didn't know who these men were or why they were here, but something was wrong, dead wrong. Why did they want her family?

"911 operator," she heard. "What is your emergency?"

In a stage whisper, she quickly reported the intruders and gave the operator her address.

Back to get Jane, she pulled her to the main-floor bathroom, secluded at the back of the house. "Get inside and lock the door behind me. Don't make a sound." One look at Jane's eyes broke her. "It's going to be okay. Trust me."

She quietly closed the bathroom door and waited to check the doorknob to confirm Jane locked it. That done, she examined the gun in her hand. It was a Glock 19 and it was loaded. Just then, a window in the kitchen shattered, and she dashed upstairs, wanting to draw the intruder away from her sister. Loudly, she scrambled up the stairs.

"Come out, come out wherever you are," taunted a menacing, singsong voice.

Adrenalin streaming through her blood vessels, she pressed her back against the wall around the corner in her bedroom, a likely place for the DA to look. She tuned her keen hearing to the stairwell. One, two, three, four, five, six... She counted the steps she heard scuffing against the carpeting as the intruder climbed toward her. Only two more steps between them. She raised her arm, perched, gun in hand.

Then he was there at the landing, and she lunged toward him, striking him with the butt of the gun as hard as she could against his temple.

Instantly, he toppled back down the stairs and sprawled out on the living room floor. She sprinted down to him and saw that he was out cold but breathing. She ran to the front porch but the other man was gone.

"Ainsley."

Startled, she looked up to see Keegan running up the walk toward her, his gun pointed in a ready stance.

"Watch out," she hollered. "One of the DAs is unaccounted for. There are two."

In seconds he was by her side, alert, tense. "Where's the other one?"

"He's passed out on the living room. I incapacitated the second one for a bit." She sent her gaze around the yard. "They had Jane." She turned quickly and walked back inside, cautiously, her gun raised. Silently, she pointed to the man on the floor. "I have zip ties in a kitchen drawer." She didn't dare lower her gun.

"I'll watch this one while you get them."

Racing to the kitchen, she was grateful Keegan didn't ask about Jane's whereabouts. She grabbed zip ties from the drawer and raced to hand them off to him, knowing he'd do what needed to be done while she looked for the missing man. He could be anywhere in the house. Panic lit in her gut.

Keegan's hand rested on her shoulder. "He's secured. Let's split up." He leaned close. "The others will be here soon," he whispered.

His warmth and strength filled her, steadying her. She lowered her lids and let out a cleansing breath. She watched him slip upstairs and she headed to the basement, warily stepping slowly down the stairs. In the darkness, she caught a shard of dark energy as it sliced through her. The other DA lurked down there somewhere.

She froze, taking shallow breaths and tuning in to the basement. It was too dark to see anything, but she could listen.

Seconds slowly passed and turned into minutes. Her muscles ached to move, to take action, but she remained still.

Footsteps, soft and deliberate, registered in her ears. Heavy breathing came closer and closer. The DA was playing it cautious, but she felt him and heard him. Ainsley wasn't going to bother with attempting to sway him to light and love, she was ready to pounce. He'd participated in kidnapping her sister, and that was crossing a line too far.

Slowly she raised the gun, poised to do whatever she could to keep her sister safe. A faint sound from upstairs, a creak from the front door opening, and a flood of radiance inside her let her know more Aeons had arrived. From below, cursing floated to her ears, and she knew the DA was fighting the light that beckoned him to accept it.

"No, no, no, dammit," he cried.

She sympathized with his pain, but all he had to do was accept the goodness offered to him.

Instead, he pounded the walls, and ran toward her, not realizing she was waiting for him. All she had to do was pull the trigger.

CHAPTER 14

"**S**top right there."

Keegan's breath caught, seeing Ainsley facing the missing DA and pointing a gun at him. Her voice solid, strictly business, hit him like a rock. He had to stop her before she did something that would alter her forever.

"Ainsley," he said gently. "You called 911, didn't you. I hear them talking. They're nearly here. The others need to leave before they arrive. Give me the gun."

She pulled back her shoulders, but didn't turn away from the DA. "They kidnapped Jane. They tried to force her to tell them where to find Mom and Dad. They could have killed her."

Keegan slid closer, his breaths slow and easy. "Yes, but you saved her. We've got the other guy secured. Braden and I will take care of this one," he said, gesturing to the man trembling in front of Ainsley. "Give me the gun."

"Don't shoot," the man cried.

Keegan's breath stilled in his chest, waiting for her to surrender the weapon. His heart went out to her, but this trajectory had to be stopped.

He heard her draw in a deep breath and let it out. Stepping beside her, he grasped the gun, leveling it on the man. "You go upstairs and send Braden down. He's a police officer."

She turned tearful eyes on him, then walked up the stairs without a word.

"You, against the wall."

"I didn't do nothing. Just let me go," he pleaded.

Keegan walked up to him. "Oh, man, don't lie to me." Swiftly, he raised his fist and walloped the man in the face, sending him spinning to the floor.

Braden came running down the stairs, hand outstretched. "Here," he said, handing a zip tie to him. "I'll get his feet, you get his hands. Let's do this before he wakes up. Nice punch, by the way."

Heavy footsteps overhead signaled to Keegan that the Auralia Police had arrived, so he and Braden left the man on the cement floor and headed to the living room. He found Ainsley sitting beside Jane on the couch, her sister's head on her shoulder. The others were gone.

Without acknowledging the policemen, he walked directly to her and Jane. "Are you two okay?" he asked, looking them over. "I see you have bruises on your wrists, Jane."

"Thanks for coming, Zane." Braden shook his partner's hand.

Their exchange confirmed what Keegan already knew, that Braden had worked on the APD force with Zane Yates for years and trusted him with is life.

"Of course." Zane nodded

"EMT are on their way in," one of the policemen said. "You both will get checked out." The policeman cuffed the men and then headed to the front door, eyeing first Keegan, then Braden.

"These guys are okay," Zane said, vouching for them.

Still, the man's suspicious thoughts in Keegan's head gave him pause. He extended his hand. "Officer, we're friends of these women. We were coming over to visit and found the intruders. Ainsley had already subdued one." He handed over the gun, making eye contact.

The officer turned to Ainsley. "You took him down?" He nodded appreciably. "What about the other one, the one we found in the basement?"

"That was Keegan's work," she answered, wearily.

"You people are quite the team." Zane eyed Braden. "Nicely done. Sorry we didn't arrive in time to do the dirty work, but I'm glad you managed. Probably no serious injuries to you two or the intruders. Do you have any idea why they broke in? Why did they kidnapped you, miss?"

Ainsley chewed on her lower lip, weighing how much to share with the policeman. Yes, she had an idea why the DAs attacked. But how to explain her suspicions that the Irish mob, the mayor of the city, and other officials were out to destroy the Aeons, the city, and her family?

The clock on the fireplace mantel ticked by the seconds. "Umm, it came out of nowhere." She shrugged. It wasn't a lie.

Jane just looked at them, hardly able to speak.

Keegan rubbed his chin and gazed nonchalantly at Braden, who was focused intently on his partner and the officers. He suspected Braden was using his ability to nudge individuals to do what he wanted.

"Okay, I'll put that in my notes." Zane nodded again. "Ladies, sir. Braden, walk out with us, Detective?"

Braden offered a reassuring look to Ainsley and Jane as he followed the officers out, then closed the door.

Keegan sighed. "Well, that was something. Are you two truly all right?"

"It was something." Ainsley hugged her sister. "All things considered, I believe we're fine, right Jane?"

"I'm shook up. Why did those men want to know our parents' whereabouts? I didn't tell them anything. I didn't tell them where to find you, Ainsley. I don't understand. Are they with the people we've been hiding from for years?" Jane shook her head. "I thought we were safe from all that terrible stuff."

Ainsley aimed her green eyes at him, and his gut wrenched; they were full of fear. He would go to her, put his arms around her just to let her know she wasn't alone, but uncertainty kept him back. And with Jane in the room, he had to censor himself. He couldn't simply blurt out the truth about her sister's life as an Aeon. "I'm sorry that happened. At least it ended well."

Ainsley smoothed her sister's hair out of her face. "Yes, it did. The officers assured us, Jane, that the men would be investigated. Answers will be forthcoming, sweetie. If we learn they are connected with the criminals we know, we'll face that when the time comes."

"You're right." Jane peered out the window. "The officers are still talking to your friend. I didn't know he was a police detective. How fortunate for us that you called him, Keegan. Thank you, too, for your help." She walked to him and hugged him.

"I don't know. I think your sister had everything under control," he said, eyeing Ainsley.

A short rap on the front door and Braden strode in. Jane quickly gave him a hug, too, and thanked him for his part.

"I'm glad we could help," Braden said. "I'm sure everything is going to be all right. The officers just wanted to get my take on what happened. Zane is good with everything." His gaze shifted to Keegan.

Braden's thoughts invaded his head, curious if there was more to the story or if the DAs had said anything useful. Keegan kept the thoughts to himself, knowing he and the Aeons could talk later about what happened. Foremost on his mind was getting Ainsley alone. He needed to talk about the gun in her hand when he saw her in the basement, needed to see where her head was in that moment. He wanted to hold her until the incident was processed.

Vaguely aware Braden was still talking, he tore his thoughts away from Ainsley.

"They bagged the gun and will try to get fingerprints from it that they can use to identify at least one of the men," Braden continued. "I told them Ainsley had taken control by the time I arrived. They have all of your statements, but I'll keep in touch with their progress. I can keep you informed."

Ainsley pursed her lips, thoughtful. Jane gave her nudge.

"What do you think, sis? Is there anything else to discuss? I'm ready to go home. I'm not going to mention this incident to Dad and Mom, unless you think I should." Her gaze moved from her sister, to Braden, to Keegan.

Keegan walked to where Ainsley sat on the couch and touched her shoulder. "It's going to be okay. Just try to relax."

"Yeah, get some rest. I'll take Jane home, if that's all right," Braden offered. He smiled widely. "Let's not have any more action like this today. Only thoughts of fairies, puppies, and kittens."

With that, Ainsley snapped out of her introspection. She stood up, chuckling. "That sounds good to me. Thanks for the offer, Braden, but I can take her home. It will give me a chance to visit with my parents. Thank you both for helping put those guys down. I mean, not down, down, not dead." Her gaze faltered, then she looked up at Keegan. "You really helped."

"Think nothing of it." There was so much to say. He could get lost in her sorrowful eyes, and he ached to open up to her. But, not now. There was so much to consider.

"I'm going to take off." Braden pulled on his jacket. "I'll see myself out. You all take care."

The air in the room was heavy. Keegan shuffled his feet back and forth, searching for the right words. Words that would heal the trauma of the day for Ainsley and Jane. Some people were good at that, but not him.

Instead, he went to Ainsley and placed his hands on her shoulder, not knowing what his reception would be. "It's okay, at least for now." He lifted her chin. "You protected your sister very well and took care of the intruders. Good job."

She pursed her lips, standing stiffly not quite an arms-length away, her eyes downcast. "It could have gone differently if you hadn't shown up. It's all my fault."

He lifted her chin. "It is not your fault. It never has been. I think we know who keyed them into where you reside." He leveled his gaze on her, suspecting she'd carried her self-blame a long time.

"Thank you." Her eyes met his.

He didn't know if she was thanking him for showing up or for truly seeing her pain. Both were needless, and he hoped she would learn that about him soon.

CHAPTER 15

*J*ane walked into Ainsley's living room in her pajamas and sunk into one of the upholstered chairs, sighing.

"Did your shower feel good?" Relief wafted through Ainsley at the small glimmer in her sister's eyes, a good sign after the incident earlier in the day. She'd run Jane to her apartment to pick up a few things, without incident, and she was ready for chilling.

"Yes, I am feeling better. Geez! I'm still shocked at what happened." Her head dropped back and she stared absently at the ceiling.

"Let's not think about it right now, huh? Unless you want to talk about it some more." Ainsley shot her a dose of light and love. It wouldn't eliminate the ordeal but it could help Jane move on.

"No, I do not." She lifted her head to look at Ainsley. "Do you?"

Ainsley thought for a minute, did she? There were things to discuss, things that bothered her, but she'd wait to talk with the others. The Aeons were who she needed to talk with. "No, not now. How about we talk about your phone call earlier, when you wanted to tell me you are considering dropping out of college."

Jane looked at her slippered feet and pursed her lips. "Man, that seems like days ago when I called you. I'm so exhausted."

Ainsley sat forward, concerned. "We could just go to bed, visit later when you're rested. How does that sound?"

Jane gave her a tired thumbs-up, so Ainsley stood and pulled her to her feet.

"Thanks for letting me stay, sis," Jane said as they walked to the stairs. "I wouldn't have felt safe my myself, all alone in my apartment."

Ainsley wrapped her arms around her and hugged her tight. "Sleep well. I'll see you in the morning."

"You, too." Jane slowly walked upstairs to the guest bedroom while Ainsley watched.

She headed to the kitchen, started the dishwasher, lost in thought, then turned out the lights, walked upstairs past the room where Jane was sleeping for the night, her door closed, and to her bedroom. Going through the motions of her usual routine helped her detach from the fear of the day. She washed up, brushed her teeth, then climbed in bed, comforted knowing her sister was safe across the hall.

She closed her eyes, but her mind swirled, replaying what had happened. It was unthinkable that the DAs would find Jane and then use her to force Ainsley to do what, exactly? She really wanted to know what Braden would find out from interrogations.

She rolled over and pulled the blankets closer. Nerves, like static electricity, chattered at her, warning not to close her eyes, not to relax.

Alone in the face of danger on multiple fronts. That's what she was. She couldn't divulge to Jane her true identity. She had to keep that a secret from everyone. Just as she'd had to keep secrets when her family had entered witness protection. And now it seemed that was falling apart, even after such a long time. Despair threatened to drop her into a dark place.

No, she couldn't let that happen. It wasn't like she truly was alone. She had her fellow light-workers. And she wasn't helpless. She had tools to take care of herself. Centering herself, she envisioned her feet going down into the ground to anchor into the Earth. Slowly, purposefully, she breathed, fully expanding her lungs and gently releasing it. With each breath her pulse slowed incrementally, and her muscles relaxed into a steady rhythm, resting into her mattress. Her brain activity slowed to a comfortable hum, and her nerves calmed. She was light, she was love, she was peace.

The pitcher's brown eyes flashed with mischief. He grasped the softball in his glove and leaned down, staring at her.

"See if you can hit my curveball," he yelled to her.

"Telegraphing your pitch, are you?" Delight bubbled in her chest, knowing better than to fall for his bluff.

He wound up and released the ball. Her body tensed and she walloped it. Without hesitation, she ran to first with all her might.

"Safe," yelled the ref.

"Yeah, Mommy! Mommy, Mommy," cried a little voice. Ainsley spied the little girl yelling at her from the bleachers and shared a glance with her sparkling green eyes, glee written all over her little face. Keegan sitting next to her high-fived with her.

Ainsley bolted up in bed. The clock on her nightstand read five in the morning. She didn't bother to turn on the light next to her bed, it was too early and her mind was still stuck in the dream. She ran her fingers through her hair and tried to focus. Lying back against her pillow, she closed her eyes. What had she seen? It wasn't clear to her if she'd had a simple dream, a flight of imagination. Or was it a vision? She rarely received pleasant visions. Typically the glimpses of a possible future alarmed her, foretelling something dire, something to try to avoid. This glimpse was far from dreadful, it brought a smile to her heart. It felt just as real as any other vision she'd had. But how could it be?

"Mommy?" The word felt foreign on her tongue. She ran over the details of the dream, or vision, whatever it was. The little girl had red hair. It was slightly wavy. She looked to be about five years old, no older.

And Keegan. His expression looked peaceful, happy.

But seriously. She hadn't played softball since high school. Where had that come from, she wondered.

Joy swirled in her body. The dream had felt real, so fun, so positive. Now, it just puzzled her, it was so bizarre.

It couldn't be real. But why couldn't it? The future wasn't set.

Personal choices made the future fluid, subject to change.

She checked the time again. Thirty minutes had passed, and she was no closer to understanding what she'd seen. But the joy, the sense of possibilities kept her awake, eager to start the day, just to experience what would come along.

Her bedroom door creaked and opened a sliver. Jane peeked in.

"Good morning." Ainsley giggled. "What are you doing up so early."

"What's so funny?" Jane stared at her. "I didn't know if you would be awake. I woke up early and can't get back to sleep."

Ainsley skooched over and lifted the covers. "C'mon in."

Jane didn't hesitate to climb in beside her and pull up the blankets. "Umm, it's warm in here."

"Were you cold?"

"No, it just feels cozy here with you." She rolled toward Ainsley and smiled. "This is nice. Especially after yesterday."

"Why did you wake up early? Worried?"

"Some. But I slept well. Better than I have in a while." She snuggled into the blankets and rolled onto her back.

"How about we talk about what you called me about yesterday before the 'incident'?"

"What are you referring to?"

"Don't play dumb. You mentioned you're thinking about dropping out of college."

"Oh. That. I don't want to talk about it."

"You can, I—"

"Shh! No heavy conversation right now. It's too nice just to be here in the quiet part of the morning. I miss you."

"Same." Waves of pleasure and memories from before went through her, but she just let them pass through. Words weren't necessary.

"What time do you want to leave for Dad and Mom's? I'm thinking we get there in time for lunch, then we can be done with them before dinner."

"Do you have dinner plans?"

"Maybe I do, maybe I don't. I love them both, but they can be a lot."

Her face sobered. "I understand. Anything I should know about?"

"Look, I've got a lot on my plate, and I don't want to weigh down Mom and Dad with all that stuff."

"Weigh me down, please."

Jane twiddled her thumb. "Well, I'm dating someone, have been for about six months."

Heaviness weighed down on Ainsley's chest. Jane was so young and had so much life in front of her.

"He's very nice, and I really, um, care about him. He's a year older than me, so he graduated last year. He's got a good job. He, he…" She hesitated. "He wants me to move in with him."

Ainsley's heart sank. "Is that why you want to drop out of college?"

"No, he wants me to finish. It's just that, he's already living a life and I'm still waiting for life to begin. I feel so ready for all that. Him, work, family." She slid a glance over to Ainsley.

She nodded. "I understand, but I can't say I agree with quitting. You're so close to being done, graduating. That diploma will make a big difference in your earning power, your independence, your job satisfaction."

Jane punctuated the air. "Blah, blah, blah."

Ainsley had to remind herself that her sister was only just barely twenty-two. Waiting half a year was an eternity for her. "I get it. Is that what you want? To change all your plans and live with him?"

Again, Jane hesitated. Restless, she ruffled the blankets. She shook her head. "I don't know. Honestly, just between us, Mathias is making me feel pressured. But I also don't want to lose him. He really wants to meet my family."

"You love him?"

"I think so." She raised her arms. "How am I supposed to know?" She rolled to face Ainsley. "Let's talk about Keegan."

"What brought him up?"

"I saw how he looked at you yesterday. He cares about you."

That caught her off guard. Her pulse raced. "That was friendship. He was simply worried. Stop changing the subject. You know I have to say this, if Mathias loves you, he'll wait for you. We're not talking about years. But you deserve to finish your education and have time to breathe after graduation. Time to decide how you feel about him. Forever is a big commitment."

Jane leaned over and kissed her cheek. "Thanks, sis. Food for thought. Remember? I don't want to talk about anything heavy. Let's keep it light today, until we get home. I'm sure our parents will do their best to pry." She sighed. "So when should we leave?"

"How about we get up and eat a quick breakfast now? We could be ready in less than an hour."

"Perfect." Jane lay still for a few more minutes, and Ainsley couldn't help but wonder what was on her mind. But she didn't ask.

In a short time, Ainsley had started coffee brewing and showered. She could hear Jane across the hall getting dressed. She pulled on a pair of dark blue Yoga pants and a white sweater, then pulled on warm, wool socks and her black tennis shoes.

She sped downstairs and set out bowls on the kitchen island with boxes of cereal. Streaks of purple and gold in the sky announced the sun's dawning. The view from her kitchen window gave her a sense that today, all was as it should be. The Earth was doing what it always did, bringing on a new day.

Jane's footsteps could be heard on the stairway and she strode into the kitchen. "I see you have the kind of cereal I like."

"I like granola, too. Help yourself, I'll get the milk."

They sat together, munching down breakfast and downing hot coffee as the day broke.

"You make great coffee. Better than Mom's. Better than the coffee shop I frequent on campus."

"We can use my insulated mugs and take it with us."

"Yumm. I like that idea. Are you ready to go?"

"As soon as I brush my teeth."

"Me too."

Ainsley stepped outside her back door onto her patio and breathed in fresh air. Jane was right, her parents could be nosy, but she was eager to see them today.

Jane walked up beside her. "You're so lucky you have all this."

"I am. You'll have what you build, too, after college. Oh, that's right. You don't want to talk about heavy stuff this morning," she teased.

Jane pulled her arm. "Let's go!"

* * *

KEEGAN DROVE into a parking space out front from Coffee Is, keeping a close eye on Benjamin. He was doing better and staying more present, but nonetheless, he couldn't be on his own.

"Does it feel good to get the monitor off?" Keegan pointed to Benjamin's leg.

"It sure does. Boy, that was a taste of reality. I told Payson I appreciated her talking to my lawyer."

"Yeah, she's great."

They walked inside and got in the short line of people ordering their morning coffee. He waved at Skye at the back of the work area and she smiled while pouring coffee into a to-go cup. Her eyes lit up when she glanced at Benjamin.

"What can I get you," the barista asked.

"Medium, black coffee," Benjamin ordered, then stepped out of the way for Keegan.

"Do you want something to eat? You ate very little for breakfast, Benjamin."

"Okay, you twisted my arm," he said, smiling. He ordered a breakfast sandwich and a muffin.

"I'll have what he's having, but make my coffee an extra-large. Let's find a table. Someone will bring us our order." Keegan nodded to Skye, who was already loading their order onto a tray.

At a table in the corner by the window, Keegan slid in across from Benjamin, and perused the room and the outside of the shop, alert for anything ominous. He tuned his hearing to their surroundings, too. Nothing to sound any alarms, but he knew he couldn't be too careful.

"Good to see you out and about, Benjamin," Skye bubbled, and set down their order. "I miss you here at the shop."

"Hey, what about me? Aren't you glad to see me," Keegan joked.

She cuffed his head lightly. "Always, but I see you often."

Skye's face scrunched up a bit, as though she was getting a reading as she looked at Benjamin. "How are you doing? Is this guy treating you right, feeding you well?"

Benjamin gave her a wry smile. "He's all right. He can even cook, a little." He glanced around the shop. "I do miss you guys, and the food." His eyes turned wistful.

"Well, as soon as you tire of Keegan and feel up to working, please come back." She stood up. "I'll let you two eat your food now. I've got to get back to work."

"See you." Benjamin took a bite of his sandwich and swallowed hard, then sipped at his coffee. "I do miss working here. I don't know why I left, do you? And what about my classes? I had started at the university." He shook his head, looking baffled.

Keegan took a drink of his coffee. "You left both about four weeks ago, when Diane mesmerized you. You'll have to make up those hours at university. But don't sweat it right now. Your main job is to get healthy." Keegan bit into his sandwich and downed a drink of his coffee, while glancing around.

"I graduated from high school. I remember that. Is that real?" Benjamin scratched his head, and took more bites of his sandwich.

Keegan weighed his words. He didn't want to demoralize the guy, but he would at some point need to face the truth. Still, he had another plan for helping Benjamin, one that would help him in a way that no one else could. "Yes, you did. Let's not worry about those kind of details for now. Let's focus on keeping you safe and getting your life back on track."

"It seems so out of focus, I don't know what to do."

"I do. Drink your coffee, finish your sandwich. Notice your surroundings. This is a familiar place for you. Sink into that familiar feeling. Savor the memories of working here with good people."

Keegan leaned back in his chair and sipped his coffee, enjoying the ambiance of Coffee Is, and knowing that, with help, Benjamin's life would become his own.

Benjamin slowly chewed the last few bites of his sandwich and drank his coffee. He clearly took the time to breathe in the aroma, and savor the flavor of his food and drink. Keegan gave him space to open his senses and ground himself in what he knew.

Finally, the light in Benjamin's blue eyes came back, and that registered in Keegan's center.

"You're right, this place is good for me. It feels familiar and comforting. Remembering it and the people here brings back reassuring feelings. I don't feel so scattered and lost."

"Good. I have one more thing I want you to do now. I don't think you know Claire Eve."

"No, the name doesn't sound familiar. Who is she?"

"She's someone the Aeons turn to when we have emotional challenges. She's a really good counselor and super good listener. She has an office above this coffee shop. I'm going to take you up to see her. I believe she'll be able to help you get more in touch with what you've been through and what you're confronting as a new Aeon. What do you think?"

Benjamin sat quietly for a few seconds, and Keegan could hear he was thinking but he tuned out. Wind gusts sent trails of fall leaves raining down outside the windows. The beauty of it exhilarated him.

"I appreciate the thought, Keegan. I haven't ever talked to a counselor before, but I'm willing to give it a try if you think it will help me."

"I do. Whenever you're ready we can go, but there's no hurry." The more Benjamin could settle into his own life the faster he'd be stronger and more resilient against Diane's intrusion.

They sat quietly, time passing gently. Conversations around them subdued the chatter in Keegan's mind, affording him peace.

"Okay, I'm ready," Benjamin piped up, interest brightening his face.

"All right, let's head up."

He led Benjamin up the interior staircase and walked into Claire Eve's office. Sunlight slanted against the warm, wooden floors from a large window in the waiting room. Plump chairs and a couch lined the square room, all familiar to Keegan.

Claire Eve walked into the room before they could sit. "Hi Keegan," she said, extending her hand. "And you must be Benjamin. I'm Claire Eve."

"Nice to meet you." Benjamin excepted her hand shake. "Aren't you called Dr. Eve?"

"No, I'm not a medical doctor, I'm a certified counselor and my first name is Claire Eve. My last name is Kelly." She turned to Keegan. "Are you going to wait?"

"No. Benjamin, you have my number. Text me when you're ready. I won't be far away."

"I'll take good care of him. He'll be safe with me." She nodded at Keegan and gave an assuring glance to Benjamin. "Come on in my office and get comfortable."

Keegan ran down the stairs and out to his vehicle, knowing he was leaving Benjamin in good hands. Walking past his SUV, he strode down the sidewalk of Old Town, his senses tuned to his surroundings. The shops that lined the area streets harkened back to another era in their quaint facades and outstanding architecture. Large windows dressed with attention-grabbing scenes promoted a casual pace and window shopping. A smile broke out on his face, taking in the variety of ways shop owners expressed their values in their work.

He strode up to Fancy This, admiring the window display of interesting antique furniture and knick knacks. He smiled to himself, but didn't enter, knowing Ainsley was on a day-trip.

He didn't dilly-dally. He had a destination, and a goal of gathering useful information about the people behind the Stillwell Project and their intentions for Auralia. It wasn't information he could simply pluck from the sky; he had to dig, just as he did when he worked in the field as a recovery agent, before he bought his bond company.

He breathed in the autumn air, savoring his surroundings from his feet on the ground to scents of nature. Until this moment, he hadn't realized he missed field work, and he had every intention of doing it well, even if he were a bit rusty.

Sounds of men working floated to him and he spied them in the vicinity of the casino construction site, surveying an open field on the edge of Old Town. Shivers ran through him as he approached, suggesting nearby DAs. Quickly, he ducked around the corner of a nearby building and crouched down, focusing on his psychic hearing.

The men relayed measurements of the property boundaries and levels to a man who sounded like the engineer.

"This is what our parcel looks like," the engineer said. "So let's make sure we map out all the features of this property."

"Of course," said another voice. "This isn't our first rodeo, dude."

"I just don't want to have any issues." Keegan heard the engineer's mind spin with fear and tension, and it made sense to him. "Make sure we set out the layout for the drainage work today."

"Aye, aye, Captain," another guy teased. "I'm going down the hill toward the river."

Another worker's thoughts were prickly to Keegan, wanting to get the work done before the boss arrived. Urgency drove his thoughts.

Keegan's legs cramped a bit, and he sent his gaze in search of a better spot from which to listen without being detected. He spotted a yellow safety helmet and vest in the bed of a pick-up truck close by, and crept up behind it, grabbed both items, and stood erect. Within his view, he saw five men working on the site, all surveyors it appeared, except for the one in charge, the engineer he deduced. He tuned into their energy, to get a feel for their perspective. Three were buzzing with the DA vibe, but two came across as simply nervous. He waited silently, perched on edge for anything revealing.

"I've got the control point set," a man called out.

"Are you sure it's about sixty feet from the road?" responded the engineer. "It has to be."

"I did the survey, so, there's no reason to question me," the man retorted. "I don't give a rat's ass what the rules demand." The man muttered under his breath, but Keegan heard him swear and deride the guidelines. He knew the guy was a problem.

Nonchalantly, he strode over to the work trailer and climbed the stairs inside. He went straight to a desk loaded with project books and documents alongside a computer with a Computer Aided Tolerance program open on the screen. He started the CAT, trying to ascertain all he could about construction details, but he was no engineer.

He bent over the pile of documents and flipped through them. Permits, plans, communications, and names, all telling a story, one that the Aeons would be interested in. He snapped pictures of documents as fast as he could, sifting through them, then pulled together the pile the way it had been when he entered.

His skin prickled, alerting him to approaching workers.

"I'm not convinced the drainage specs are correct," one worker said.

"Well, we know what has to be done, so just do it. Our job is to make sure this project gets done and on time," said another, his voice harsh, his vibration dizzying.

"I know, I know. Don't you think the engineer will notice the discrepancies?"

"Don't worry about that. I told you," he warned. "The only one we need to be accountable to is the boss."

Steps up the stairs to the trailer alerted Keegan he was in the wrong spot at the wrong time. He stepped swiftly into a tiny bathroom and shut the door just as the two men he'd heard opened the outside door and walked in.

"Boy, am I ready to sit down and have a drink," said one.

Shifty laughter broke out between the two and Keegan could hear rummaging.

"I assume you're not talking about coffee," the scary one said. "You get the glasses, I'll pour."

Keegan worried his lip, forming his plan. His search for information was done for today. Now he had to get out of the trailer without getting killed. It sounded like the men were settling in for a long break, and either they would be inside the trailer for a while or the engineer would be coming in, too, to get them back to work.

He turned on a faucet for about twenty seconds.

"You hear that?"

"Yeah. Hey," yelled the other man. "Who's in here?" The door handle rattled. "Come out of there."

Keegan pulled back his shoulders and opened the door. "Hey, guys. What's up?"

"What are you doing in here?" The biggest of the two took a step toward him.

"You know, I had to drain the main. You got a problem with that?" Keegan narrowed his eyes and emanated peace and happiness toward the two.

"I know who you are," said one of them, peering at him.

"I doubt that, but go ahead. Tell me who I am." Keegan stood solid and stern, unafraid of his odds.

"You're an inspector. We weren't expecting you until next week."

"Well, I'm here today. I've been watching your work and going over permits and data. I'll be giving the engineer on this site my report when I get back to the office and process the information." Without moving, he stared down the men. The smaller one looked away, as though he wanted nothing to do with the present situation. The other one glared as seconds passed.

"Step aside," Keegan demanded, tensed for a fight, but strengthening the flow of peace.

The dangerous DA, throbbing with darkness, moved out of way and dropped into a desk chair to take a sip of his vodka, without a word. But he kept his eye trained on Keegan.

Keegan gave him a side-glance and nodded at the other man, then stepped outside and headed toward Coffee Is, awareness prickling his back that he wasn't safe yet. He slipped around the corner where he'd confiscated the vest and helmet and dropped them back in the truck. As he put the site behind him, the easier he breathed.

Back in the main part of Old Town, he shook off the heavy, slimy feeling he'd picked up from the DAs. Hope stirred inside him that his contact with them and the energy he'd sent their way would support their choices toward a better life.

One could always hope.

CHAPTER 16

The drive to Ronen, the town where her parents lived, was not Ainsley's most favorite drive. Just short of two hours away from her house, it was long and boring, with nothing but fields of corn and soybeans to look at, with the occasional combine bringing in a late harvest. Still, she didn't mind. Sometimes boredom and bucolic were welcome changes from the thoughts that typically chatted on and on in her mind.

"Did you tell Dad and Mom we were coming? They don't know I missed class yesterday, thanks to the kidnappers." Jane scrunched up her face.

Her voice was flat. Ainsley's eyes squeezed, suspecting her sister was numb. She wished she could talk freely about her life as an Aeon. Anything she would say to reassure her, though, might seem dire right now. But they wouldn't stay that way. Not if she and her fellow lightworkers had anything to do with it. Which they would.

"No, I thought I'd surprise them. As for missing class, that's your business." She grimaced. "Do you think I should have called? Should I call? Should you?"

"No, we're not far from there. They'll be happy to see you." Jane bowed her head. "I don't know if I will be able to keep it together when I see them. I might start crying again, on account of what happened."

"Don't worry about it. We're going to talk, all of us."

"Wow, I hope they don't take me out of college."

Ainsley smiled to herself. It had been less than a day since her sister had mentioned dropping out of college and already she thought differently? "No, they won't. You're well into your last year." She reached over the console between the front seats and patted her sister's knee. "Parents are always worried about their kids. But we have to live our lives, despite their fears."

"I so agree," Jane said, with zeal.

That zeal made Ainsley question if Jane was feeling pressured by her parents in some way; if she was struggling with more than average young adult frustration.

"Anything you want to talk about?"

"No, well, they want me to follow in their footsteps. You know, become an accountant like them and join the family business." She gave a forced laugh. "I'm their last hope."

"Right. I didn't fulfill their dream. I took a different path. And you can, too."

"It's my last year of college, remember. I can't switch majors now. Besides, it would break their hearts." Her voice dropped off.

"Don't settle for someone else's dream. Don't do that to yourself. It's not too late. Yes, it would take you longer if you changed, but Jane, you've got the rest of your life. I think they'd understand."

"I don't."

"They would." Ainsley sat quietly, letting Jane mull over her thoughts. The scenery, while boring, could also be calming, and she drank it in. Her sister had the right to make her own choices, but it was so hard for her to watch her make a huge mistake.

The silence was rich with unsaid words and unexpressed emotions. She glanced at her sister and noticed creases in her brows.

Jane sighed. "I'm getting nervous," she whispered.

"Why? It's just Mom and Dad. Nothing to be worried about."

"There is so much pressure to do certain things." Jane wrung her hands.

"All you have to know it's what's right for you. Filter out the other stuff."

"That's not a simple thing to do." Jane frowned again.

"I know, but you can find your way." Ainsley wanted to refrain from adding to Jane's pressure, but this conversation was important. She was loathe to make the final turn onto her parent's road out in the country. "How about I keep driving and we continue talking? Dad and Mom will still be surprised no matter when we arrive."

"Thanks, sis, but I just want to get there. I'm tired of riding." She sat quietly again, and Ainsley let her.

"Okay. I understand."

Suddenly Jane twisted to face her. "I appreciate your thoughts. I really do. I know you think you're unavailable to me often, but I don't feel that way. I can always reach you when I need you and you are my rock, sis." She shot Ainsley a sweet smile.

"You are so beautiful, inside and out, Jane."

"I know," she beamed.

"You goof. Next turn, Dad and Mom's."

Ainsley parked in the driveway, hoping her parents were home and realizing she should have called ahead. She'd just turned off the car when her mom came running out.

"Ainsley, I wasn't expecting you." Theo, her mom, nearly knocked Ainsley over and wrapped her in a hug. "It's so good to see you." She eyed Jane. "What are you doing here? Don't you have class today?"

"Not today, Mom." She headed up the walk and into the house, her mom's arms circling her waist.

A familiar scent wafted to Ainsley's nose. A smile broke out. "It smells like home."

"It's so good to have you both here. Can you stay for lunch?" Her mom walked through the living room to the kitchen and into the family room where her dad, Asa, was sitting at his desk, his back to them.

She tiptoed up behind him and wrapped her arms around his neck before he noticed their entrance. "Hi, Dad. What are you working on?"

"Oh, you startled me. I've got my nose stuck in books and didn't hear you come in. Hi honey, so good to see you. You, too, Jane."

"Jane and I had dinner together last night and we just decided to drive out here this morning."

Her mom gave her a stern look. "It's been quite a while since you've made that drive, Ainsley. I'm glad you remembered the way."

"Mom, don't nag Ainsley. She's here now, isn't she?" Jane went to the fridge and peered inside. "I'm getting hungry. We had breakfast early."

Her dad chuckled. "Help yourself to whatever you like. Would you want me to make my famous grilled cheese and tomato bisque for lunch?"

"Oo, yum." Jane rubbed her stomach, then grabbed a stick of string cheese and a bottle of water. "Yes, Dad, please."

"Sounds good to me," Ainsley added.

"Let's sit for a while and chat." Her mom settled into the couch and patted the spot beside her. "How was your drive, girls?"

"Don't ask," Jane joked.

"What do you mean, dear?" Her father knitted his brow.

"Driving through farm fields is not the most exciting thing to experience." Jane punctuated her sentence with a grin.

"Oh, you're joking." He chuckled. "I like it out here in the middle of nowhere. It's peaceful."

"Oh, Dad, I know you do." She rested her head against his shoulder.

"How's school going, Jane?"

"Mom, don't worry about my classes. I'm doing just fine." She lowered her gaze. "Did I tell you I'm taking an art class?"

"Whatever for?" Her mother laughed. "Tell us about your new boyfriend, Jane. I'm eager to learn all about him."

"Don't change the subject, Mom. I'm taking an art class because I like doing art. I like all kinds of art. This class is a survey of visual arts. I'm doing well."

Her mother shared a glance with Asa. He gave a quick shake of his head.

"I'd like to see your work, dear. Tell us when you have a show," he suggested.

"I will." Jane crossed her arms over her chest and nodded.

The conversation continued for a while, and Ainsley sat back and listened to Jane share her thoughts primarily on drawing and painting.

Her mother shook her head. "I never knew you had an interest in that sort of thing, much less talent." She gave Jane a pointed look. "Just don't let it interfere in your studies."

"Don't worry, Mom, I can manage." Jane's voice gave Ainsley a smile in her heart. It was firm, but gentle.

Theo slapped her knees. "How about lunch?"

"Yes, that sounds good, Mom." Jane walked directly to the kitchen and stood at the counter.

Her mother pulled pans from the cupboard while her dad gathered ingredients from the fridge. Twenty minutes passed with small talk, catching up, and sounds of her dad cooking up his specialty. It warmed her heart to watch her family interact in their family way.

Chewing her sandwich and spooning her soup as her family sat around the table in the dining room, Ainsley waited for the right opening to bring up difficult topics from the past. Did she really need to? What was the point? Was it worth the risk of conflict?

Then she stared at Jane, watching her animated expression as she chatted with her parents. Eight years younger than her, Jane had been only four when the family had gone into Witness Protection. She probably didn't have memories of their life before. She had no memories of the average, ordinary, safe life they'd enjoyed, before.

Ainsley's resolve sharpened. Yes, she had to be brave, if for no other reason than Jane deserved that much. The conversation needed to give her space with their parents to discuss what was in her heart.

Still, she waited. As they finished eating, she rose and gathered dirty dishes and carried them to the kitchen, where she loaded the dishwasher, half-listening to the nearby, light-hearted chatter.

Chairs moved out from the table across the wooden floor.

"Hey Ainsley, come join us in the living room," her mother called.

Ainsley froze, a vision taking over. She saw a dark gray SUV driving fast down the same road they'd traveled to get to the house and she saw two men inside.

"How far away did you say this house is? It feels like we've been on the road forever."

The man driving the vehicle pointed. "It's straight ahead, just a few more miles. Cool your jets, man."

"I'm just excited to get there and get this business taken care of. These bums have been a thorn in boss's side for too long."

"Yeah, I'm eager too."

Ainsley shivered, as the two men laughed. Malicious intent vibrated darkly all around them. She knew what their intentions were and she knew they were close.

First, she checked her phone. Sure enough, she'd gotten an alert. She sprang into action and raced into the living room.

"We're blown," she hollered. "We have to get out of here, now."

"What?" Jane jumped off the couch, her eyes wide. "What's going on?"

Her mother and father stood stiffly, frozen like scared rabbits, knowing what was happening without being told.

"C'mon, we have to move. Men we don't want to meet up with will be here in minutes. Get in my car. Now!" she yelled.

"What shall we take?" her mom asked. "I'm grabbing my purse. Should I get food and clothes?"

"All you need is your coat, Theo." Her father's voice was kind but stern. He brought her mom her jacket and helped her into it. He took her hand and Jane's, and walked outside.

Her pulse racing, Ainsley ran out to her truck and started the engine, as they climbed in to the king cab. With the last door closed, she tore out the driveway without hesitating for a direction at the road, she just turned and gunned it.

Escape from imminent danger had been practiced over and over as a regular activity in her childhood. When a day came that agents came to their door, they'd grabbed their go bags and exited their home as fast as they could, no questions asked except for, Where are we going? But the destination had always been the same: one of their safe houses. When the FBI had told them it was safe to relocate permanently, her parents had thought ahead and purchased a safe house close to their new home to make it an option in case danger returned. When an enemy is a criminal organization, you think things like that. So that's where she headed to now.

It had never gotten easy to uproot all the times with the threat of danger on their heels, and the trauma of those times haunted her still. It probably did for Jane, too. Her stomach clenched, wishing beyond wishes that she could have prevented it all from happening again.

"We're going to be okay. We made it out in time, I think." Ainsley stopped chewing on her lower lip.

"Why do you think someone is coming for us," Jane asked.

"Yes, why, Ainsley?" her mom turned to her dad. "Why didn't we ask this question before we left? What's going on?"

"Now, now," Asa said, shaking his head. "I'm certain Ainsley has her reasons." His head pivoted to peer out the back window. "I don't see anyone following us."

"What does that mean?" Jane's voice wobbled.

"I'm sorry. I didn't have time to waste telling you, but I got a notice from an agent that the agency had noticed suspicious behavior near your house. I can't give you an explanation." Though she'd told them of her Aeon identity long ago, she knew better than to bring it up again and divulge her ability, but she'd told them the truth. Anything more would only lead to more questions on a topic long set aside.

"Well, okay, now we know." Her dad squeezed her shoulder. "What did the agent tell us to do?"

Hmm, she thought, anxiety creeping up her spine. Dark energy vibrated harshly in her body, telling her to get to safety asap. She didn't know what to do, and yet she had to appear to have a plan. Geez!

"We can go to a public place for the moment." Her eyes vigilant on the rear-view mirror, Ainsley grasped at straws. "Jane, look up nearby restaurants on your phone."

"There's a coffee shop two miles away. Will that do?" Jane bit at her nails, her eyes darting from her phone to Ainsley and back again.

"I'll make it work." She was already driving beyond the speed limit. But a speeding ticket might be just what they needed. Could she be so lucky?

She shook her head, knowing she had to make her own luck, knowing no one was coming to rescue them, there wasn't time to wait. It was up to her.

She knew the way like the back of her hand, and finally, she turned sharply onto a side road lined with tall trees and fields of lanky weeds blowing in the breeze.

"No, you're taking a wrong turn," Jane cried out. "The coffee shop is back on the main road."

"I know, but we can't do the expected. We don't know who to trust." Less than a mile down the road, with a sharp twist of the steering wheel, Ainsley wheeled into the modest house sitting at the back of a large unkempt lawn. She pulled behind the house to hide the truck, keeping a watchful eye on the surroundings and attuning to energy in the near area. So far so good. She wondered how long her family would let her be in charge. "Okay, let's get inside."

Her dad pulled a key from his pocket and unlocked the back door. It had to be pushed hard to open, but it gave way. Ainsley led the way inside, cautiously, slowly.

"We haven't been here in a while." Her father eyed cobwebs hanging in an archway into another room.

"It's kind of sad." Jane explored beyond the main room, opening doors down a hallway and looking inside each room. "I think it's kind of creepy here."

Her mom flipped on a light switch and the dining room lit up. "We have electricity." She moved back into the kitchen and turned on the faucet. And we have water. We're okay."

"It's cold in here," Jane muttered. "I never liked it here. How long do we have to stay here?"

"I don't know. I'm working on that." She tuned inside, intentionally seeking an image of the whereabouts of the DAs who were pursuing them. Immediately she saw the same gray SUV she'd seen in her mind's eye before. It drove fast, speeding through a small town, passing apartments, a church, restaurants. And a small coffee shop on the main drag. Relief sifted through her. But how to tell her family she knew all was well and they were safe here? Worse, how could she be certain the danger wouldn't return? How had the DAs found them in the first place? They'd been schooled so well in being observant, vigilant, careful with who they trusted.

"I'm going to check the furnace," her dad offered, and disappeared to the utility room.

Her mother dragged out a bucket from a cupboard. "Let's all pitch in to clean up this place." She found a sponge and some cleaning supplies, then turned on the faucet to fill the bucket. "Let's get busy. The sooner we clean, the more comfortable we can get."

Ainsley grabbed a broom and began knocking down cobwebs. Her father found another one and went about sweeping the floors while her mother wiped off counters and cupboards.

But Jane objected. "This is not how I planned to spend my day. I have to get back to school."

Ainsley paused. "It's safer here, Jane. I'm hoping this isn't a long stay. But we have to take it in stride."

"Yeah," Jane muttered.

"Someone is driving up to this house." Her dad was peeking out the window through dilapidated blinds. "Should we hide?"

"Yes," Jane said, her voice high and scared. She ran to the kitchen and shoved a rug to the side, ready to pull up a floor trap door, the same they'd installed years ago as a way to hide in the basement.

Ainsley still was feeling into the energy around her and it didn't feel invaded, it felt supported, full of light. "No, we don't need to. Jane, it's okay." She ran out back just in time to see Keegan's SUV drive around and pull to a stop with Benjamin in the passenger seat.

Her heart leapt at the sight of Keegan's friendly face.

"Ainsley, are you all right?" he shouted, jumping out and running to her. "I heard the DAs coming after you and your family. Are your sister and parents inside?" He searched her eyes. "I came as soon as I could. I hoped you were here. I had to bring Benjamin, but I'll take care of him."

"They're fine. So am I." All of her reached out to him energetically. She couldn't hold it back, and she felt his energy respond. "Thank you for coming."

He came at her, wrapping her in his warmth and nuzzling her neck just below her ear. "I'm sorry it took so long. I was afraid I'd be too late."

She continued to lean against his shoulder. "No, no, you were right on time. I took care of everything. I didn't know if I could but I did. The last vision I had indicated the danger had driven by us. I was trying to determine what to do next." Tears, unbeckoned, filled her eyes.

"You're a strong, resilient woman, but you don't have to go it alone. I'm here. I want you to know that. You haven't always had back-up. I know that. But things have changed. You have support, willing, meaningful support."

"Who is this man, Ainsley?" Her mother stood in the back doorway, her stern tone loud and clear. "How did he know where to find us? And who is that young man," she asked, pointing to Benjamin."

She stepped away from Keegan a few steps, a little shaken by his words challenging her beliefs from way back to twelve years old.

"This is a good friend, Keegan Barnes and that is Benjamin Clover. He's okay. Keegan these are my parents, Theo and Asa Durham."

Her dad put out his hand to Keegan and the two grasped hands for a quick handshake. "I don't know what your involvement in all this is, Keegan, but I see my daughter trusts you. Has she apprised you of our situation?"

"Dad, just to make everything clear, Keegan is a very good friend and knows about my past with Witness Protection. We've been working together with some other friends to determine who is, I mean, was, responsible for the threat to our safety. To learn if anyone new is after us."

Her dad looked over Keegan warily, and Ainsley had to stifle a chuckle. He knew nothing of what she was sharing or that Keegan had put his life on the line to help them out, but still her father was suspicious of an unknown man popping into their lives. He was ever the father, and that warmed her heart for him.

Her mother cleared her throat and glared at Keegan. "Can we move past the introductions and history lessons?" She shoved her hands down onto her hips and took a stance. "This isn't our first rodeo. We know what we're hiding from, and I for one am eager to ensure our safety."

Jane scoffed. "Mom, why are you always so melodramatic? Keegan and Ainsley are simply letting us know he's someone we can trust. Let's give him a minute. Let's go inside. Can that guy come inside, too?" she asked, peering at Benjamin climbing out of the vehicle.

"Let's go," Ainsley said, and they walked in the house.

"I'm sorry if I come across brash," her mother spouted as they took seats in the living room. "I could be more gracious if I were safe somewhere, now."

"Of course, Mrs. Durham. I want that, too," Keegan said. "Is this not your safe house?" He shot a bewildered glance at Ainsley.

Her mom sighed heavily. "Yes, it is. I guess I'm a little unnerved. I thought all this was behind us. We live with danger at the back of our minds, but I'm just as afraid today as the last time we had to live here, years ago." Tears filled her eyes. "Do you remember those times, Jane? You were so young."

"I do, but not well. I get the shakes, though, thinking about it." Jane wrapped her arms around herself.

"Okay, everybody take a big breath. We're all together, this is a safe place, and we have help." She nodded to Keegan. Benjamin just smiled.

"Does the FBI know we're here?" Ainsley's dad started pacing.

"I'll take care of that," Keegan offered, sharing a brief glance with Ainsley.

Her muscles relaxed into his support, knowing she could trust him. He knew not to contact the agency yet. And they both understood that no one outside the Aeons could be trusted for now.

CHAPTER 17

$\mathcal{K}$eegan rolled over on the couch in the living room and startled awake. He sat up abruptly, surveying his surroundings. Reality settled in as he remembered the happenings of the day before and that he was waking up in the Durham's safe house. He yawned and scrubbed his head, threw off the blankets he'd slept under, and quietly walked past sleeping Benjamin, curled up in a sleeping bag on the floor, on his way into the kitchen. Opening cupboards, their emptiness told him he better go out for food. The only thing he could find was cans of beans and packages of beef jerky. The prospects in the refrigerator and freezer were just as bleak: butter and bottles of water. The freezer had only ice cubes and a bag of frozen corn.

Quickly, he grabbed a pen from his truck and scribbled a note: Gone to get breakfast and coffee. Be back ASAP.

Speeding down the road to the nearby town, reluctance burned in Keegan's gut. He hated to leave the family alone, even though he knew Ainsley could manage without him. As he drove into the town outcropping, he noticed a bin outside a used clothing store and was tempted to grab some clothes but didn't follow the urge. He couldn't take time for himself at this point and he didn't know anyone else's size.

His attention tuned to every passing vehicle and the energy he encountered, his insides churning with adrenaline. When he spotted a breakfast joint, he pulled into the parking lot and strode inside.

"Do you do take-out?" he asked the first worker he spotted.

"Yes, have a seat, sir, and I'll take your order." The young waitress smiled and pulled a pad from her pocket. "What will you have?"

"Six orders of scrambled eggs, milk and orange juice, and six black coffees," he spilled out. "Oh, and can you give me some cream and a hand-full of sugers?"

"Can do. That will be ready in a few minutes."

"Umm, an extra tip if you make that fast," he added. It was worth a try.

She gave him a thumbs-up, and swirled away.

Keegan thrummed his fingers on the table, and swept his gaze around the diner and out to the surrounding area. He tuned out the noise in the room and focused on what he could pick up outside. When he didn't hear anything alarming, he called in the troops.

Hey all, some dangerous people have discovered where Ainsley's family lives. You know the story. They've moved to a safe place and I'm with them for now. We're all fine, but we could use back-up. I don't think it would be good for them to see you all come charging in to the rescue. Just send us some good vibes and use your abilities and skills in a way you see fit.

It didn't take long before responses lit up his phone, assuring him the group would be there energetically, supporting the family's safety. He couldn't suppress the grin that pulled up the corners of his mouth.

A little while later, the waitress arrived, a big bag in one hand a drink holder in the other. "You look happier. Can you manage this all by yourself?"

"I can get it." He paid and handed over an extra tip. "I appreciate your fast service."

Pulling out, he knew he should pick up some groceries at the little convenient mart he spotted, but there were things to discuss before he invested in a bunch of food, so he headed out of town.

Thoughts circled in his brain, as he tried to settle on a plan to keep Ainsley and her family safe, but primarily get them back to their lives. Too many unknowns could factor into the equation. Who was in charge of the organized crime organization taking revenge? Was Diane behind this attack on them? How could his work exert more of an impact for good?

His cell phone rang and he answered it with his hands-free app. "Hi Ricki, what's up?"

"Hey, your dad is here at the office." Her voice was low. "He needs to speak with you. When are you coming in?"

"Something has come up and I'm busy right now. Just tell him that, okay?"

"I did. He's going to wait here for you, so…"

"Sorry about that. Tell him to call me. I'll try to get him out of your hair. I'll be out touch for a minute. I'll check back in when I can."

"Thanks, boss." Relief lightened her voice. "Will do."

He blew out a long breath and refocused his thinking on solving the problems facing Ainsley. And her family. It wasn't like the Aeons were superheroes. Their abilities were limited, but together they could influence the outcome and quality of life for her if they could affect change in the path forward.

It was a challenge to go deep with the problem while awaiting a call from his father, so he put that possibility on the back burner. Instead of waiting for input from the others, he needed to step up and get things covered on his own, in partnership with Ainsley, of course. The realization coursed through him, strengthening his intentions. They could do this. And maybe through the process of securing the family's safety and quality of life, Benjamin could be involved and learn more about his own path.

His phone rang again. Seeing it was his dad, he fought back anger. "Dad."

"Son. Your secretary told me to call you."

Keegan didn't mince any words. "Why did you drop by my office?"

"I need to talk with you. I thought I could catch you there. I hardly see you anymore."

Without trying, his father's thoughts entered his head. I hope he goes for this. I really need him to help me out.

Keegan cleared his throat. "I'm working, Dad. What do you need?"

"I need to see you."

"Well, I'm not going to be in the office today. I'm working. Can't we talk right now?" Less than a mile from the safe house, he wanted to get *this* over with.

"Okay, screw it. Here it goes." His dad coughed. "I bought your business loan from the bank."

"What? Why did you do that? How did you do that?" If it were possible, he would have reached through the phone and grabbed his dad by the collar.

"I did it last year because I wanted to—"

"Own me? Control me?" Keegan turned off the road, dust flying up around his vehicle, so angry he had to stop. Suddenly, he got suspicious, defensive. "Where are you?"

His dad was silent.

He picked up sounds from the background: a train whistle in the distance, heavy traffic, music piped from shops, he deduced. He must be in the city, near or in the downtown.

"Don't get all riled up. I thought I could help you out, maybe take care of your debt, you know, so you'd be free of it. I have a buddy who works at that bank. He made it happen for me."

"Thought?" Keegan gritted his teeth. "You thought? You had a buddy?"

"Don't worry, I've been covering your payments, but, well, I've gotten into some trouble. I'm going need that paid in full. And if you choose to continue with disloyalty, you'll be forcing me to bring in your brother in on the project I'm working on."

Keegan could imagine his dad getting into trouble, probably with gambling debts. "Disloyalty? You mean you're still demanding I keep quiet about your affair and your criminal activity. I'll have you know I've never said a word to anyone. Not that it's right not to." Seething, he could hardly take in what his dad was telling him. How could he not have known how far his father would go to get back at him for 'disloyalty,' for distancing from him? And his father knew just how to twist his arm. He would never allow Jayce's life to be ruined further. "When?"

"Yesterday. And I want it in cash."

CHAPTER 18

*A*insley sat in the kitchen, holding the note she'd found from Keegan. She couldn't do anything but stare at it. It wasn't that her parents had neglected her. They'd been loving. And it wasn't that the group of Aeons hadn't made her feel accepted and seen for who she really was. She'd known Keegan well as a fellow Aeon and appreciated his unique skills and abilities, but he frequently stood at the perimeter of interaction. Throw him a soccer ball and he'd jump into the game and invite the neighborhood. But he was a thinker and a straight-talker. He wasn't shy, just thoughtful, as in always going deeper.

But coming to help her and her family during this threatening time and going the distance to make sure their needs were addressed touched her heart in a way she'd never expected nor experienced before. It threw her. She didn't know if she could trust the gesture to be genuine and without strings, or if she should be on guard.

So she was just numb.

Stirrings from her parents came from down the hall. She stared out the kitchen window into the backyard. A layer of leaves lay on the lawn and needed to be mulched. Funny she'd not given the house much thought over the years and it seemed like her parents hadn't tended to it either. But there was a time when this place had been their refuge for months. Until they'd been given the okay that they were no longer in danger. The man her father testified had been found guilty and was going to prison for life. But the authorities had been wrong, apparently. The man her father had put in prison wasn't a threat, but his criminal organization was still after them. Maybe they simply renewed their revenge or maybe they were being threatened by another mob and therefore needing to illustrate their strength. It was only conjecture. She didn't know, but the thought prompted determination to harden in her bones. This would be the last time they'd run and hide.

A warm vibration began humming in her body, informing her an Aeon was nearby. Slowly, she stood and walked outside, braced for the refreshing, autumn air. Keegan pulled up and parked, giving her a quick wink. She strode to the passenger side of his SUV as he ran around to that side and opened the door.

"Hey Ainsley. I took longer than I'd expected, but breakfast is here." He leaned over the seat to retrieve it.

"Here, let me help." She reached out for him to pass over a bag and his hand brushed hers. It sent pleasant sparks up her arm, and she paused for a split second. She'd been avoiding any kind of close relationship for so long, but something inside her responded to his touch anyway. "Got it. I smell something yummy."

"I hope it's a breakfast you all will enjoy. I didn't want to take time to get supplies and more food." He cocked his head. "Or maybe I was being optimistic."

His mischievous smile relaxed her anxiety. She walked beside him through the leaves and into the house. Despite the danger all around, she felt a sense of peace and calm. His optimism was contagious.

Inside, they were greeted with enthusiasm and smiles. They all grabbed a seat at the table and dug into the breakfast.

"This is great coffee." Her father beamed. "This was really thoughtful of you, Keegan."

"Yup, Delish!" Jane shoved a forkful of eggs in her mouth.

It did Ainsley's heart good to see her family's happiness, even if just for a moment. How long will it last? She frowned, unable to prevent the niggling thought stabbing her heart.

"Ainsley, snap out of it." Jane snapped her fingers.

Startled, Ainsley stared back at her sister, her introspection broken. "Sorry, I didn't hear you."

"I asked you if we could go to shopping for supplies. We came here with nothing."

"No, it's not safe for you to leave the house."

"Could we at least make a run home? We need things. I need things." Jane's expression drooped. "I need my shampoo, hair dryer, laptop. And food. What are we going to cook?

"I'll go. First Ainsley and I need to make a plan," Keegan said. "You can't stay here indefinitely."

"That's right." Desperation and frustration drained her patience. But Jane was not wrong. "The plan ahead needs to include a way to get you back to normal. I just need a little time to strategize." The situation was challenging but not dire. She knew that because she'd checked. I admit, there's not much here in the way of supplies, but we'll work it out." Her temper flared. The life and death circumstances they faced made thinking of shampoo and laptops trivial.

"You're right. You're always right," Jane pouted.

"Ainsley and Keegan are protecting us." Her mother scowled at Jane. "Let's have a little perspective."

Jane stomped out of the dining room into her room and slammed the door shut. It hurt Ainsley's heart to see her upset. The situation was bad enough without them turning on each other. She held strong to the stream of love she was directing to her family in hopes it would alleviate Jane's fears.

The room got quiet. Ainsley grounded herself and sent peace and acceptance to Jane and her parents, and to Benjamin. He could use a little help, too, considering how quiet he remained.

Softly, he spoke up all of a sudden. "I don't want to intrude." He cleared his throat. "Jane is worried about missing her classes. She doesn't want to get behind. I know it may seem irrelevant to need her laptop in light of the surrounding danger. But she could do her schoolwork if she could use a computer. Right? A little bit of normalcy wouldn't hurt, would it?"

Ainsley stared at Benjamin. "I hadn't thought of that. I guess I'm hoping we're not left here emptyhanded for very long."

"I'll go talk to her," her mom offered.

"No, I will. This is a very scary predicament. I don't blame Jane for being upset."

She wiped her mouth with her napkin and headed to Jane's room, knocking lightly on the door. Waiting for a response, she heard Jane talking, and opened the door. "You're on the phone?"

Jane covered the phone. "Quiet. I'm talking with Mathias. Don't say anything to Dad and Mom, or—"

"Hang up.

"What?"

"Hang up now. Tell him you have to go." Her heart pounded erratically. How could Jane be so reckless?

"Mathias, I have to go. I'm sorry. I'll call you later."

Ainsley stared at her, unbelieving. She tried to suppress fear and anger. "I didn't mean to jump all over you, Jane. I had a reaction. You haven't known Mathias long enough to know everything about him. We don't know who we can trust right now."

Jane popped to her feet. "Are you saying Mathias might hurt us? How could say that. You don't even know him."

"Exactly. I don't know him."

"Well I do. I trust him." Her eyes flashed angrily. "You have no right to judge him. I don't need your permission to talk to him."

Ainsley's heart went out to her. Jane wanted things to be normal so badly, she wasn't using good sense. She breathed in deeply and relaxed her shoulders, sending patience and understanding to her poor, confused sister. "I know this is hard. I wish I could make it easier. It's important for now that we keep ourselves insulated. From everyone outside our family."

"What about Keegan? Benjamin? Why are they okay?"

"I've known them for a long time and I know all about them."

Her gaze softened. "I hate this. I really hate this. We don't deserve this kind of life. We did nothing wrong."

Ainsley pulled her into a hug. "No, you don't. None of us did anything wrong. I'm hoping this time confinement and abnormal don't last long."

Jane rolled her eyes. "I know all the clichés. This won't last forever. We have to make the best of it. At least we're alive and we have each other."

"You do know the clichés." Ainsley laughed and Jane joined in. Seeing her smile made things better. "I'm glad you still have your smile."

"Oh yeah, that's one too." She plopped on her bed. "Don't say anything to Dad or Mom about all this. I think I've given them enough to worry about for now, what with my art class and all."

"Don't worry. I won't. It's your story to tell."

Ainsley closed the door behind her and turned her attention to Keegan, still sitting at the table with her parents. "Shall we brainstorm now?"

He slapped the table in a staccato beat. "Let's go out to the kitchen."

"No." Her dad pushed away from the table. "Let's go, Theo. They need some privacy."

She watched her parents grab water bottles from the fridge and their books from the living room and go to their room down the hall, love for them filling her. This mess was hard on them, too. She could see it in the creases in their foreheads and hear it in their voices. Even so, they were remaining calm and, for the most part, patient. "Okay, let's do this." Ainsley slipped into a chair opposite Keegan at the dining room table as he pulled out his phone and Benjamin sat quietly beside him.

"Before we get started, I wanted to talk to Ainsley alone. Benjamin, can you give us a minute?"

"Sure." He grabbed his jacket and walked outside.

Ainsley frowned. "What's on your mind?"

"I haven't had a chance to talk to you about what happened at your house with the DAs, and I need to."

"Oh yeah, what exactly about?"

He measured his words. "When I came up behind you in the basement you were aiming a gun at one of them." He stared at her for a moment. Her eyes full of questions touched him. "Would you have shot him, killed him, if I hadn't stopped you?"

She looked away, running a finger over the table in circles. "I don't know. I wanted him eliminated, stopped in his tracks so he wouldn't hurt Jane."

"I understand that. I'm unclear what would have been the right thing. I know for myself I took training on how to use and care for a gun, but I've never shot anyone. I've never carried a gun because I haven't wanted to be in the position of deciding who should live or die. That's just me."

She laid her hand on his. "I'm glad you stopped me. I don't know what is right about shooting someone, but I think I would protect someone I love."

"You'll figure it out. We've all said at one time or another that just because we believe in light and love doesn't mean we're push overs. We get in our punches. But our power lies in using our abilities and focusing light and love to raise vibrations to help others make good choices."

"I know, and I agree."

Her gaze captured his, and he paused to tweak a lock of her hair. She smiled, hitting his heart hard. "I'm going to get Benjamin." He stepped outside and retrieved Benjamin, who laid down on the couch. Uneasy that he had any answers, back inside Keegan changed the subject. "Here, take a look at these pics." Keegan handed his phone to her, nodding to the screen. "Just scroll through."

She scrolled through the photos, reading the documents, forms, and plans.

"Read anything of interest yet?" Keegan asked as he slipped beside her.

"Where did you take these?" She passed the phone to Benjamin.

"I visited the construction site of Principle Group's Stillwell Development project early yesterday. I had to act quickly, but I tried to get as complete a picture as I could of what's going on." He pursed his lips. "It's not pretty, is it?"

"No. decidedly not." Knots in her gut twisted. "This looks like a very active crime scene. Not that I'm an engineer."

"I'm not either," Benjamin said.

"Nor am I, but I don't think we have to be to recognize that the drainage plans pose pollution issues to the Wherryite River. We need to talk to the rest of the Aeons to alert them that action is required."

Benjamin squinted at the screen. "I see that the company is under investigation for not adhering to state and federal construction laws. We should all talk soon." He yawned. "Sorry, I'm beat."

"Take a nap, why don't you," Keegan suggested.

"Yeah, I guess I will, if you guys don't mind."

"Of course, not, kid." Keegan tousled his hair, and Benjamin took to the couch.

"We all need to talk, ASAP," she said, shaking her head back and forth. "The gall of these people, stepping over laws and restrictions all in the name of power and greed. And how about the list of names? It's a lot to take in."

Keegan stretched his arm across the table and stroked her hand. The feel of her soft skin distracted his thoughts.

She lowered her gaze, staring at his hand moving across her skin.

"We're going to stop this project. It's what we're meant to do." Ainsley looked at him, stilling his mind.

"I know. We have too," she said.

He took his phone from her and sat back, leaning against the back of the chair. "Let's call in the cavalry." He bent his head to meet her eyes. "Are you ready to do some business?"

"I sure am." She rose to her feet and walked outside, Keegan following her.

He took her hand and she grasped his, then they stood together in the backyard, breathing in deep breaths, their eyes closed as they concentrated on sending out their energy to their fellow lightworkers.

The streaming energy filled Keegan's body. Power glimmered through him from inside himself and from Ainsley. They created a circuit of unmistakable light and love the Aeons would receive without effort. The message would land with them instantly, with no time passing. He knew that was the way of energy, and smiled to himself.

"We've got this," she said, her eyes still closed.

"Yes we do." Keegan responded with wrapping his arm around her waist.

She dropped her head to his shoulder and he took in her warm scent. It lifted the energy even higher, and trust bloomed inside his heart. This was not what he had intended to happen but it was what he needed. Maybe hope could be the best of things for her and her family after all.

Keenly aware of his expanded heart, Keegan turned Ainsley into his embrace. That she received him, opening to him at a trusting level, stood as a miracle in his book. He cupped her face in his hands, her skin soft against his, and leaned toward her waiting lips. Softly, he pressed his lips to hers.

With no holding back, she leaned up against him and kissed him back, passion flowing between them. He let her in, felt her warmth and acceptance, and something inside him broke open.

He pulled back, breathless and alive in a way he couldn't remember. He stared into her sparkling green eyes and let out a sigh. "Whoa."

She laughed. "I'll say. Whoa."

He lurched toward her, eager to taste again of her sweetness, her desire, her acceptance. She met his lips with hers, pressing hard against his mouth and inciting fire in his belly. He ran his fingers through her long tresses, and she moaned just slightly.

"Oh, I'm sorry."

Dazed, Keegan moved his hands to Ainsley's waist at the same time she gasped. "We can resume later," he whispered in her ear. He took a side-step away from her, her eyes lingering on him.

"Jane." Ainsley's voice came out hoarse and low. "We just—"

"Don't explain." Jane stood motionless, ankle deep in neglected grass. "I didn't mean to interrupt. I came looking for you to apologize. I'm sorry for coming down on you. You didn't deserve that." Abruptly, she pivoted to the back door.

"Wait," Ainsley called, running toward her. She grabbed her and hugged her.

While the two of them talked, he overheard Ainsley assure her sister she cared about her feelings and would always be there for her as he walked past them and headed to the back door.

Just as he reached for the doorknob, two vehicles pulled up behind the house.

CHAPTER 19

"Get inside," Keegan hollered to Jane and Ainsley.

"Wait, wait," Jane yelled, pointing to one of the cars.

Men in both vehicles hung out of the passenger windows, guns raised, one aimed on the women, the other on him.

He hurtled in front of Ainsley and Jane just in time to allow them to escape inside. Instantly, he dropped to the ground, burning pain sizzling in his shoulder and blood dripping onto the ground.

Swiftly, he jumped up and retreated into the house, slamming the door closed and locking the deadbolt.

But he knew those measures wouldn't stop the people outside who were determined to take them down.

Ainsley stopped moving. "You're hurt."

"It's nothing. We need to get moving."

"Did you see who they are? I saw Mathias. He was pointing a gun at us." Jane's voice quivered. "He's one of them. I don't understand."

"We don't have time to talk about it right now." Ainsley looked from Jane to Keegan.

Keegan tried to calm Jane, whose emotions churned just under hysteria. "I don't know how those people found us, but we'll find out. Right now we have to hide."

Jane made an effort to follow his orders. "Now can we get into the basement?"

"I don't think that's a good idea. That would be the first place they'd look. You all go upstairs," Ainsley ordered. "Dad, Mom, Jane, Benjamin, go!"

"What about you." Her mother's lower lip trembled and tears wetted her eyes.

"Don't worry about me. Keegan and I will handle this."

Keegan nodded. "We can't waste any more time talking. Up with you all." With that, he ran to the kitchen and lowered the kitchen shades. He grabbed knives, a rolling pin, and the one gun he'd seen in a kitchen drawer earlier.

He sensed Ainsley in another room, gathering potential weapons, he supposed. He nearly ran into her as she flew into the dining room at the same time, reaching for a heavy glass vase, the same one he was after. He put down his supplies and grasped her shoulders.

"We can do this." He knew it in his heart. No other outcome was inside him, other than protecting the family, to protect Ainsley.

Her eyes pierced his, and his heart went out to her. She had so much at stake. But so did he. "I'm not about to lose you just when—"

She put two fingers to his lips. "I know. Same for me."

Steady pounding at the back door resounded through the house. He grabbed the gun. "You send a message to the Aeons to let them know Dark Aspects are here, so be wary."

"I will."

She closed her eyes briefly, and he felt her focusing on her message, sending it out as fast as she could.

Keegan dashed to the kitchen window and snuck a peek through the blinds.

His heart pumping hard, he saw Diane out back and Barry Russell standing beside her.

"Harder," Diane chanted to the men at the back door. "Get inside there. Hit harder."

"This door must be reinforced," Russell shouted. "Or they'd have already knocked it in."

Keegan dropped the blinds, readying to shoot if the door gave way. He glanced around the room, wishing he had more time, to prepare, to protect the others. Nothing stood out to him as an effective weapon to stop the intrusion.

He nodded to himself, knowing what he had to do. He didn't hesitate.

He laid the gun on the counter and strode across the kitchen. He stood for one nano-second in front of the door. The beating against it rattled the windows and drowned out all other sounds.

He saw Ainsley out of the corner of his eye, at the same moment Jane ran up to her.

"I'm going to help," she said, and grabbed the rolling pin. "I'm not afraid anymore."

AINSLEY HEARD her but just barely. Her feet moved numbly toward Keegan, but he was already pulling the door open. So swiftly, he was out and being wrestled to the ground.

Over the din, she heard him holler, "Close it and lock it!"

Then he was down and she felt his energy diminish. Her heart crashed to the bottom of her gut. "No!" she yelled.

Jane restrained her and she pulled against her sister's hold on her. "Let me go!"

"No. Stop. Keegan wants you to take care of yourself and our family," she said. "We'll have our chance to make it right. Mathias used me. He's dead meat," she declared.

"She's right," Benjamin said. "Listen to Jane."

"They'll kill him. I'm not going to let that happen." Ainsley strained against Jane's hold.

Just then cold air from outside wrapped around her and she stared into Diane's stern face.

"No we won't kill him. Not yet," she said. "But you and your family are coming with me. Someone important wants to see you."

Her father's voice rang in her ears. "Stop right there," he commanded Diane.

She threw back her head, releasing a loud laugh. "You're a funny guy." She turned to the one man not dragging Keegan to the truck. "Get them in the vehicle, now."

Ainsley saw her father pull Jane to the living room and upstairs, faster than she'd seen him move in a long time. The door upstairs slammed and the DA Jane said was her boyfriend lifted her up and carried her outside, while she struggled, flaying at him with all her strength. Silently, he stuffed her into the backseat of the truck beside Keegan.

His eyes were closed, his body slack. Urgently, she checked his pulse. Thank God, he's alive. She checked his pockets and pulled out his phone, making sure it was working, and slipped it into the pocket attached to the front seat. She touched his face fondly. "Keegan," she whispered. I'll find you."

Her heart breaking, she climbed out of the truck while Diane and Barry talked to the DAs. They hadn't yet corralled her family and she had put the gun in her waistband, just in case.

Slowly she dropped onto the ground and slid around the side of the truck, shielded by it. She opened her senses, hoping beyond hope the Aeons were getting close.

Bingo. Strengthened by their energy, she raced to the front yard and tore inside, cursing from the others following her all the way.

"Get her!" Diane screamed. "Ainsley, it didn't have to be like this. We just wanted to talk."

Disbelief and revulsion shot through her, knowing Diane's emotions were out of control. At any minute, she could use her powers of telekinesis to fracture them all into bits and pieces and scatter them on the wind. How could she stop her?

In in an instant, Ainsley locked the door and took a stance, ready to do whatever she needed to keep her family safe.

Footsteps up to the front door alerted her that danger approached. Carefully, she stretched up to look through the peek hole in the door. What she saw took her aback.

Diane stood out on the step, drooping, tentative. The expression on her face touched Ainsley. In the moment Diane thought was private, she had let down her guard. Defiance had wilted, replaced by a tiny bit of longing, honest longing.

For what, Ainsley didn't know. But she could guess. The love and protection of a family she'd never had, the kind of family her own father and mother had offered her and Jane in these moments of danger. Softly, she streamed light, kindness, and hope to Diane. If those elements could reach her heart, they offered the best option for self-love that could truly contain her pain.

Ainsley couldn't wait for Diane to move in the direction of positive choice. She had to let go of control over the next move. She ran upstairs to the secret closet her parents had installed the first time they lived here. Inside the room where she prayed she'd find them, all was quiet. She knocked softly on the hidden door inside the closet and the small door opened a crack.

"It's me," she said.

Her mother opened the door farther. "Come in here, quick."

"No. I just wanted to check on you. Jane is secured in the other closet with Benjamin. My back-up is arriving soon. Keep quiet until I return when it's safe."

"No, come in here with us," her mother hung onto her arm.

But Ainsley broke loose and tuned her out. She ran back downstairs, knowing she had to keep moving. Keegan was paramount in her mind.

Commotion outside grabbed her attention. She checked through the window and spied Cooper and Braden in fist-fights with DAs, while Skye and Payson wrestled with the remaining DA. No sign of Diane and Barry or the other DA. Her breath caught in her chest. The vehicle missing was the one Keegan had been in. Her knees weakened. It wasn't supposed to be this way. Good people were supposed to win, not get into worse trouble. They weren't supposed to be betrayed by a trusted person, as Mathias had inevitably done to Jane. She unlocked the back door, aiming to join in the fight outside, but before she could, the fighting ended.

"We're here," Skye shouted as she and Payson ran into the kitchen. "We've secured the DAs. They're out cold. Are you okay?"

Payson slipped her arm around Ainsley's waist, holding her tightly. "I've got you."

Ainsley straightened, grabbing a breath. "I'm fine. Thank you for coming. But Diane and Barry Russell kidnapped Keegan."

"Oh no, what about your family?" Payson glanced around. "Where are they?"

"They're all right. But Keegan got shot and beaten up." Her lower lip trembled. "I couldn't stay with him. I had to take care of my family."

"Of course. That's your job right now." Skye hugged her.

Ainsley brushed aside both Payson and Skye, and ran upstairs. "I'm letting my family know they're safe. For now."

"I'm coming up, too," Skye called up.

"I'll keep an eye out down here," came Payson's words.

"C'mon out," Ainsley told her parents, then ran to the other closet. "It's okay, Jane. You and Benjamin can come out."

Benjamin led, looking calm. "We're okay." He left them alone.

Gingerly, Jane stepped forward. "Are Dad and Mom all right? How are you?"

"Here, let's go downstairs. Your parents are already down there." Skye ushered Jane down, allowing Ainsley to collect her thoughts.

She sat on her bed, staring at the floor, immersing herself in high vibrations to settle her nerves. Breathing in large, calming breaths, she found resolve still strong. As much as she feared for Keegan's life, he had all the support of the Aeons.

No one, especially not Diane and the Irish Mob were going to keep her from finding Keegan and getting him the help he needed.

She ran down to find all the Aeons gathered in the living room with her parents and sister, sipping water from bottles and appearing to be resting from all the drama that had just enfolded.

"Join us," Payson said, gesturing her to take a seat beside her.

She stood longer, assessing her mom and dad and Jane. She heard the remaining vehicle outside. "The other DAs. They're getting away. I thought you'd secured them."

"Let them go," Benjamin said. "We'll deal with them another time."

He was right. She crouched down in front of Jane. "Are you okay?"

Jane shifted from staring to focusing on Ainsley. "Yes. I'm sorry I wasn't any help, but I wanted to be." A tear drifted down her cheek. "And I'm sorry I trusted Mathias. You were right. I shouldn't have let him get close. I just don't understand why he would do such a terrible thing."

Ainsley pursed her lips. It was hard to watch her family go through such distress, but she believed in them. This wasn't the first time they'd persevered, after all. "You couldn't have known, Jane. You showed your strength just by your willingness."

"Ainsley's right," her mom spoke up. "It wouldn't do any of us any good to have you taken, too."

Her dad nodded. "Let's figure out how to help Keegan."

"No, we need to figure out who is behind this mayhem. We know that Jane's boyfriend—" "Former boyfriend," Jane interrupted.

"Former boyfriend told Diane where to find us." Ainsley took a seat beside Payson. "Maybe there's a mole in the FBI."

"That's a strong possibility. I'll get my laptop and work on that angle," Cooper said, eyeing Braden. How about you and I work on that."

"Sounds good." Braden walked outside with Cooper.

Ainsley saw them from a window talking. Between all of them they would figure out their next move. Hope rose for a swift resolution. "Meanwhile, we need to move you guys to another spot."

"Can we go home?" Jane asked.

Ainsley slanted her head. "Not yet, sweetie. Soon, I think."

"There isn't going to be anywhere safe." Jane hung her head.

"She's right," Payson said, giving Ainsley and Skye a pointed look. "Why don't we work on finding them a place until we can eliminate the threat."

"Sure. Upstairs?" Skye gestured upward. "We'll let these guys make a list of supplies they need so we can get them before we move them."

"A good plan." Jane perked up. "I can do that with Dad and Mom."

Minutes later upstairs in her bedroom Ainsley sat at a desk and faced her laptop screen, beginning a search for rental homes within her parent's price range in a safe and isolated spot. Restlessness twisted her muscles. She tapped her fingers against the wooden desktop, struggling to stay seated.

"Why are you still here?" Skye asked. "I know you want to be out looking for Keegan. And that makes a lot of sense. I meant that Payson and I can do this work on securing a safe house for your family without you."

Ainsley combed her mind for an answer. "They're my mother, father, and sister. My parents kept me and Jane safe during the years of living in the Witness Protection Program. Shouldn't I be here taking care of them?"

Skye looked at her through soft eyes. "We know the FBI isn't involved in this fiasco, Diane and the city leaders are to blame. We know that Braden and Cooper are using their abilities to find Keegan's location. We know Keegan's life is at stake and that the two of you are becoming closer. Your connection is strong. You're the best person to follow that connection and find him. It's okay to leave the rest in our hands, knowing we'll take good care of your family."

"Are you sure that's the right thing, for me to leave and lean on you all to stand in for me?" Guilt and misery boiled in her belly, feeling torn.

"Go."

CHAPTER 20

*A*insley retrieved her sunglasses from her purse and shoved them on. At mid-morning, the sun shone brightly. On the road after telling her family goodbye and assuring them she was entrusting their safety to her "friends," Ainsley sat behind the wheel of her truck, doubting herself. She'd found Keegan's location, she thought, using her GPS and his phone's location. But about a mile down the road, she'd spotted it lying on the side of the road. One of the DAs must have found it and tossed it out the car window.

Drat. She pulled off onto a country side road and parked, wrestling with self-doubt, guilt, and wondering how she'd find Keegan. She knew why she was so mixed up, it was the years of living under the cloud of possible death, hers and her family's. The constant questioning of who was coming through the door and whether a car pulling around their vehicle brought a loaded gun. But dang it, it was past time to get it through her head that the danger of those times was different from now. She was strong, she had the Aeons, and she was doing everything she could to protect not only her world but the city of Auralia, for the sake of the larger world. And that mattered.

Pain, anguish, fear twisted inside her, but she stayed with it, knowing she had to if she wanted to create her best life, much less save Keegan.

Her mind dazed as her eyes fixed on the windshield, no longer seeing the soybean and corn fields around her, but rather the moment she watched her father testify against the hit man he'd seen kill another man.

Her young self trembled and held her breath, listening to her father tell the chilling story he'd happened upon while jogging in the park that day.

"I saw up ahead a man pleading for his life from another man," her father said, glancing at the defendant and then looking away.

"Is the man you saw pleading for his life in this courtroom today?" the prosecutor asked.

Ainsley froze. Her father and mother had prepared her for the hearing and she had insisted on sitting in on the procedures despite their dismay at her choice. But seeing the man and his scarred face and clenched teeth eyeing her father with a hard stare made her pull inside herself. Overwhelm flooded her brain and she felt herself go numb.

"No, he is not."

"Go ahead, tell the jury what happened next."

Her father cleared his throat. "I saw the other man, the man with the gun, shoot him and the man who had been pleading fell to the ground. Blood poured out of his head and pooled on the ground around him."

"What did you do?"

"I didn't know what to do. I just stood there, trying to gather myself together. Then I ran as fast as I could to get away before the other man could shoot me, too. I thought about my wife and my two young daughters."

"So is that man you were running away from in the courtroom today?"

Ainsley stared at her father, fear rising in her throat. She didn't want him to die because of his honesty. What would be wrong with a little lie?

A hush fell over the courtroom, and she knew what he would do. He'd talked to her about the importance of honesty and respecting your own values, even if it was a hard way. But as she watched him weigh his answer, she wished he would take the easy way.

"Mr. Durham, answer the question," the judge said, his kind voice.

"Yes, that man is here. He's sitting right there," and her father pointed to the killer, his finger shaking just a little.

"Had you ever seen that man before that day in the park," the lawyer asked.

"No, never."

"Do you know the defendant's brother or anyone in his family?"

"No, no one in the defendant's family." Her father's voice trembled, and Ainsley sank in her seat at the back of the courtroom.

She let out a breath and the vision shifted.

She saw a dark room and Keegan slumped on the floor.

"Wake up." A man walked into the darkness surrounding Keegan and kicked at him.

Ainsley held her breath, fear tightly squeezing her lungs.

"Get up, I said."

She jumped and lost the vision. The man's energy scratched under her skin, alerting her. He was DA. Her eyes closed, she twitched, and she intensified her focus.

Keegan moaned low.

"People want to see you." A second man marched in and the two of them yanked Keegan to his feet. The second one in the room grabbed his head by his hair and Keegan's eyes opened. "That's more like it. Now get walking."

Dragged along faster than his feet could carry him, Keegan stumbled. His eyes strained to see. She blew out a long breath and tried to discern where this place was by the surroundings as the men carried him down a long hall, but the darkness was only dimly lit by small, overhead lights.

Through an open door at the end of the long walk, they dropped him into a straight chair in a room with a single bright light hanging from the ceiling. Dark figures lurked at the back of the room, and Ainsley shivered. Hostility permeated the atmosphere.

Another man walked in the room, smirking. "Barnes. Not the person I really wanted to see," he said, emphasizing 'really', "but you'll do for now."

Keegan pulled himself erect. "Well if I'm not your top priority, I'll be on my way."

"Sit down." One of the DAs shoved him hard back in his seat.

"I understand you recently visited my construction project on the Wher-ryrite River. What did you find there?" the man asked.

"Who are you?" Keegan was gathering strength.

The man huffed. "I ask the questions. But just to be fair, I'm Deglan Furey."

Keegan attempted to stand.

She winced and the vision closed. Everything in her scrambled to get it back. But it was gone. She sent light and love to Keegan. But it couldn't be all she could do.

She chewed on her lower lip. Who was that man? She squinted, trying to ring out every bit of information she could that would clue her into his location.

Her memory jostled, and she knew she'd heard a train whistle in the background and a distant rumble of a train riding fast on its rails, sweeping past. Her eyes closed, and she heard the roar of a grain elevator running, familiar to her only because of her experiences of a line of safe houses located on the edge of Auralia. She remembered that elevator so well.

Her eyes snapped open. Keegan wasn't in the city.

But who was the man she'd seen? Could he be the Big Boss of the Irish Mob? The one they'd gotten an inkling of from Diane's computer?

Her blood chilled in her body.

Just then she got something. Call it a vision, call it an insight. Whatever it was, she dropped it and pulled back onto the country road. Not completely convinced she was doing the right thing, she gunned the accelerator and coursed through the short distance through the country to the nearest grain elevator situated near a railroad track she knew of. Only two miles away in the middle of nowhere, she couldn't get there fast enough.

Her phone rang and she heard Braden on the other end.

"Cooper and I haven't found a location for Keegan. We couldn't find his phone. Where are you?"

"I'm only about a mile and a half from where I think Keegan is being held. I'll send you the coordinates. Come quickly."

"Will do."

"I'm on my way to a grain elevator. That's where he's being held, I believe."

Braden chuckled. "If you wait until we get there we can bring reinforcements."

"I can't wait." Urgency rolled her stomach over and over. "Besides, you need to take care of my family and Benjamin."

"Skye and Payson have that covered, don't worry. We've picked up Benjamin. He can help out."

"Really? Well, Benjamin is coming along fast if you're ready to include him in on a rescue."

"He's made for this, Ainsley."

"Just get there fast." She hung up before Braden could protest further.

What she'd seen froze her blood. It was just a vision of what could happen, she told herself. It didn't mean Keegan's fate was sealed. She shook her head. No! It didn't mean Keegan was dead.

"Hang on, Keegan. I'm almost there."

KEEGAN'S FACE HURT, his body hurt, but he was not out of the game. Resistance and resilience seethed inside him. He grinned at the man standing on the other side of the room. "So you're the big boss, huh? I'd shake your hand but I'm all tied up," he joked. A wallop landed hard against his face, sending him to the floor. The man who threw the punch pulled him up and slammed him back into the chair.

"Sassing won't get you anywhere." Furey crossed his arms over his chest, glaring at Keegan. "This can go easy or it can go hard."

Keegan chuckled through his fat lip. "You really think threatening me is going to loosen my mouth?"

"It should, if you're a smart man. Are you smart or are you simply dumb?"

Keegan stared into his fiery eyes. "Is your name really Furey, as in fury? That supposed to scare me?"

Frustration flooded the room, satisfying him that his approach was getting the best of this jerk.

"You know what to do," Furey directed the big man beating the crap out of Keegan.

The big man and his younger cohort dragged Keegan to a large room and hoisted him to hang a foot off the floor, his hands above his head. The ropes around his wrists burned his skin and his arms ached bearing his full weight.

"What were you doing on my construction site? What did you find?" The man gritted his teeth, waiting for Keegan's response as seconds ticked by.

Furey nodded to the hitter.

Keegan grunted as the hitter slammed his fist into his gut.

Furey hit his balled hand into his other palm. "This guy, he can do this all day and all night, but let's get to the point. Tell me what I want to know."

Furey's angry expression didn't faze Keegan. "Take me down and remove the ties and let's see who lasts the longest."

Another round of slams into his body took a toll, but Keegan wasn't about to talk. He was listening. And what he heard gave him a second, maybe third, wind. Furey was steaming mad, but also thinking hard about what Keegan knew and who he'd told.

Furey's phone rang. "What? Where?" He frowned. "Did I say you could stop?" he said angrily to the hitter.

Keegan opened his senses to Ainsley, searching for her whereabouts. Within moments, he got his answer and knew she was not in trouble: the message didn't regard her. Exhaustion made him breathe hard but relief sifted through him. Furey's energy, weak and agitated, clued him that something was up and his beating wasn't over.

He tried to capture both sides of the phone conversation, but he couldn't. Exhaustion wore on him. He breathed heavily.

"There's someone outside making noise."

"Check the security cameras."

"I have, sir. I didn't see anything out of the order."

"Check again." He turned away from the phone. "I told you to get him to talk," Furey raged. "I want submission, not banter."

"I will check again, yes, boss."

Keegan filled himself with peace and joy, then, gleefully willed it toward Furey. With luck, it would distract him from his problems long enough to let Ainsley make her move to help him escape.

Pain throbbed throughout his body, but hope grew. Anticipation took over for what could happen next, and he waited calmly while the hitter picked up brass knuckles from his tray of weapons. He braced for what was to come, confident of his stance.

Furey put down his phone and raised his hand. "Wait." He eyed the door. "What's that noise outside?"

"It sounds like cars running, Boss."

Furey's eyes flashed. "Well, go check it out!"

Keegan dangled from the ceiling rafter, continuously streaming positive energy to Furey and eyeing him for signs it was doing what he intended. The man was a hard and fast criminal, but all odds were in Keegan's favor that the energy would exert an impact on the present dire circumstances. So when Furey started coughing and scratching his neck, it didn't alarm Keegan. Light and love in a DA could elicit discomfort.

"You know," Furey started, grappling with his coughing and scratching, "You and I are marked different. But we're also alike. I know your story, so you know mine, as well."

Keegan focused his senses on Furey, getting understanding. "Your ancestors are Atlantian. That's how we're the same. But you have chosen to belong to Dark Sides. That's how we're different."

He nodded, and a grave, sinking feeling registered in Keegan, and awareness of Furey's truest identity filled him. He wasn't simply a mob boss, he was Dark Sides itself.

"I'm going to take you Aeons down, all the way down, and Dark Sides will win in Auralia. Then nothing can stop it for claiming the world."

"You only think so," Keegan declared. "It's not going to happen." He gave all his might to love, light, and acceptance, streaming it to Furey.

Furey's pupils widened, filling his eyes until they looked completely dark. He clawed at his neck and convulsed into coughing.

All Keegan had to do was wait and see how far Furey would devolve. And meanwhile, Ainsley would have a fighting chance of finding him and getting the two of them out of there before Furey ordered his killing.

That he wasn't wild about.

CHAPTER 21

*K*eegan heard a loud boom outside and felt it shake the building. Alone in the large warehouse room, he suspected but couldn't know for sure that the noise was about Ainsley's rescue attempt, imagining she created a distraction with an explosion somewhere on the grounds. As wasted and bruised as he was, he rallied his body and mind to prepare for her entry. There wouldn't be much time to escape, as he'd gathered that the facility was loaded with DAs belonging to Furey.

He chuckled to himself at his thought of Ainsley blowing up something, then immediately regretted it, as his pain sliced through him. Maybe if his brain weren't mush at this point he'd be able to work it out, but he wondered who was in charge. For a long time it had seemed that Diane was under Barry Russell, and Tim Brody and all of them were under Farrod. Now, it appeared all of them were under Furey's thumb. But weren't all of them just backstabbers, looking for the biggest pot? It seemed to him that criminals could never count on other criminals not to stab them in the back given the right circumstances.

His head lolled back, his physical strength ebbing. How long had he been here? He had to hang on. That's what Ainsley had said to him energetically. His thoughts wandered, and he envisioned what could be if he survived this day. He wouldn't hold back any longer how he felt about her, that if he admitted it, he had strong feelings for her. He wanted a relationship. He'd tell her the truth about his brother and father, which could mean total rejection, from her and the rest of the Aeons. But he wouldn't give up without a fight. He hadn't committed crimes or gotten entangled with DAs for any reason, much less for personal benefit.

Coming clean was the only way out of his isolation and aloneness. The clarity strengthened his resolve to survive. He struggled against the ropes around his wrists and feet, trying to wrest free.

From outside the room, he heard commotion and voices.

"Get the fire hose out of the case," one man yelled.

"I'll get an extinguisher," came back another.

A rumble of feet running fast pounded the concrete floor as groups ran by.

Just then Furey, Farrod, Brody, and Russell walked in, resolute. Diane marched in behind them, her face impassive. Keegan closed his eyes, waiting.

The three conversed in a huddle, and he listened in.

"Shall we leave him to die here?" Russell asked. "Does he matter much?"

Diane cleared her throat. "Remember, he's only one of the six Aeons. The others won't relent just because one of them dies. In fact, it would be the exact opposite. Losing one of them would make the others more resolved to stop us."

A faint whiff of smoke wafted throughout the room and alarm slid up and down Keegan's spine. Helplessness quickened his pulse.

"I'm not letting this ass hole off easy. He knows too much, I'm betting." Furey's voice was more growl than statement to Keegan's ears, and he let loose a laugh.

"Perspective is everything," he said as loud as he could, before coughing fitfully. "I heard an explosion. It smells like fire in here. Rome is burning. Your threat to me is a moot point." A wave of weakness swept over him, and his head dropped to one shoulder. Oh what

165

he wouldn't give right now for a knife, a shard of glass, hell, a glass of water.

"Shut up!" Furey punched Keegan's stomach, eliciting a groan from him. "Whether we leave you here to die or move you, you're a dead man if you don't tell me what I want to know."

Keegan gritted his teeth. This was not the end of him, he just knew it.

"Let's go," Russell urged. "Authorities are going to arrive. We're going to have to explain what's going on here."

"It's a grain elevator. It's going to explode," Diane said, pacing. "Why haven't we left already?"

"Our success with Auralia is paramount, and you all know that." Furey pounded his fist against the wall. "Without Auralia, we have nothing. I think Diane, you're right. We can't just leave this guy here. Take him down and bring him to the car parked behind the business office. I'll be waiting, so be quick about it." He pointed toward the hitter and the younger guy in the room, then walked out with Russell, Farrod, and Brody beside him.

Diane stayed behind, staring at him. Keegan sensed something in her. Something he couldn't recall noticing before. She was having a moment of remorse. Just a little bit of softening.

"You two go get me a gun and a fire distinguisher," she ordered.

"But the Big Boss told us to bring him to his car," said one, pointing to Keegan.

"Do what I say," she spit out. "Now!"

They left hurriedly, and Keegan's determination and prediction solidified.

He mustered all the strength he could to stream love and acceptance to her, not to manipulate her to save him, but because choice was the way for her to find peace. He sighed, watching her begin to fall to pieces.

She shook her head back and forth, her gaze pinned on him.

"What's up, Diane?" he muttered.

She lowered her gaze.

"How about giving me a hand?"

Just then the men returned with what she'd asked for. "Hand them over," she said, reaching out.

Keegan held his breath as the unbelievable happened. The men put the gun and fire extinguisher to Diane's hands. She instantly slammed one, then the other in the head with the fire extinguisher in rapid succession. They fell hard to the floor, out cold. She raised the gun, on alert.

"You killed them?" he hollered.

"No," she said, stepping up to them and nudging them over on their backs. "They'll need an ambulance, not a funeral home."

"What's the gun for?"

"Self-protection." She turned to him, pulling a knife from her boot.

"Now what?" he asked, still sending love to her. It flowed freely as she seemed to go with it.

She yanked a chair over to him. "Here, put your feet on this chair." Then she pulled another chair close and climbed up to cut the ropes.

Wary, guarded, he lowered down and away from her.

At that moment, Ainsley dropped down from a low ceiling rafter. "Back away, Diane," she demanded, holding up a gun aimed at Diane.

"I just cut him down. Don't tell me to back away. Where have you been?"

Ainsley ran to Keegan, wrapping her arms around him and crying.

"Ouch, ouch," he mumbled through his fat lip.

She ran her fingers tenderly over his face and kissed his bruised face, eyelids, head, and finally, touched her lips to his. "You're alive."

Tears trickled down her cheeks. He held her close, breathing in the scent of her skin, loathe to ever let her go.

"We don't have time for this," Diane declared, her hands on her hips.

"What about them," he asked.

"One of them is Jane's old boyfriend. I'd like to take them with us, just to give them their due." Ainsley gritted her teeth.

Moans from the floor warned them she was right, and Ainsley directed Keegan to lean on her.

Diane pulled in a deep breath. "Let's just get out of here."

Ainsley regarded Diane warily. "You need to explain to me what's going on here," she said. "Keegan, what's she doing?"

"Not now," Diane said. "You can take your chances on your own, or you can follow me. I know the fastest way out of here."

"So you say." Ainsley took stock of Diane's energy. It felt different, but what it meant she was unsure. "I need an explanation."

"Suit yourself. I'm getting out of here before others find us, not to mention I'd like to avoid the fire underway in the facility. I suppose that was your doing."

"It was. It's a grain elevator. I just dropped a match."

With that said, Diane strode to the door and turned in the opposite direction down the hall from the direction Furey and his men had gone.

"I'm speechless," Ainsley said. "What do you think, should we follow her?"

"I know the other Aeons are around. Let's find them," he suggested.

Slowly, step by step, Ainsley walked Keegan toward where she expected to find Cooper, Skye, Braden, Payson, and Benjamin. Clearly, they were each sending out their positive energy, like a beam for them to follow. Within minutes, they found a door out of the building and the Aeons watching over it, their vehicles at the ready.

"Is this how you got into the building unnoticed?" Keegan asked.

"No, I climbed up a ladder to the roof. From there I found an access door to the ventilation system. I followed my sense of you to the room they were keeping you in." Ainsley leaned her head against his shoulder, and her warmth, compassion, and affection soothed the pain throughout his body.

"Here, let's get you in to a vehicle." Payson said, helping Ainsley get him into her truck. "We'll get you to the hospital, Keegan."

"I'm fine. Just give me a few minutes to catch my breath," he objected. "Our work isn't done. We have the Big Boss within walking distance. We need to pin him down."

"Not today." Cooper shook his head, peering into the vehicle and patting Keegan's leg. "You've done enough for now."

"That's right," Braden added. "There's still much to do. Right now you need a doctor and rest, and we need to regroup."

"Your aura shimmers with pink, indicating your stress, which is understandable," Skye explained. "There's also muted yellow and vibrant green and lavender. It's diverse, but primarily tells me you're in pretty good shape. Just let me give you a dose of my healing touch for a few minutes."

"I'm not going to say no, Skye." Keegan chuckled.

Ainsley's gaze darted from one Aeon to another. Her heart raced. These moments would help Keegan, but every minute they didn't run put them closer to danger. Finally, she closed her eyes along with them to be present with the healing process. She filled herself with light and streamed it outward.

Keegan's eyes popped open. "Oh, oh. Healing time is over."

He was right. The sound of running feet and vehicles racing closer punctuated the general sentiment of everyone's point. Keegan pulled himself erect to see what he could see, but Ainsley jumped to attention, pulling a gun from her waistband. She aimed at the two approaching vehicles, taking out tires on one, then the other. They careened into each other, turning over on their sides.

"Good shot," Payson shouted, then ran to her vehicle. "Let's go!"

Limping, but already feeling strength returning, Keegan went to Ainsley. "What are you doing?" he hollered, grasping her shoulders. "Get in the truck before you get shot." He made a circling motion with his arm and limped back to Ainsley's truck as the others climbed in vehicles and peeled out the back road, escaping into the rural landscape.

Before leaving, Ainsley cupped her mouth over Keegan's ear and whispered to him. "Don't think I'm going to rest until I know exactly Diane's disposition and what came over her."

CHAPTER 22

*A*insley concentrated on keeping up with the vehicles ahead of her as the Aeons drove fast and furiously away from the grain elevator. She expected them to drive into town to the hospital for Keegan. But safety and anonymity were their immediate goals. It looked like Cooper in the lead was taking a back way into town.

She kept glancing over at Keegan. He half-slumped against the passenger door, his head kinked awkwardly against the headrest, his eyes closed. His silence was okay, considering what he'd been through. Evidence of a beating was clear on his face, but she imagined it had encompassed his entire body. A little rest would be good for him. She was glad he could do so.

Restlessness squirmed in her body with the need to hear an update about her family. There hadn't been time to talk before they'd split up into twos in the three vehicles, she understood that. But it didn't mean they weren't on her mind.

Dusk slipped around them, dimming the rolling hills and open fields whizzing by, dotted by occasional farms and homes set back from the road. If things hadn't been so dire, she could have been cheered by the pastoral countryside.

Soon they ended up on the edge of town. No one was taking time to talk now.

"No, I need to, stop," Keegan uttered in his sleep, shifting in the seat a little. He chuckled to himself. "You just wait."

Ainsley smiled, curious what was happening in his dream.

All at once, he jerked awake, like he'd had that dream of falling. "Oh, sorry. I didn't mean to go to sleep."

"It's okay. I've just been playing follow the leader."

He peered out the window. "Do you know where we are?"

"Just outside of Auralia." It made her heart happy to hear him able to talk and apparently have a clear head.

He nodded. "So as far as you know, there is no plan for where we're going?"

"Yes there is. The hospital." She gave him a side-glance. "How are you feeling?"

"But I'm not going to any hospital. Call them and let them know I'm hungry. Let's stop for food."

"What? How are you feeling?"

"Like I've been run over by a Mack truck, three or four times. But I'll be better soon. Where's your phone?"

"I'll do it." She made a group call to the other Aeons, letting them know their new destination was a restaurant.

All she could think about was the brief moments they'd been able to embrace right after his rescue, and how dear he felt to her. The thoughts sent tingling up and down her body and in private parts that hadn't been moved in such a way for a long time. Her heartbeat sped up, but she tried to ignore it all—the attraction, the racing pulse, the anticipation—timid about expecting much from him in return. The pattern set up in her years ago protecting her from pain automatically moved in place.

"I'm okay." He reached over and touched a spot on her forehead. "I see you saw some action before you dropped in to rescue me."

She winced. "Yup. But I'm okay too. What went on while you were waiting for help?"

"I met the head of the Irish mob. He knew I'd visited the construction site on the river and pressed me for information. I think he had a stake in getting back at me for daring to investigate what he's up to. Plus, he clearly didn't want details of his plan to get out."

"No one would blame you for telling him what he wanted to know, Keegan."

"His name is Deglan Furey. And he got nothing out of me. And thanks to you, I made it out alive." He dropped his head against the seat and sighed. "I must say, Diane had a part in keeping me alive, too. Which blows my mind." He reached out across the console and rested his hand on her shoulder.

His touch spurred peace and joy in her heart. "I want to hear all about Diane's unexpected actions, but you can rest now and tell everyone about it when we stop."

He slanted a smile at her. "It was the darndest thing. One minute she was all about following orders from BB." He cracked another grin. "Then the next time I saw her she took action to protect me from further danger. With no explanation."

"Furey, the Big Boss." His hand still warmed her shoulder. She moved hers to cup it. "I'm sorry you went through that."

"Me too." He shook his head, then yawned, and ran his fingers through his hair, catching on a spot knotted with dried blood. "Ow."

She raised his hand to her lips and brushed it with a gentle kiss.

"Now that feels nice." He slowly caressed her cheek, his eyes beaming.

She was grateful he wasn't reading her mind, but she blushed at her thoughts of kissing him all over.

Love streamed from his heart to hers, and gratitude filled her. "I have a theory about Diane," she said, refocusing on the problem at hand.

"I'd love to hear it." He slipped deeper into the seat and closed his eyes. "After years of her move toward Dark Sides and seemingly relishing individual power, she randomly softens? I don't get it. It's hard to trust her."

Sitting there musing with his eyes closed and his dark hair all tousled, Keegan looked vulnerable, approachable. If circumstances were different, she was fairly certain she would lean over and kiss him, gently, so as not to hurt him, but definitely leaving no questions unanswered.

She shifted uneasy in her seat and remained quiet, in case he fell asleep again.

"I haven't forgotten that you came to my aid a few days ago when DAs ambushed me. You kicked ass. I didn't know you had self-defense skills," he said, sighing heavily and sitting up straight. He grabbed her gaze, his eyes twinkling in the darkness surrounding them.

"Glad I could help. I didn't want you to go it alone."

"I appreciate that." He stared straight ahead. "You know, I haven't been forthright with our group. That bothers me. What bothers me more, though, is that I've kept things, important things, from you, Ainsley." He turned his gaze on her and she nodded.

"I figure you have your reasons."

"Yup, I do. At least I thought so. Until now."

"You don't owe me anything. We're in this together. All of us."

He scrunched up his face. Shadows made it difficult to see his expression, but she sensed his nerves wriggling inside him, and she wanted to be there for him without invading.

"I thought I was doing what was best, but I see differently now. Let's just say, you all deserve an explanation, but I want to start with you. Just hear me out, please."

"Okay." Her eyes trained on the road ahead and the others' vehicles, she opened her heart to Keegan, no holds barred and no expectations.

"I got a phone call from my father this morning. He and I don't see eye to eye on a lot of things. There's history that is hard to get past. He informed me that he'd taken on the bank loan I have for Best Bond Company. He claimed he was trying to help me out. I know him better. He's putting the screws on me because of a thing that happened a few years ago, I know. But he's probably out of money and in trouble with gambling. He wants me to pay him the loan. This week."

"What? That seems just wrong. Why would he do such a thing?" Her insides instantly flamed.

"He's not a good person, Ainsley. That's the problem. He's profited from working with DAs. I've known about. I've also known about an affair he's been having for a long time. He asked me to keep it a secret from my mother because it would ruin her, he said." He wrang his hands together. "And I complied. But I dropped out of his life as soon as I could. Didn't want anything to do with him."

"I can understand that. What's the problem?"

"My father is a criminal, and he's pulled my brother into his criminal world. I'm an Aeon. I fight for justice and peace and love. I've been ashamed of my father. I've been afraid to fess up to having a family member who could, and would, given the right opportunity, use me to get to the Aeons if it meant it would give him more power and financial gain. He would leverage me, using my mother's life or my brother's."

Speechless, Ainsley scrambled for words. Aeons were fallible humans. No one expected them to be perfect. But Keegan was right. Having someone close who would jeopardize their mission if opportunity arose, put them in a dangerous spot.

"You see my point, don't you?" He dropped his head in his hands.

"I see that your father misunderstands love, especially the love of a father for his son."

"I can't let him further ruin my brother's life." He pounded his fists on the dashboard. "I feel ashamed. It's taken me so long to see that I'm not helping or protecting my mother by withholding the truth about my father. His infidelity is disgusting and hurtful, but it's not the end of the world. It's another story when it comes to his criminal activity."

"Yes, you're right. What does it all have to do with your brother?"

"That is another secret I've been keeping." He scrubbed the top of his head. "Dad got my brother involved in a one of his schemes and Jayce ended up doing jail time, not my dad, my brother. He's out now, it was a short stint but it was a felony."

"It sounds like your dad is close to crossing the line into Dark Sides. I'm sorry to hear that."

"I should have protected my brother. We were close, but I didn't know what he was doing. I should have."

Ainsley took a minute to weigh her thoughts. "Yeah, well, couldn't we all say that about our family members? I know I could when it comes to my sister. I bet you tried to intervene on your brother's behalf, but our siblings have wills of their own."

"I don't know about anyone else, but I do know I've been neglectful of my brother. My dad came between us and I let him because I wanted nothing to do with him. But I should have been stronger and less concerned about myself, more involved when it came to Jayce." His voice got quieter. "I stuck my head in the sand. I couldn't bear to look, to see what was really happening."

"What happened? How did your father get your brother in trouble with the law?"

"My father owns a lot of properties. He has run into trouble off and on throughout his career due to a variety of crimes, but he protects himself. One way he does that is through shell companies and rubbing elbows with other criminals, otherwise known as prominent DAs. That protection eluded Jayce. Good old Dad left Jayce out to dry when the Internal Revenue Service looked into a business he put in my brother's name. Jayce took the fall for him for tax evasion charges."

"Whoa. That's cold." Ainsley shivered.

"I'd warned my brother to stay out of my father's business ventures, but he learned the same family loyalty plan I'd been indoctrinated in. Loyalty to my father at all costs. When I learned about it there wasn't anything I could do for Jayce. He was in prison for six months."

"That seems harsh."

"The government doesn't mess around. I can't help but wonder if my dad's reputation attached itself to my brother in the government's eyes,"

"How could your father do such a thing? How could he put your brother in that position?"

"He's a stone-cold narcissist and a criminal mind."

175

"Not a DA?"

"Not that I've detected. Still, it's always a possibility." He shrugged.

Ainsley pointed ahead. "Looks like you're going to get that meal," she said, as the other vehicles pulled into a parking lot at a small restaurant.

"Good, I'm starving. I haven't eaten in hours and it's getting late."

CHAPTER 23

Slow walking in to the restaurant while the sun hung low in the sky, Keegan noticed a couple of the others were limping. Under the lights, their cuts and bruises stood out as testaments to their combat with the DAs earlier. A hard knot tightened in his gut. This wasn't the first time they'd suffered battle scars, but it hadn't been for his sake before.

At their request, the waitress seated them in a corner at a large, round table. Perfect for discussion. Dimly lit, the dining room was cozy, but nearly empty. The aroma of French fries and hamburgers filled the air. Keegan's stomach growled.

He lowered into a chair, feeling his injuries but trying not to show it on his face.

"You okay," Benjamin asked him, grabbing a chair beside him.

"Yeah."

"Good. I need my mentor."

They quickly perused the brief menu and ordered, all looking eager to catch up. Drinks were brought, and he downed his water.

"Miss," he beckoned the waitress. "Could you refill my water, please? Better yet, just bring us a couple pitchers." He shot her grin.

He sent his gaze around the table, assessing facial expressions. "Everyone doing okay?" he asked.

"We're not dead, right?" Cooper quipped.

Ainsley raised her water glass. "Here's to not being dead."

They chuckled, clinked glasses, then got quiet.

Keegan let out a long breath, relieved and grateful. "Thanks to you all for keeping me alive. Our fight is not over, but these moments alone and safe are beautiful to me," he said.

"Speaking of keeping people alive, what happened with my family?" Her gaze darted back and forth between Skye and Payson.

"We found a rental house in a neighborhood in Ronen not far from their residence. You know, hiding in plain sight. They're all right," Skye assured her.

"We took everything they'll need, too. They're probably taking a breather right now." Payson nodded, assuring Ainsley.

The waitress began setting their plates in front them until each had their food. "Anything else I can get you folks?" she asked brightly. She waited while they concurred that they were set. "Okay, then, I'll check on you later."

While the others dug into their sandwiches and burgers, Keegan collected his thoughts. "First off, I want to let you all know that Principle Group's plans include bulldozing Old Town and replacing it with new buildings for apartments and retail."

Gasps and groans went up, but he kept talking.

"I think we all suspected something like this. I found evidence that the company will manage the new small businesses, making them ripe for laundering money for the Irish mob, along with doing the same at the casino. The Irish mob is behind everything—building the casino, razing Old Town, Dark Sides taking over Auralia—and the city leaders are in cahoots with them. I met the head of the mob. He made a reference to me not being the Aeon he'd wanted taken. I think, you could help me with this, that he wanted Ainsley and your family." He paused and took a bite of his club sandwich.

"Why?" Skye asked, her forehead creased.

"What do you think, Ainsley?" he asked.

"Revenge. Plain and simple. For putting his brother in prison." Ainsley took a sip of water. "The FBI released us when the brother was jailed. We thought the threat was over. It's weird that years later Furey has come after us again."

"I don't think he ever just gave up. He couldn't find you because you all had taken great pains to protect your privacy," Braden said. "He had to be very careful because of his own criminal behavior. But he discovered Jane at college, and planted a mole. I'm sorry, Ainsley. He still needs to be eliminated."

"Well, that's not all of it," Keegan continued. There is a problem with the jobsite. It has drainage and pollution issues. They're trying to ramrod permits and reports through the powers that be, and looking to void any court injunctions. But that's a slow process."

"So we're on a tight timeline. That's not new news," Braden said. "Nonetheless, now we have concrete evidence?"

Keegan nodded, his mouth full again.

"Who do we know in the Auralia government who can follow the process through and make sure there's no naughty business?" Payson asked.

"The right people in the city are already following up, so there's a good chance the court will at least put a hold on the destruction project. I can check in with the head of the Plan Committee, but Braden has that connection." Keegan eyed Ainsley. "Is there any talk amongst the present business owners about what's coming up? I know you and Skye are circulating a petition."

"There's a lot of despair because Principle Industries is such a large conglomerate," she said. "Hope is weakening. I've been trying to help them remain upbeat, but what they believed was impossible appears to be happening."

"It's understandable that a company involved with Furey would create chaos and doom. Furey admitted to me that his ancestors were Atlantians, the dark ones."

"Keegan, you may have buried the lede. Furey admitted his connection to Atlantis, where all Dark Sides began?" Cooper scratched his head. "That is an important detail."

"Sorry. My brain is mush, remember? I don't think it changes our approach. We fight darkness with light. So we will continue to meditate jointly to raise our combined good will. That's something. Although it may be discouraging to watch Dark Sides continue to cause havoc, what we're doing is powerful and promises to have lasting influence on the balance of light and dark. We're making foundational changes in lives. Believing is part of our strength."

Determination sparked in Payson's eyes. "Did you learn anything else in your visit to the site?"

"That's about it. I didn't have much time to investigate." He lowered his gaze, preparing to lay everything out.

"Not complaining, Keegan," Payson added. "Thanks for checking it out. You've done a lot to further our cause. I'm grateful."

He sighed heavily. "I'm afraid there is more for me to tell you. I haven't been forthright with you all and I'm sorry. I've been a coward."

"What? You're nuts, bro." Cooper gave him a once-over.

"No, it's the truth." He told them about his father's disposition as a not-quite-DA-but-almost and his brother's time in prison. Shame ached inside him as he finished revealing all the dirty secrets he'd kept from them.

Silence permeated the group and they stared at him. If he could make it all disappear, he would. He hated how much he'd screwed up.

Braden laid his hands flat on the table. "Being an Aeon doesn't mean you're not human, Keegan," he said, his voice low. "You didn't want to talk about something painful. We get it. No judgement."

Cooper nodded before shrugging. "I'm certainly not perfect. Are you,?" he asked Skye.

"Well, I used to be." Glints in her eyes gave away that she was teasing. "Of course not. You know me—"

Keegan interrupted. "It's not simply that I thought I needed to be perfect. It's that I let myself be compromised. I could have been responsible for the downfall of each one of you. That was irresponsible." He dropped his gaze again. "I was afraid I'd lose you. And, to be honest, I wanted to protect my family, especially my mom and Jayce."

"Each one of us has had to face issues from our lives that are less than desirable," Cooper said. "You're not alone in that. There are always reasons behind our actions, though. That's why we work on ourselves, so we have more clarity and inner peace."

"Right, Dr. Cooper." Keegan sighed. "I'm joking at you putting your counselor hat on, but I'm taking your words seriously."

"Would anyone like pie?" The waitress stepped up to the table, holding her tablet. "We have six different kinds. Homemade right here."

"I'll say," Braden spoke up. "Do you have apple?"

"Yes we do. We have apple, blueberry, coconut and chocolate cream—"

"I'll have blueberry," Skye said.

"I'll have chocolate cream," spoke up Payson.

"And so will I," Cooper said.

"All three, sir?"

"No, just the chocolate cream."

"You got butterscotch?" Benjamin asked.

"Yes, sir."

"Count one slice for me." He smiled disarmingly at the waitress.

With the rest of the others' pieces ordered, Keegan's insides filled with gratitude for the moments. The talk of dessert lifted the mood, and he got his second wind. "Boy, you guys are great. I appreciate your support, but I know now that my belief about loyalty to my family has been off. I can love them and want the best for them, without believing I have to take care of them."

"Are you saying you've had a Superman complex?" Braden joked.

"Doesn't every man?" Ainsley added, a mischievous smile lighting her face.

Keegan pulled her hand into his and held it up to his lips, silently capturing her gaze. Warmth spread between them, healing like a salve.

Skye cleared her throat. "So, you two, huh?"

"Looks that way," Braden said. "It's about time." He chuckled.

"Enough, about us." Ainsley pulled her hand away, smiling widely.

"I hate to interrupt this love fest, but shouldn't we get on the road soon?" Cooper suggested over his last bite of pie. "I think Braden has scraped every molecule of his apple pie off his plate."

"I have one more thing to say before we get going." Keegan pulled in a deep breath. "Diane was in the room with Furey and his boys when I was getting the crap beaten out of me. She was her usual vicious self. Until at the end, when it appeared she was having a change of heart. She helped me out when it looked like it was going to be the end of me."

"Get out!" Braden shouted, then demurred. "I mean. I don't understand."

"Me either." Keegan rolled his eyes. "She clobbered two DAs, released me, then left, without any explanation. But I felt her energy shift, so I know something changed. And Ainsley has a theory I haven't heard yet." He gestured to her.

"I think it might have been a combination of factors." Ainsley pursed her lips.

"What factors? I'm simply stunned," Payson said.

"I know. So was I. I couldn't believe it. I believe the energy we've been streaming out touched her deep enough that she was moved, emotionally. And when she witnessed my family's dynamics and how they cared about each other, she started questioning her own lack of love. Or something like that. I don't know. It's just a theory."

"It's not a bad theory." Skye stared up at the ceiling. "I'd like to assess her aura, if I get a chance. But what are the implications?"

Cooper chimed in. "People can change. It's what we've been working on very vigorously. Why should we be surprised when our efforts pay off?"

"Yeah." Payson scratched her head. "Because, she's been very bad, very dark, very resistant to light, love, and peace. She tried to end me. And you said she attacked two men."

"Well, she had a gun but chose, key word there, to merely knock them out. Ainsley and I didn't stick around to check on them but they weren't dead. We were kind of in a hurry to get out before the Big Bad Boss and his men returned. Life and death on the line."

"Oh, so now Furey is the BBB, not simply the BB?" Ainsley laughed. "They were moaning, so I wasn't concerned."

"Okay, where are we going next. We escaped, but what's next? We can't just all go home tonight." Skye took a sip of her water.

"No, we can't go home."

"We go to my place," Payson said. "I've got great security, remember, thanks to you guys. And there's plenty of room. I'm sure ZuZu the cat won't mind all the company."

CHAPTER 24

*a*insley followed the caravan to Payson's house out in the countryside, but she knew how to get there. It was one of her favorite places, with all its up-close nature, and it was only about forty-five minutes away from town.

She eyed Keegan in the darkness in the car. There were no streetlights shining the way out here, just moonlight. She didn't mind that he'd been quiet since they left the restaurant. The silence between them was as comfortable as her blankets on her bed, and peaceful.

A few miles farther, Keegan sighed heavily.

"Are you all right," she asked.

"Yeah, just relaxing. How are you?"

"Worried."

"Your family, right?"

"I should check in with them. It's been hours since I saw them." Guilt weighed in her heart, knowing she hadn't been in touch since morning.

"You've been busy, you know." Keegan gently twirled a lock of her hair between his fingers. "You should have let me drive so you could call them. I didn't think of that. My brain might still be mush."

"No, you should rest. I just know how hard it is to be in unfamiliar territory and not know if anyone is paying attention."

"I get that. But they're grownups. It's not exactly like what it was for you when you were very young."

His sentiment soothed her anxiety. "You're right. I fall into the old pattern without thinking. Having to watch out for danger and the lives of people who are important to me is natural."

"I think it's okay to believe others can take of themselves, but I completely understand. I'm the one who has been shielding my family from the best people I know." He dropped his hand to her thigh and rested it there.

His touch sent her pulse racing, at the same time that it reminded her she was not alone in the events of her life anymore. She could believe in goodness and light, and let down her walls. She'd been having regular interaction with the Aeon group for years, and yet the walls had remained, keeping her safe inside, but also stuck in her old beliefs.

"You're quiet," he noted.

"I'm just thinking about you." The smile that stretched across her face couldn't be contained.

"Me? What about me?"

Words rose, but she weighed them, wanting to say just the right words that would convey her true feelings, and he remained silent.

The lights ahead she'd been following kept up their pace, but she knew they were not far from Payson's house. What could she say to Keegan? That he'd given her the space and time she'd needed to expand like no one ever had? That her heart danced in her chest just thinking about his warmth, his kindness, his thoughtful nature? Or that she'd dreamed of a future with him and now that was all she wanted out of life?

No. All of that could send him away faster than she could think. Better to take it down a notch. Feel her way, step by step.

"I was thinking how brave you've been to keep fighting the fight against darkness and despair," she said.

"Aww, thanks, Ainsley. Right back at you."

In the faint light she saw him bow his head and braced herself.

"You're the brave one," he said softly. "You're always candid and honest. I can count on you to tell like it is, and that helps me be a better person."

His hand slipped inside hers as it rested it on the console between them, and she closed her fingers around it. "Thank you. That means a lot to me."

She slowed her vehicle to match the caravan's speed, as they turned up in to Payson's gated driveway and waited as she punched in her code, then drove up the drive.

Energy between her and Keegan sparked like lightning. Their eyes met and he leaned close, kissing her hard and earnestly. She pulled back, breathless.

"This isn't over," he said, his voice hoarse. "But we have to go inside now." He broke out chuckling.

She laughed along with him, savoring joy that spilled out of her, eager to see what would happen next, when the old ground rules completely fall away.

"I DON'T KNOW about all of you, but I'm beat." Payson dropped her things on the living room floor and sank into a nearby couch. "Feel free to get snacks out of the kitchen and just generally make yourselves at home."

Braden sat beside her and pulled her into the circle of his arms. "Do what I do, raid the cupboards or the fridge and settle in front of the TV as you want. Security is on. We're safe here. I've got to feed the cat." He picked up ZuZu and took her to the kitchen.

Keegan kept his gaze on Ainsley. Standing at the sliding glass door, she looked entranced by the nature outside. He couldn't blame her. Trees circled the large pond, highlighted by a small waterfall. Hesitant to intrude on her musings, he stood back on the other side of the room, captured by the curves of her body.

"I'm not hungry," Skye offered. "It's still early, but I'm tired, too. Payson, where do you want me to sleep tonight?"

"There are three bedrooms and two couches that aren't too bad for sleeping."

"Well, make that two bedrooms. One belongs to me and Payson." Braden's head leaned against the back of the couch, and Keegan noted the dark circles under his eyes. He rubbed his own eyes, then quickly stopped, as pain shot through his head. "Ow."

Ainsley turned to face him, consternation crossing her face. "What happened?" she asked, eyeing him.

"I forgot for a minute that I have a black eye." He grinned at her, his heart flipping erratically in his chest at the beauty and warmth of her face. Figuratively, she brought him to his knees with the touch of her hand on his face.

"Take it easy on you," she said quietly, pausing her gaze on him.

"I'm fine," he nodded, heat spreading throughout his body. He rubbed his fingers over his mouth. "Do you have cold drinks in the fridge?"

"Yeah, help yourself." Payson rose and led him to the kitchen. "Are you sure you're all right? You got quite a beating." She held open the refrigerator for Keegan to see the selection of cold drinks.

"I'll have water," he said, grabbing a water bottle. "I'm sore, but it's not fatal." He heard Ainsley in the other room excuse herself to call her family. "I think I'll turn in soon, but a shower would feel good. Is that okay with you? If it's all right, I'd also like to take one of the couches."

"Of course. There's a couch in my office downstairs and one in the den on the main floor."

"I'll take the downstairs one. That sounds good." More than anything he wanted Ainsley by his side in bed tonight. That was a long shot, he knew.

Payson sauntered back into the living room and relaxed beside Skye.

"That couch is a hide-a-bed," Braden added. "There's a full bath connected to her office, too, so you can shower in there whenever you want." He leaned against the island and took a swallow from his water bottle. "I tell you, Diane has me perplexed. I don't know whether to be

187

encouraged by her coming around even just a little or to run and hide."

"I get that." Keegan narrowed his eyes. "It's too soon to know what's true. I think whatever she's doing will play out. We have to remain careful, though, just to be sure we don't get destroyed."

"Yeah." Braden nodded for a long few seconds, as though weighing the thought. "I can't let anything happen to Payson, man."

"Of course not. I'm right there with you." He looked for Ainsley. "I don't want anything to happen to any of us. But each of us, including Payson, can take care of ourselves." He patted Braden's shoulder, then headed back to the living room. He didn't see Ainsley, but he could hear her talking in another room, so he eased into a chair and put his feet up on a stool. Conversation glanced off him and he drew inside, pondering what Braden had said.

Diane had been lethal, no doubt about that. She'd been so clear that she'd wanted nothing to do with the Aeon mission, yet she'd chosen differently. Probably saved him from further beatings and who knew what else? It blew his mind.

"What do you think, Keegan?"

"Huh?"

"Hello, Keegan. Come back to earth."

So focused on his thoughts, he hadn't been paying attention to conversation around him. He stared blankly at the others, and finally realized Benjamin was talking to him. "What do I think about what?"

"I was saying that I think I know what my special ability is. It's claircognizance. Do you see that in me?"

"Hmm. What are you basing this on? What's your evidence?"

"Do you remember what I said a few days ago when you first told me about being an Aeon?"

"Remind me."

"You told me I was an Aeon and I told you that what you said about being an Aeon really fit, like I knew somewhere inside of me that it was true, and really lined up with what my life was about. That knowing, we could call it, was my claircognizance. A gut feeling that is more than a simple idea."

Benjamin stared at him wide-eyed, so sure of what he believed that Keegan wanted to agree. "Okay, that's a start. Prove it to me more."

"The feeling of knowing is something I've always had. I know when a friend is coming over to my apartment. Sometimes I know what someone is going to say before they do. I have known when I'm going to get a job. I could go on. Do you want me to?"

"Okay, you sound sure of it. Now how would this ability contribute to the Aeon mission in Auralia?"

All eyes were on Benjamin and the only sound in the room was that of the clock ticking on the fireplace mantel.

Benjamin's eyes danced. "It just so happens I've been thinking about that. Ainsley," he said, twisting to face her. "Remember that at the first safe house I told you Jane was concerned about missing her classes and falling behind? That wasn't mind-reading; it was something I knew in my gut. It was intuitive knowing."

"I remember that." Ainsley nodded. "I thought she'd told you that."

Benjamin chuckled. "I let it slide. I didn't think you'd believe me. No one ever has believed in my ability." He paused, slanting his head. "I'm not sure, but I feel something more to it, but I'm not sure what it is."

"If so, it will express soon. It sounds right on to me," Cooper spoke up. "It's similar to my empathy, only I feel their emotions."

"It sounds right to me, too. Keep us informed." A smile popped out on Keegan's face, unbeckoned. "I told you you'd figure it out. So the important thing here is that I was right."

"Oh, yeah. That's what's important," Payson joked. "With that, I'm going to get to bed. It's been a long, brutal day."

"I trust you all can find your place to sleep tonight," Braden said, standing and stretching.

"I've already called the couch downstairs in Payson's office." He eyed Ainsley, his breath catching. "That's where I'm heading to right now."

"Ainsley, you and I can take one of the bedrooms. What do you think?" Skye grabbed her things and waited.

Ainsley gazed at the floor, then met Keegan's eyes before turning to Skye. "Sure, I'll share a bedroom with you. I don't snore."

Skye laughed lightly. "Nor do I."

"That leaves the other couch for me." Benjamin eyed the couch in the room.

"I'll get you all blankets and pillows, just give me a minute." Payson walked toward the hall closet.

"Hold up, Payson. I'll help." Braden followed her.

"Me, too." Benjamin trailed along behind them, surveying what was visible of the house.

"That leaves one remaining room for me," Cooper said. "Going once, going twice, it's mine."

Braden tossed him some bedding and Cooper joined the exodus to the various sleeping splace, leaving Benjamin to the living room.

Down in Payson's office, Keegan opened the hide-a-bed and made it up, then stripped down to his naked and stepped into the shower. The water sprayed over his head and body, easing the soreness in his muscles. He stood there savoring the fluid motion of the water, letting it do its magic. Soap sudsed in his hands and over his body and face, easing away the day and the blood that had dried on him. His face uplifted, he held his breath under the spray and scrubbed clean, one-hundred percent more himself than before. The softness of the towel against his skin as he dried off soothed him. Naked, he settled into the bed, appreciating its spaciousness. All he really needed now was Ainsley, but he knew there was little chance of that happening tonight.

CHAPTER 25

*a*insley was first into the shower and first under the covers. Lights went out more than an hour ago. Now, staring at the ceiling, she listened to Skye's soft breathing beside her in the bed, so she knew she was asleep. She didn't want to disturb her by tossing and turning, but she was wide awake.

She checked her watch again and sighed quietly into her pillow. The night stretched out before her with no sleep in sight. It wasn't that the bed was uncomfortable or that she wasn't tired. But her brain wouldn't quiet down, and worse, her body tingled with something that definitely was not sleep.

Again, she hunkered down into the covers and tried another time to soothe her mind with deep breathing. In, out, in, out, in out.

Oh who was she kidding? It hadn't worked before and it wasn't working now.

She peered into the darkness. The forest surrounding Payson's property kept light from penetrating. It would be great for sleeping. If she could fall asleep. But her problem wasn't too much light, and counting sheep wouldn't help.

She slowly lifted the covers from her side and slipped her feet out to touch the floor. Still dressed, she sat perched stiffly on the edge of the bed. Nothing but silence met her ears. Was what she was considering reckless? Was it even wanted? Dare she chance it? She'd have to walk downstairs and get past Benjamin.

No. She swiveled her feet back under the bedding and resigned to trying again to sleep.

Who was she trying to kid? Her heart knew for sure that what she entertained was wanted. All it took was a little sneakiness and little courage.

She eased out from under the blankets and crept down the stairs slowly, inching her way down to the lower floor, grateful for carpeting and non-squeaky steps. Silently, she walked to Payson's office and cracked open the door. Her breathing in the silence thundered inside her head, so she held her breath as she tiptoed into the room and shut the door behind her. Step by soft step she approached the hide-a-bed where she expected to find Keegan. She dropped her clothes to the floor and knelt beside the bed, reaching out to shake him.

"Ainsley," he whispered.

She had to suppress a shriek. "Keegan, you startled me," she whispered. He wasn't asleep.

"What took you so long?" His eyes glistened in the low light of the computer router across the room.

She put her hand over her mouth to giggle. "I'm here now."

Propped up on one elbow, he ran his hand through her hair. "What do you have in mind?"

"You have to ask?"

He opened the bedding and she began to crawl in, but he grabbed her and tucked her close beside him. She sighed, feeling the rightness of it, while Keegan pressed kisses to her skin under her ear, then her shoulder and down her arm closest to him. Her skin tingled appreciatively, and she giggled quietly.

"Oh, you're ticklish?" He paused, his face above hers, barely an inch away.

"Very." Her breath was coming fast, and she felt suspended, waiting as the weight of him along her naked skin seared deliciously. "Are you okay? I mean—"

"I know what you mean." Gently, he brushed his lips against hers, then instantly pressed a hard, driving kiss that sent her heart racing. "Yes."

Eagerness swelled inside her, dizzying her mind. Pulling her on top of him, she felt the hardness of his torso against her. His hands ran up and down her body, caressing and exploring all of her, titillating her senses. She nuzzled into his neck and set kisses down his chest, his abdomen, his thighs.

Keegan moaned, and she smiled to herself as she moved up higher on his body and he took her breasts in his hands, his mouth, slowly and deliberately savoring, as though he never wanted to stop, but then intense and fast. Lost. In his fondling. As she'd never been lost before.

He kissed her lips again, and when she pulled back, she opened her eyes to meet his gaze, steady and expressive.

"Ainsley, you're so beautiful." His voice hoarse with emotion stunned her speechless.

He paused for protection. Then with one, swift move, he rolled on top of her and she opened to him. He teased her body, entering slowly, then drawing out. Her eyes stared at his muscled and glistening body as he held her in his clear blue eyes. He nodded and she returned it.

He thrust inside her and she arched to meet him. "Keegan," she breathed.

Together they rocked, matching tempo for tempo, heightening her pleasure with every move. Coming to crescendo together with him, bliss and ecstasy rippled through her.

"Oh, Ainsley." His head dropped against her shoulder, his breathing deep and fast against her face. He lay there, still and silent, and she held him in the most intimate way, her arms across his back, caressing.

He slid beside her, his arm draped over her body. A kiss to her shoulder, then he chuckled. "Oh my," he said, breathing out a sigh.

She let out a long breath. "Oh yes, most certainly."

They laughed quietly together, hugging and turning to face one another. He traced the contours of her mouth, then kissed her quickly.

"Do you think anyone heard us?"

"No. I think we were controlled in our out-of-control state."

"Me, too." He rolled to his back and she did as well. "Regardless of if anyone heard us, they're going to know what's going on with us. They saw us together earlier."

Filled with contentment and peace, Ainsley just continued to lie quietly, listening to him and taking him in. "I don't want this moment to stop," she said. "It's been, dare I say, special to me." A warm blush crept over her in the dark. Maybe it was too soon to admit such a thing.

He propped up on one elbow and ran his fingers down between her breasts and resting on the curvature of her waist. "These moments are precious to me. It's probably too soon to say this, but I've held back out of your sphere for a while, afraid to get close but wanting to."

She smiled up at him. "I had no idea. We've been silly. I've felt the same, us being sort of coworkers and all. But for you, it probably was more of a problem because if you got close to me, you might have been putting yourself in jeopardy in the eyes of the Aeons, right?"

"Yes," he said softly. "I was messed up."

"Aren't we all?" she mused. "But you know better now. It's a new game."

"Yes. And I've got game, don't you forget." His eyes sparkled playfully.

"Never." She cuddled in close to him. "I can't stop sighing."

"In consternation?"

"In delight. I'd like to lie here all night, just fall asleep beside you. But I probably better get back upstairs."

"Oh, not so soon. It's not nearly morning." He snuggled her close and pulled the blanket up around them. "How was your family when you called?" he went on, tenderly running his hand up and down her arm.

"I talked with just my dad. He said they were fine at the rental and had enough supplies for a few days. It sounded like they were secure, but anxious."

"It's understandable they'd be nervous. You'll see them tomorrow."

She glanced toward the desk and read the clock. It said they still had time. "It's two-thirty."

"Stay. So what if the others find out we had intimacy?"

"Hmm. Well, is this the beginning of a sure thing? What if things go sour? Won't everyone feel uneasy?"

His finger swept down the bridge of her nose. "I have high hopes. Plus, we're all Aeons. We all have been working on getting our heads on straight, but we can handle a lot. Just earlier, when I confessed to my poor decisions, no one kicked me out."

"I don't know if I'm ready to make that kind of announcement, casually or formally." She chewed on her thumb nail. "There's nothing wrong with testing the waters, is there?"

He hugged her. "Nothing at all."

Reluctant, Ainsley slipped out of bed, dressed, and gave Keegan one last kiss. "Sweet dreams."

He kissed his finger, then touched it to her cheek. "You too."

She tiptoed in her bare feet up the stairs and into the bedroom. Chills went through her as she got under the cold bedding. It had been so warm and cozy in bed with Keegan. A smile lifted her lips thinking about the evening with him.

Skye's breathing again told her she was the only one awake in the room, and relief fluttered through her. The idea that Keegan wanted to out them was sweet, but it gave her nerves a shake. Everything with him was so new, and she had a lot of experience with things not working out. Her gut clenched. If she were to have a lasting, meaningful relationship ever, she would need to truly get that those days to come to an end, and maybe they were very close this time around.

She rolled onto her side, relaxing into the soft bedding. Thoughts of Keegan and their time together danced around her brain. His kisses, his touches, his gaze on her, all exquisite moments. She couldn't help but sigh, and let her thoughts continue, committing them to memory.

Her body got softer, her thoughts quieter, lulling her into stillness.

AINSLEY'S EYES squinted and she sat up abruptly in bed.

"Good morning." Skye sat on the other bed, pulling on her shoes, and tying them up. "Sorry if I woke you."

Rubbing her eyes, Ainsley got out bed and opened the blinds. "No, not a problem. Is anyone else up?" Sunlight slanted into the room.

"I know Cooper, Benjamin, and Keegan are. Cooper and I are going for a run. Take your time. Yesterday was exhausting." She smiled, then winked.

Ainsley's heart skipped a beat. "What was the wink for?"

"Oh, nothing. I'm just happy."

"I know it wasn't nothing. You're up to something."

"No, I'm not. But you were." Skye chuckled.

Ainsley dropped back onto the bed. "Does everyone know?"

"No one has said anything about you two, but it's been clear that you two care about each other." She slanted a grin. "Don't worry. Your secret is safe with me. And girl, I'm happy for you two. I'm just saying, you don't need to hide it. You both deserve a little something, something with each other."

"Have a good run." Ainsley dug her toes into the plush carpeting and smiled from deep within her. The world remained the same as it was yesterday, with good and not-good struggling for power. That knowledge burned inside her. But today, he cared about her. That knowledge bolstered her faith and hope in possibilities that the Aeons could triumph in their mission.

But she grabbed her phone and punched in her dad's phone number rather than dwell on her personal happiness. As usual, there was work to do and there were people to attend to, including her family.

"Hi Ainsley," her dad answered. "Where are you? Are you okay?"

Tension in his voice urged her to stay on task. Their lives were at stake, that hadn't changed with a different address. "Hi, Dad. You sound better than you did last night. Does that mean you slept well?"

He sighed heavily. "I did. Your mother didn't fare so well. Are we going to see you today?"

"I'm planning on that. I need to touch base with my shop. I had some business to attend to last night, so I'm sorry I couldn't make it to your house. I'm hoping nothing else dire crops up. Do you guys need anything I can bring you?"

"Skye and Payson got Jane's stuff, including her laptop, with strict instructions to stay off line. We've got food and other essentials. But thanks for asking."

"Okay, sit tight. I'll talk to you later."

The conversation ended but her thoughts lingered. Could she hope for an end to her family's dangerous threats, at long last? She was going to do all she could to make that happen, she vowed.

Chatter from the kitchen floated down the hall, reminding her of the time. Dressed in the same clothes she'd worn yesterday, she was glad she'd at least been able to shower, and wondered what she could find for breakfast. Stopping at a mirror in the hallway to give herself a quick look-over, her stomach did flip-flops. Would Keegan give away their secret or even acknowledge their feelings from last night?

CHAPTER 26

"Jayce, you have to stay away from him. He's only going to bring you down."

"Dad needs my help and he said this deal would be the best way to build my assets."

Jayce's voice in his ear, saying the same thing he had two years ago when Sully messed him around, made Keegan's stomach lurch. "Well, chalk it up to bad advice." Keegan bit his tongue, trying to remain calm with his brother, despite the frustration ramping up his blood pressure. Turned away from the others, he spoke as candidly as he dared, bearing in mind that Jayce was sensitive. He didn't want to turn him off, but the situation with his father threatened Jayce's freedom, again.

But he heard the others greet Ainsley as she walked into the kitchen, and turned his eyes on her. She met his gaze, and nodded. His heart skipped a beat, and he slanted her a grin. He watched her get cereal and take a seat at the kitchen island beside Payson.

"What? No!" He whirled around again to face the wall. "Listen, please hold off from making a commitment until I can talk to you in person."

"He's our dad, Keegan. I'm not going to let him down. I can take care of myself. Besides, things are different this time."

He listened to Jayce's side of the argument, his gut twisting. "I know that line. I've heard it myself. Just give me some time. Maybe tonight or tomorrow. Okay?"

"Okay. I'll hold off. For a little while. But Dad is under the gun."

"I get it. Talk to you later." He disconnected, hopeful but cautious.

"I didn't mean to listen in, but it sounded like you have family issues going on, Keegan." Braden took a sip of his coffee.

"Yes, dear old dad is at it again. He's trying to pull in my brother to work with him and apparently Jayce hasn't learned to keep dad more than an arm's length away."

"He's young. He'll figure it out soon. But I'm sorry to hear that. It's so hard to watch a loved one make poor choices."

"Yes it is. I want to intervene, protect him. Dad has already used Jayce and then let him take the fall. I don't want to see him hurt again. I blame myself for not being around to take care of him, to show him a different way of living."

"I think we're all dealing with guilt in some form. Me, too. I haven't been very hands on at APD work for days. My partner Zane is shouldering the workload." Braden rubbed his temple. "It's all part of being an Aeon, I guess. I know Payson feels out of pocket. It seemed like the first thing everyone did this morning when they got up was touch base with their regular work."

"Yeah, I talked with my office manager earlier. I'm lucky she knows the business well and keeps things running in my absence." Keegan glanced around at the others as some were on their phones and others were working on their laptops and still others were conversing. His gaze centered on Ainsley staring outside. He couldn't blame her. It was beautiful out behind Payson's house, and at the moment the sun sparkled on the still pond and autumn leaves drifted down gracefully in the forest.

ZuZu brushed against his leg and he bent down to pet her. "Payson, was your cat a little spooked last night by all the commotion? I didn't see her much after we arrived."

Payson looked up from her laptop and chuckled. "She likes company but she hid last night in my bedroom. It's her safe space and we arrived after her bedtime. She was ready to hit the sack. I see she's warming up to you?"

He rubbed ZuZu's head and patted her on the back, but all the while his thoughts remained on Ainsley. He knew well what he wanted; tell the others or show the others they were hooking up. But he wanted to respect her need for time and space.

For the moment, all was quiet, with everyone apparently tending to their separate chores. Suddenly noticing his leg bouncing, he tried to sit with his impatience and not explode. Between wanting to talk with Jayce, to face off with his father regarding the loan, tackle the situation with Ainsley's family and the mob and the Principle Group's casino and Stillwell project, as well as address Diane's strange behavior, he felt pulled in multiple directions but marching in place.

Inside his head, words took shape.

"Mayor, please, you must consider my concerns. The casino and Stillwell Project are endangering the river and the community. Reports indicate problems with drainage that would lead to pollution. We need to halt construction, at least until compliance is met."

"The project is underway. We're not going to shut it down." The mayor dismissed the input.

""But Mr. Mayor, you've got to understand, the city would risk legal liabilities if we don't enforce state and federal laws for construction sites determining storm drainage runoff control. Already, community residents are preparing to protest the casino and new construction to place of Old Town. You must—"

"Stop telling me what I must do," Mayor Farrod interrupted. "You just make sure the project passes scrutiny."

"Sir, surely you don't mean—"

"Just do it. Whatever it takes. Higher-ups than you want this done. Shut the door on your way out."

Keegan recognized the person speaker was Braden's friend at the City of Auralia, Reid Curtis. Hearing him warn the mayor boosted his spirits. The Aeons weren't alone.

But as the voices stopped, Keegan focused back on the setting around him. First in his sight, Ainsley, watching him from across the room. He smiled, and she returned it, warming his heart. She raised her open hand, gesturing to the rest of them, and he interpreted her message.

"Excuse me." The room got attentive. "I just overheard a conversation between Farrod and a possible ally, Reid Curtis."

"Doesn't Reid work for the City of Auralia?" Cooper asked.

"He does. And he's a friend of mine," Braden piped up. "I worked with him before. In fact, I sent him out of town when he stood in direct line of fire with Diane and her cronies."

Keegan nodded. "It sounded like he may need our protection again. It appears the mayor is telling him in no uncertain terms to push his projects through."

"What else did you hear?" Ainsley rested her elbow on her knee and leaned in.

"It's as I told you already. The casino and other nearby project are not squaring with government regulations. There are problems with their CGP."

"CGP?" Benjamin asked.

"Sorry," Keegan said. "Construction General Permit. All projects must meet National Pollution Elimination Discharge Systems requirements. These regulations come under the local, state, and federal Clean Water Act. It can take up to ninety days from submission to get approval."

"What happens if a project goes forward without a proper permit?" Skye twirled a lock of her long, dark hair.

Keegan drummed his fingers on the countertop. "Shut down and hefty fines. Things I doubt the mob cares about."

"But, I doubt they would want the attention," Braden added. "That must stand for some kind of a deterrent. If they knew and went ahead anyway. And woe be unto the inspector who catches them on it."

"Good point." Ainsley shot Keegan a wry grimace. "Maybe the info should go to the FBI. I happen to have an in with one of those agents."

The silence was deafening, and Keegan chuckled. "Sorry, Ainsley.

That idea fell like a lead balloon. And I can't say as I blame anyone. Do we really want to get close to a government agency?"

Ainsley rubbed her chin, thoughtfully. "Right. I'm seeing padded walls and locked doors in our future were we to come close FBI scrutiny. Sorry guys. Breathe, breathe," she laughed. "Can Skye and Payson use this information with their community outreach?"

"Ooh, I want to." Skye's eyes widened. "Can we get a copy of the documents you photographed to verify the pollution problems at the construction site?"

"They're on my phone, so I'll just text them to you. Will that work?" Keegan asked.

That would be perfect," Skye said.

"How's your petition drive going?" Cooper asked.

"Fair. A lot of people we approach don't want to get involved. But we're not easily dissuaded," Payson said. "We've been in touch with a local journalist, so we're hoping to get some press covering the next meeting of Advocates for Community Empowerment. Top of the agenda is discussing a protest at Old Town against the Stillwell project and the casino. Anyone else attending that meeting? It's tomorrow afternoon at the Community Center.

Braden raised his hand. "I am."

"I would but, I'm sorry, I need to relieve poor Iris," Ainsley said. She's held down my shop while I've been taking care of my family and doing Aeon work the last few days."

"No apologies. Take care of things," Keegan said. "Your shop is your livelihood."

Ainsley frowned. "It is. But I've been wondering about it. I've always believed Fancy Is to be important to the community in keeping it grounded. Now I'm wondering, am I doing enough to support our mission?"

Keegan chewed on his lower lip, wondering why Ainsley felt unsure of her contribution to the mission.

Payson scooched closer to Ainsley and put her hand on her shoulder. "What's going on to make you question something you've believed in for a long while? It's a beautiful spot of history, community, and serenity."

"It's not like I fight justice like you and Braden," she answered. "Or help people get resolution to a crime or a second chance at a new life, depending on the circumstances, like Keegan and Payson. I don't serve people nutritious food and offer a place to gather with friends, and offer healing, like Skye, or counsel people in need like you, Cooper. I just sell antiques. It occupies my time, but is it enough?"

Helplessness and uncertainty stabbed Keegan hard. How could he help Ainsley? He wanted to go to her and wrap his arms around her. But she wasn't a frail woman. She could sort out this dilemma herself, couldn't she?

Around the room, words of encouragement and support were given. He held back from joining, not because he didn't care but because he supported her strength.

"I appreciate all your encouragement," she said. "This is something I've been mulling over. I have to sit with my feelings and learn what's best."

Payson and Braden exchanged a glance. "We both have work we need to address," Braden said. "What up for the rest of you?"

"I think we all need to remain vigilant." Cooper shook his head. "DAs aren't going away for good just because we had success rescuing Keegan and had a night holed up here. And we can't neglect the issue facing Ainsley's family."

"Thank you. But I can take care of my family today."

"I know you can." Cooper's lips tightened. "But you don't have to do it alone. I can help out today. And the next day. But we probably should address the biggest concern. Furey and his intention of destroying Auralia and all of us, including your family. I know we keep talking about it."

"Give it a rest." Ainsley started pacing the living room floor. "I don't mean to be rude. But we had one night of rest. We've been doing a lot to raise awareness. We've been over and over assessing our efforts. You all have done a lot. Let's not forget that."

"I'm with Ainsley." Keegan dared to say he agreed because it seemed so right. He strengthened his sense of light and love, spreading it to the group. "I'm going to do what I do. I'm going to raise my awareness of the energy of truth and strength. Fight the fight at my personal level. Address the needs of Ainsley's family today. Set my family straight. And support all of you with my abilities."

His eyes met Ainsley's and slowly, deliberately, she closed the space between them, taking his hand and sitting beside him. His heart fluttered erratically, and he knew it wasn't from heart disease. Warmth spread through him.

"What's this?" Cooper's smile stretched across his face.

Payson's hand went to her mouth and Braden chuckled. "You two have something you want to share with us?" he asked.

In his head, Ainsley's voice came to Keegan. *Tell them.* He searched her face. "Really? Are you sure?"

She tossed her hair out of her face and nodded vigorously.

Wrapping his arm around her shoulders, he pulled her close and couldn't suppress a spontaneous smile. "We're together, officially."

Benjamin jumped up from his seat on the floor. "I knew it."

CHAPTER 27

$\mathcal{K}$eegan led Ainsley by the hand out of the living room and downstairs to Payson's office. They needed to talk, privately, she knew, so she went willingly. She dropped onto the still open sofa-bed and he flopped down beside her. Her pulse skipped a beat and she nestled close to him.

"So," he started, "we told everyone we're a couple." His eyes gleamed, setting her heart on fire.

"We did."

"I was surprised to hear your message. What changed your mind?"

She took a moment to gather her thoughts, but meanwhile, enjoyed the tender touch of Keegan's fingers tracing a path up and down her arm. He melted her fears, her misgivings, her guardrails. And she was grateful for that. It had been such a long time since she could remember feeling completely relaxed like this. But she couldn't deny that somewhere in the back of her mind was an expectation: When will the other shoe drop? She didn't want it there. It was just so automatic.

"You know the other day when we were attacked at the safe house and you sacrificed yourself?" Her eyes stared at the ceiling.

"I'll never forget. Why?"

"After I confirmed my family was safe, and that the others had them covered, I drove like wildfire to find you. I had a sense of you, and it felt like you had died."

Keegan's hand paused mid-air for brief moment, then resumed caressing her arm.

"I had to get to you, to stop that from happening. I'd dropped your phone into the pocket on the backseat, so I knew I could track the vehicle to where you were taken."

"That was smart. I didn't know that." His voice was low, serious.

She rolled on to her side and peered into his eyes, fear warring with emotion. "Well, someone found it and tossed it out the window on the side of the road. Anyway, my visions aren't predictions, but they can be. And they're not anchored in a particular time. Unbeckoned, a tear meandered down her cheek. Keegan gently brushed it away and kissed her cheek. He waited quietly for her, not rushing her or pressing her to continue. "Not knowing, I had to get to you. Had to protect you. I knew then just how much I felt for you. But a part of me was afraid, afraid to believe that you could care about me in the deep way I long for. That you wouldn't simply be another part of my life that goes away."

"So that was the real reason you wanted to hold back from the others?"

She sighed. "It was the reason beneath the fear of disrupting the group."

He rolled her head to under his chin and hugged her. "You're an amazing woman, Ainsley. You have such a keen understanding of yourself and others. It is truly a gift to me. I have parts that want to hold back, as you know. Afraid of being ignored, used, rejected. It's good that we are allowing those parts to speak to us, rather than repressing them. I guess we could call them our dark sides. Shining light on them helps us heal and be able to have more joy and happiness. Do you think?"

Bliss filled her from head to toe. No one other than her counselor Claire Eve had ever talked to her like that. And no family nor friend had truly seen her this way before. "You mean a lot to me. I'm just grasping how much. But I don't want to move too fast or skip over anything."

"What do you mean, skip over?"

"I want us to take our time to get to know each other better. I'm not a surface person."

Like bubbles, Keegan's laughter was light and airy and delightful. "I know that about you. I like deep thoughts, too."

"I've been learning that about you."

"You know. I didn't die. Not in the way you thought from your vision. But metaphorically, parts of me that no longer fit me did die while I was in captivity. I realized my feelings for you were solid and my fears were preventing me from owning up to them. I had to release those ancient parts that used to protect me, because they were standing in the way of being with you."

"I don't like to think of you dying in any way, but I get what you're saying."

Just then, she heard someone calling them.

"I guess we're wanted upstairs." Keegan dropped his head onto her belly. "Do we have to go?"

"I suspect if we don't, someone will invade us down here eventually." She rolled him over and climbed on top of him. "This has been nice. Thank you, Keegan." Softly, she pressed her lips to his, savoring their closeness for another moment.

"That was sweet." Keegan smiled as she pulled away.

She rolled off him, then stopped short. *Her focus shifted, and she saw the inside of Fancy This, everything smashed and thrown about. Laughter, sickly and menacing, came to her. DAs grabbed merchandise and flung it to the floor. Precious, beautiful pieces breaking apart and crumbling to smithereens. Her heart cried out. "No! No!" Then the worst of it happened. The DAs grabbed Iris by the arms and threw her down.*

"Stay down," one demanded. She tried to rise, but he shoved her down and stomped on her hand. She hollered, but tried again to get to her feet.

Ainsley held her head between her hands as the vision closed. "Wait, I need more," she cried.

"What is it, Ansley?"

She looked at Keegan, standing in front of her and he pulled her to her feet. "My shop. Iris. I have to go right now."

"Wait, I'll go with you."

She couldn't run fast enough up the stairs. She grabbed her jacket and purse and headed toward the door.

"Wait, what's going on?" Payson tried to stop her.

Turning from the door, Ainsley faced her friends as Keegan ran to her side. "I had a vision. I don't know if it's happening right now, but the vision showed me that my shop was being ransacked and Iris was being attacked. I have to go."

"I'll drive you," Keegan offered.

"You don't have your vehicle," Skye reminded him, as each one gathered their things and ran to their vehicles in the driveway. "Are you okay to drive Ainsley's truck?"

"Yes."

"You ride with one of us, Keegan, Ainsley." Braden stood at his vehicle, dangling his keys. "Benjamin, you're with me and Payson."

"I'm driving. Keegan, Ainsley, Skye, you're all with me." Cooper slid in behind the wheel in his electric SUV, giving them just enough time to climb in.

Braden led them both out of the gate and down the road toward Old Town, wasting no time.

Nerves inside Ainsley fired over and over, straining to learn the truth: Iris was badly hurt or she was perfectly fine. It was all too much. Her parents and sister under fire, then Keegan, and now Iris and Fancy This?

She watched the passing fall scenery outside the window, trying to settle her mind, her heart, her soul. Keegan sitting close beside her grabbed her hand and held it. She squeezed his, and shook her head. "If Iris and my shop have been attacked, it may Dark Sides amping up pressure on us."

Keegan nodded. "That's a good point. It also could be a distraction, trying to divert our efforts away from Dark Sides. Keep us busy on other fronts."

"As far as my brain is concerned, it's working. My thoughts are scattered. I'm inundated."

"Understandable. It is a lot to manage all at once."

Skye turned in her seat. "Whatever we find when we get to your shop we'll be grateful for your vision. Insights are always helpful to our cause."

"Skye is right," Cooper said over his shoulder. "Your abilities are important to our work. Remember that."

"Thanks." Ainsley bit her lower lip. Regardless, she had decisions to make about her shop and her role as an Aeon.

The rolling road ahead remained clear, with no appearance of any interference. As they drove closer to the city, traffic increased but nothing warned them that DAs were near or danger loomed. Peering over Cooper's shoulder, Ainsley prepared for the worst as they approached Old Town. "Pull in the parking lot behind the building when we get there," she said.

Minutes later, Cooper slowed the car and made the last turn into the area, and Ainsley held her breath. As soon as the vehicle stopped, she flung open the car door and ran to the back door of her shop, with Keegan right behind her.

"Hey, wait for me, wait for me," he called, catching up with her. He tried to hold her back and go in first, but she blocked his way.

She stepped inside and tore across the floor. Debris littered the main showroom floor. "Iris, where are you?"

"I'm right here." Iris walked out from one of the adjoining rooms, holding her right hand in her left.

Ainsley walked to meet her. "Oh, Iris. Are you all right?"

"I'm so sorry, Ainsley. I tried to stop them. I tried to call the police." Iris swiped at tears running down her face.

"Whoa, look at this place." Braden stepped carefully into the room with Payson by his side. Benjamin, Cooper, and Skye followed.

"This is a such a travesty." Payson bent to pick up a broken vase. "Ainsley, I'm sorry. What happened here?"

"I just couldn't stop them. There were two of them and they were strong." Iris sunk to the floor and Ainsley joined her, hugging her.

"It's not your fault. I'm sorry I left you here alone. I should have heeded your warning. You told me a man had threatened you here." Ainsley rocked on the floor, lost in anguish.

Quietly, Skye snapped photos of the mayhem, while Cooper took it all in, his expression sorrowful.

Keegan crossed his arms over his body, striding from room to room.

Ainsley stood up and righted a chair, helping Iris to sit. "How did your hand get hurt?"

"I was trying to stop the men from destroying things and one of them threw me down and the other one stepped on my hand. I think it's okay, but it's sore."

Cooper gently took her hand, turning it over and inspecting it. He moved her fingers one at a time. "Does this hurt? How about this? And this? Well, I don't think there are any fractures, just bruising. But I suggest you get it looked at by your doctor, just to be sure. Today. One of us can drive you."

Skye tapped Ainsley on the shoulder. "I'll send you these photos. You should call your insurance representative." She took hold of Iris's hand. "I'm sorry this happened. Could you tell me more about the attack?"

Iris relayed the same details, but Ainsley knew what Skye was doing, giving her a dose of her healing touch. Then she walked her to Cooper's vehicle to take her to ER. It meant a lot to Ainsley, but it didn't take away the pain.

Cooper's conversation with Iris and talk between the others went on around her, but Ainsley paid little attention. She surveyed the four rooms, fisting her hands. Anger built inside her. "How dare they tear up my shop and attack Iris." She gritted her teeth. "How long are we going to put up with this stuff. People are getting hurt. Auralia's treasures are being destroyed. Bad people are doing whatever they want and no one is stepping up to stop it all."

Braden shook his head. "The police force is fighting crime. But it takes more than traditional action to stop the diabolic threat the city faces."

"There must be another way." Powerful determination flooded Ainsley. The warmth of light, love, and peace streamed through her.

"What do we have here?" Diane walked in the front door and swept her gaze across the main showroom. "I've never been a fan of your shop, Ainsley. But I'm sorry this happened."

"What are you doing here?" Keegan marched up to stand face to face with Diane, staring her down. "What do you know about his? Did you have a part in this?"

She pursed her lips and seconds passed silently, as she blinked rapidly. "Are you accusing me of something, Keegan?"

He spread his arms wide. "You showing up right after this mess happened is a little too coincidental. So yes, an explanation would be great."

She hung her head. "I can understand you all thinking I'm behind the attack, but I had no part in it. I haven't," her gaze shifted to Iris, then back to Ainsley. "I haven't been in touch with those people since the warehouse incident. You do remember who, um, helped you out there, Keegan, don't you? I promise you, I'm disentangling myself from the people who did this and other diabolical things happening in the city."

"That doesn't explain why you're here now." Payson rested her hands on her hips.

"I'm here to help." Diane rolled her head around her shoulders. "I overheard Mayor Farrod and Deglan Furey discussing how they would interfere with the city's investigation into pollution problems at Principle Industry's casino and Stillwell construction site, and how Keegan posed a threat to its success. I heard them dispatch men to Fancy This to cause havoc. And I heard them discuss their plan to get revenge on the Durham family. There is an expectation that such interferences would cause you all to lose hope and feel helpless. Weaken you."

Ainsley marched up close to Diane, her eyes flashing. "And you didn't think to alert us?"

"I couldn't get away. I'm here now."

"A little late." Ainsley pivoted, then paused and turned back around. "This attack isn't weakening my resolve. It's only strengthening it."

"Mine, too," Keegan added. Around the room each Aeon agreed. But Diane stood silent.

Payson crossed her arms over her chest. "I don't know what to think about you, Diane. You've done everything you could to promote the growth of Dark Sides in Auralia, and suddenly I'm to trust that you have switched sides?"

Diane sighed heavily. "I know, I know. I've been terrible for many years." She cocked her head to one side. "I want another chance. When I participated in the attack on your family, Ainsley, I saw the love your parents had for you and your sister. You had Keegan. It made me mad, at first, jealous that I'd never had that. And I'd been jealous of you, Payson, because you had Braden. It hurt so bad. But I also felt the love you all have penetrating my anger. It devastated me to think I'd been out to hurt you and Keegan. Then, at the warehouse yesterday I saw and heard the hatred and greed in Furey, and I saw how it had driven me for years, since I was young. I sought power and control to relieve my feelings of worthlessness, my feelings of guilt for what I'd done. But I also saw that not one of you had ever given up on me. I've fought light and love tooth and nail, that's true. I have no excuse except that I've been terribly messed up. But your efforts to offer me a way out of darkness have penetrated my pain and anger. That's all I can say." She raised her hands palm up to the ceiling. "Give me a chance. I'll prove myself to you. I want to help you, Ainsley, with protecting your family, if you'll let me."

Anger seethed inside Ainsley. "I'm not letting you near my family."

"I get that. But I can work behind the scenes, somehow persuade Furey it's not in his best interest. I don't know exactly how, but I'm willing. I want to make up for what I've done."

Ainsley heard something different in Diane's demeanor. A sense of sorrow and remorse that allowed her to consider possibilities that could benefit her family and the Aeon's mission.

"I can only speak for myself," Cooper said. "But don't we need to discuss this?" He gave a pointed look in Diane's direction. "Without her in the room."

Ainsley raised her chin to Keegan, who in turn nodded. "We can do one better, Cooper."

"Oh, yeah." Braden nodded.

"Yes. It is better," Benjamin chimed in.

Payson chuckled. "What are we waiting for?"

"What's going on?" Diane looked from one, to another, to another, of the group.

Each one stood around Diane and closed their eyes.

Ainsley centered herself, opening her senses, already suspecting what the others knew too. Seconds passed quickly, in time with her heartbeat. Light, love, peace, and strength undeterred by darkness flowed freely throughout the room, the building, out into the community and beyond.

No darkness buzzed under her skin. It took only sixty seconds, one minute, for the truth to shine out beyond a shadow of a doubt. She opened her eyes and watched the truth dawning in all the Aeon's faces. Light had grown in strength.

Diane truly was one of them.

CHAPTER 28

The morning got away from Ainsley. After talking with her insurance agent and hanging up the closed sign in her shop, she and Keegan and Benjamin drove back with Braden and Payson to her house to pick up Ainsley's truck. With Payson promising to return Benjamin back to Keegan's place, Ainsley drove Keegan to get his car at the first safe house.

She stood opposite him in the back yard, holding tightly to his hands. His grasp and tenderness in his eyes raised goosebumps on her arms. Silence stretched between them. There was much to say but words escaped her.

"Everything has changed," he said, almost as though reading her mind but she knew he wasn't. They shared the sentiment. "It's been a rough few days. What am I saying? It's been weeks, months, years. I don't know if I'd change any of it, because it's the path that has brought you to me. Please be safe out there today."

She wrapped her arms around his neck and lifted her lips. Without hesitation, Keegan's hungry mouth kissed her hard, determined, demanding, and passion ignited in her heart. She couldn't have asked for anything more. "You too. Pressure is on us all. Keep your guard up." She stood on tiptoe and pressed her head against his. "Please stay in touch."

Reluctantly they stepped apart and she waved to him as he drove away, then climbed in her vehicle and followed her GPS to the house her family was staying in for now, her thoughts scattering. Diane's admission to wrong-doing and her energy shift had been not only completely unexpected but miraculous. She shouldn't have been so surprised. It was something the Aeons had been hoping for and working on for years, sending Diane light and love at every chance. It almost made the destruction of her shop less awful.

On top of that, the possibilities of a growing relationship with Keegan lifted her hopes for love in her own life that she'd never expected.

But before jumping into anything more, she had to square away her family's safety, permanently. How? She didn't know. Her nerves rattled, wondering what she'd find at the new safe house today. With every hill and every swerve in the road she grew closer to finding out, and she eagerly pressed the pedal farther down to arrive as quickly as possible.

Her GPS announced her destination was just ahead and her heart rate sped up, anxiety making its mark. She slowed to enter the neighborhood. The house she drove up to sat far back on the lot and a line of tall trees nearly blocked the view. She turned up the driveway and parked in front of the garage, trepidation filling her gut. What ifs compounded in her brain, but she quickly marched up to the front door just as the living room drapes fell back in place, letting her know someone inside was watching.

She raised her hand to tap on the door but it opened before she could.

"Ainsley." Her mother's arms grabbed her and walked her inside. She shut the door closed. "It's so good to see you."

"It's about time." Jane looked up from her laptop, smirking. "Where have you been, sis?"

"Oh, Jane, give your sister a minute to sit down and breathe before you start picking on her." Her dad dropped his book on the end table and strode over to hug Ainsley. "You've been busy, I bet. Thanks for coming."

She slid into the nearest chair. "I came as soon as I could. It's great to see you're all doing well. It's been rough out there. We came close to losing Keegan. But you don't need to know about all that. What can I do for you?"

"What? Keegan almost died?" Jane stared at her in disbelief. "That's awful." She nodded her head from side to side. "We're as best as can be expected, being stuffed away here. Not that I'm complaining. I know it can be worse. I'm just so weary of this lifestyle. It's not something I'd choose."

"Are you keeping up with your classes?"

"Yes, dear sister. But my social life is nonexistent." Jane frowned. "Can we expect to get out of here and back to our lives soon?"

"I'm working on it. What about supplies? What do you need?"

Ainsley listened as her family list their needs, wishing she could eliminate the threat to their lives today. She wasn't about to give them more hope, just because Diane promised to help out. That would be a fool's option, but still she hoped.

"I'll run get these things and be right back, making sure no one is tailing me. Keep your vigilance up, as always."

"Are you going to spend some time with us when you get back?" Ansley's mother asked. "Maybe have a late lunch?"

"Yes. I'll spend the night and stay as long as I can." She didn't want to tell them about the travesty at her shop. They needed only good news or no news at all.

* * *

WHICH WAS MORE PRESSING, Keegan wondered, getting face to face with his father or face to face with Jayce? Both needed immediate attention, a situation his nerves were well aware. Urgency sent flares off in his body to do both. Maybe he should rock, paper, scissors it. Nah.

Easily, he decided on seeing his brother first. A quick call to Jayce and an equally quick drive and he rapped on his brother's apartment door. The complex still looked shabby and cheap, but he knew it was the best he could hope for.

The door opened and Jayce motioned him inside. "It's a good thing you called ahead. I was about to leave for the office. Have a seat."

"Thanks." Keegan perched on the edge of a chair. He couldn't relax. His visit was serious.

Jayce slumped into the other empty chair. "What brings you to my humble abode?"

"I haven't spent much time with you lately. I miss you." He hadn't lied.

Jayce squared him with his gaze. "Okay. Yeah, I guess you've been busy with work, huh?" He eyed him closely. "What happened to your face?"

"I got into an altercation. "

"That's a fancy word for fight, Keegan. What happened?"

"It's not important. I'm fine."

"You don't want to say." Jayce frowned. "I'm not your little kid brother anymore, ya' know."

"Yah, I know. That's not why I'm here." He looked down at his hands, searching for just the right words. "I should have taken better care of you back when Dad pulled you into his mess. I know you're grown and all that but I wish I could have kept you from taking the rap for him."

"Hmm" Jayce stared him. "I did what I had to. It wasn't your doing."

"That's what I mean. You didn't have to. It wasn't your doing. Dad got himself into financial trouble, not you. He got you into the real estate business, then falsified business records and financial statements, not you. He rightfully deserved to go to jail and he let you take the blame for him. I know that."

"What's your point?"

"I don't want it to happen again. I'll take care of you."

Jayce fisted his hands. "I can take care of myself."

The minute he'd said the words, 'I'll take care of you,' he knew he

217

shouldn't have. "I know, I know. But I want you in my business. You've got the four-year Business Degree. I could use your help. If you want, you could even work under my recovery agent license, get your own license in time and work in the field."

"Be a bounty hunter?" He eyes widened. "I don't know. Dad is—"

"Stop thinking about Dad," Keegan interrupted. "He will always survive. Trust me. I know him and I know his type." He leaned closer to Jayce. "I help people, Jayce, put their lives back together, whether they're a perp or someone seeking closure as a victim. Tell me you don't want to work with me or get your own license or help people."

Jayce looked away, staring out the window.

Something crashed above their heads in the apartment above, and a baby cried, followed by hollering between two people. Jayce shrunk down in the tattered chair. Keegan's heart clenched and he streamed light, love, and hope to him, wishing only for the right and perfect thing for his brother. He sat quietly, waiting for a response. They were different from each other. His brother wasn't him, wasn't an Aeon either. But he was a good young man.

"Do you need an answer right now?" Jayce asked.

"I don't want you to think too long about it. Know that I'm not offering you a busy-work kind of job, I'm going to be able to pay you well. And the job would come with benefits."

Jayce looked away again. "I couldn't get a job after my stint in the pen. No one would hire me, even with my degree. Dad set up a business for me," he said softly. "I was grateful. I didn't know."

"You didn't know Dad was a criminal or didn't know he'd leave you dangling when the law came?"

Jayce faced him. "Neither one."

"I tried to tell you."

"I know, but he was my dad."

"Yeah. I get that. I've done my share of protecting him, too. Not anymore."

"If I work for you, do you think we could still hang out more, I mean, after work, weekends?"

Keegan jumped up and ruffled his brother's hair. "You bet. How about you come over sometime this week and we'll watch the Lions' game?"

"I'd like that." Jayce hugged him and smiled. "Thanks for this."

"Of course." He paused. "You know what I think we should do? I think we should have Mom over to my place for dinner. Just the three of us."

Jayce grimaced. "That would be tricky if we leave Dad out."

"A mom has the right to visit with her sons, right?"

"That sounds good to me. You set it up and let me know, okay?"

"I will."

On the drive through town, Keegan's mood lifted. Sure there was a whole load of not-such-great things to attend to still, but his time with Jayce had been productive. He checked his watch, noting it was past noon, and cemented his intentions for his next stop. He'd thought he done everything he could to keep his brother safe from possible harm from Sully, but it turned out he failed. He had to live with that. But as he made his way toward his father's place of business, he had every intention of making sure things were different now. He pulled into a parking space, climbed out of his jeep, and marched inside.

"Dad," he called, bypassing the secretary. "Dad."

"You don't need to yell, son." His father walked out of his office, frowning. "I hope you're here for a good reason. You know what I mean."

Keegan strode past him into his office and sat in front of his father's desk. "I have a very good reason, but it's not what you think."

Sully stopped short, then pulled the door closed and took a seat behind his desk. "As long as you have my money, I don't care why you're here."

Keegan straightened his shoulders and peered into his father's eyes. He pushed an envelope toward him, but remained on the edge of his seat while his father opened it.

A smile lit up Sully's face and he nodded, holding the check. "This looks good."

"Consider us squared, then."

"Uh, yeah. Is there something more?"

"Yes." He leaned over the desk and pointed his finger in his father's face. "You will stay away from Mom and Jayce."

"What are you talking about?" His father's face reddened.

"I believe I was clear. You are never to go near either of them again. No visits, no phone calls, no business endeavors that involve them. If you do, I'll give the authorities proof of your crimes. Your crimes," he said, emphasizing *your*.

His father stood. "You're threatening me?"

"It's an agreement. A business arrangement. One that carries consequences for you if you break it. Effective now." He rapped on the desk.

"You can't order me around."

"Can. Am. And just so you know, I gave you that money, not because you're entitled to it but because I want you completely out of my life. So this is it. The last time I'll see you or talk to you unless I find out you've broken the agreement, because we both know you've already broken the law and the hearts of people I love."

"Hold on! You think you're better than me. You always have, just because you think you're special." Sarcasm framed his words. "You're full of light and I'm just dark. Fine. Stay away. See if I care."

Keegan patted the desk twice, then walked back through the door and out to his jeep. With a lighter heart, he headed to his house to check on Benjamin. He wanted to entertain only positive things about Diane, but he would be wrong to trust her fully, especially with Benjamin on his own.

The trek across town to where he lived took about thirty minutes. Impatience to get there as soon as possible ran through his blood vessels like lightning. He turned onto his street and up his driveway coming to an abrupt halt. Sure enough, Diane's vehicle was parked in the street out front. Without acknowledging her, he strode briskly to his front door and closed the door behind him, locking it.

"Benjamin," he called.

"I'm up here." His voice carried down the stairs.

"I'm coming up. You decent?" Keegan ran up the stairs two at a time to find him sprawled on his bed, watching television. "Hey, you good."

"Yup. I saw Diane outside a few minutes ago. Did you know she was coming over?" He stood up and leaned on one foot.

"No. I didn't expect her at all. Do you have a gut feeling about her?"

"She wants to make up. I don't want to talk to her, not yet."

"Yeah, I wouldn't want to either after what she put you through. I'll check her out. I can handle her. I have things to say to her. You can stay up here. I'll close the door and you lock it."

Before he got to the bottom of the stairs he heard a knock at the door. Taking a moment to center himself, he then opened the door to Diane. "You want to come in?"

She gave him a dismissive wave and walked inside. "I want to talk with you." She handed him her coat, dropped into the couch, and crossed her legs.

"Come on in." He gestured a welcome with a shake of his head and laid her coat over the back of the couch. "What's up?"

"Sit down," she ordered.

"This sounds like the same Diane I've known for years. Demanding. Bossy. Rude." He eased into the upholstered chair. "What do you want?"

She shook one of her legs up and down rapidly and said nothing for a couple minutes. She ran her tongue over her dark red lips, avoiding his eyes. "I have a couple of ideas of how I can help out the cause and get back into the group's graces."

He measured his reaction, not wanting to offer hope that wasn't there for her or give her the feeling her help was loaded with suspicion. He laced his fingers behind his head. "Shoot."

"As a city leader, I have knowledge of Project Stillwell that no one else outside of a few members of an inner circle are privy to."

"And by city leader you also mean you're a member of the Irish Mob's inner circle and card-carrying member of Dark Sides in Auralia, right?"

She cocked her head and rolled her eyes. "You don't have to highlight those things. I'm coming to you with this proposition because you've been the kindest and most open Aeon to me lately."

"I haven't heard any proposition yet."

Diane let out a long sigh. "I propose that I persuade the head of the Irish Mob, the Mayor, and the Economic Director, as well as the project director to relax their timeline, thereby giving Old Town and the community more time to fight against the project."

He curbed his reaction to her suggestion, waiting for the other shoe. "What's the other idea?"

"I'll convince Furey to drop his vendetta against Ainsley's family."

"He's been on the attack for years, and they only had some years of relief when he didn't know where they were. How are you going to stop him?"

"The same way for both. Threaten to out him to the authorities, and show him how bad for business it would be."

Shock and disbelief rocketed through Keegan's brain. Dare he trust her? "You do realize that for years, years," he emphasized, "Diane, you've been fighting for the bad guys. You've hurt the Aeons over and over. Now you profess to be on the side of good and suggest you would intervene on behalf of what's best for the community. Am I getting that right?" He heard his voice getting louder, but couldn't help it.

"Yes," she said, punctuating with hearty nodding. "I'm all in for the side of what's right and perfect for my fellow Aeons, the community, and the world, if it comes to that." Earnestness filled her eyes. "Look, I said, I know I've been all wrong and proud of it. I've done wrong things for all the wrong reasons. I wish I could erase it all, but I can't. All I can do is this, right now, and hope that it works out well for us."

"And by us, you mean, Aeons." It was so hard to take her at her word.

"I mean Aeons. I want to work on the side of good. Unequivocally and for the rest of my life. Even if you all don't let me in to the group, I'll advocate for the people of Auralia." Her voice dropped. "I have absolutely no right to ask this, but please believe me."

222

He held up one finger. "Wait. I need to think on this. I'll have to ask you to leave and I'll get back to you."

"I expected as much." She pulled on her coat and headed toward the door. "Don't take too long, Keegan. The others I've been working with aren't going to hold off long on their project."

"Don't do anything without talking to me again."

She opened his front door and stepped outside. "I won't."

CHAPTER 29

*a*fter talking with Ainsley about Diane and her proposition, Keegan still had reservations, but work called. He set his thoughts of Diane on a back burner and grabbed Benjamin to drop off at Skye's café. The young Aeon had good coloring in his face and clarity about who he was and what he wanted to do, beginning with getting back to work at Coffee Is. When he brought it up to Skye, she'd concurred. With her ability to see and assess Benjamin's aura, she'd attested to his good health, so as Keegan walked inside with Benjamin, she opened her arms wide and hugged him.

"I'm so glad you're here. Are you sure you're ready to put on an apron and man the orders?" she asked.

"Where's my apron?" Benjamin walked behind the counter, hands open and eagerness written all over his face. "You bet I'm ready."

Late afternoon was settling in as Keegan stood near the door, watching Benjamin interacting with customers. Happiness spread through him, and naturally his light, love, and joy flowed. With a light heart, he sped away to work he'd been away from for too long.

Pausing a moment to take in the sun low in the sky, Keegan collected his thoughts in the parking lot at Best Bond Company. He'd been relying on Ricki to manage the day-to-day of his business the last couple of days, but expected her to be done for the day. His brain went on to making lists of what to catch up on, as he raised his hand to punch in the code to unlock the door. He hesitated, his peripheral vision catching that the door was slightly ajar. He swung it open. Shock rocked through him with his first steps inside.

Ricki's desk area looked as if it had been hammered with a sledgehammer. Her computer, little twinkly lights, files, everything was scattered across the floor.

He ran to his office, and leaned against the doorway, dismay and fear pounding inside him. All his things—desk, computer, shelves, memorabilia—all of it in shambles.

He pivoted to the storage room and found it, too, a mess. Heaving a sigh of relief, he found his safe locked and its contents inside, including his gun. Luckily, he'd gone for the impenetrable version of a safe.

The enormity of the malice behind what had been done in his business could barely sink in. The logical part of his brain overrode the emotional parts of him that wanted to exact retribution, and he called Braden, Detective Braden.

He drifted from one room to another, surveying the destruction, all the while carrying sadness and empathy. Only a very unhappy and chaotic person could conceive of this kind of destruction of property. He didn't want to use his ability to hear what he already knew. He didn't want to dip a toe in it. Diane had been right about Dark Sides ramping up pressure on the Aeons, attempting to prompt hopelessness in them and render them useless in the fight against darkness in Auralia. Instead of harboring animosity toward them, Keegan raised his vibration and made himself more available to clarity and courage.

Strengthened, he started sorting through his things in his office. Ricki needed to be told, but he couldn't have her in the building and speak freely with Braden when he arrived.

He sat down among the piles he'd already built and called Ainsley. The phone rang in his ear, and he realized, this is what it felt like to need someone. His parents, too busy with their work and too inattentive to lean on, had not given him that foundation. Was it right to need someone?

"Hi Keegan." Ainsley's voice was breathless. "Sorry it took me a minute to answer. I've been sweeping."

"Me too." His heart went out to her, dealing with the aftermath of the break-in at her shop.

"Don't you have cleaning service at your work?"

"Yes, but," he hesitated. He didn't want to pile his problems on her shoulders.

"What's going on?"

"My business was broken in to. Just like yours."

She gasped. "Oh, no. Keegan. I'm so sorry. Have you told the others yet?"

"I called Braden and he's on his way. I need a police report to give to my insurance agent."

"Yeah, I know. So, DAs have been busy. Looks like we're making progress."

He chuckled. "Yeah, they must be hurting."

"Hang in there. I'll be right there."

"Keegan?"

Hearing Braden call him, Keegan walked to the outer office, and found not only Braden, but Benjamin, his hands in his pockets, both surveying the mess.

"I picked up Benjamin on my way here," Braden said.

"Geez." Benjamin shook his head. "This makes two attacks on Aeons in one day."

"One long day," Braden added, walking through the building, taking notes and snapping photos. "I assume you weren't here when your place was hit, right?"

"No, I got here a little bit ago. This is how I found it. No one was here." Keegan kicked at a broken chair. "If they think this will stop me from doing my job or addressing their influence in the city, they underestimated me."

"You got that right." Braden clapped his hand on Keegan's shoulder.

"And me." Ainsley strode through the room up to him and grabbed him by his shirt, yanking him close. She stared into his eyes and he saw her concern. Something more, much more, then mere sentiment and sexual attraction raced through him. Could he? Did he? In the midst of so much hatred and darkness, love bloomed?

He caressed her cheek and rested his forehead against hers. The others stood nearby, but the closeness he felt with Ainsley was intimate, just between them.

"I'm sorry this happened, Keegan," she said.

"Me too." He made a fist. "This is going to stop."

A tear traipsed down her cheek. She leaned in close and whispered, "Do you know what it would mean to my family to have Furey off our backs, finally, permanently, after all this time? I don't even know how to imagine that kind of freedom."

He pulled her aside. "I know. It would mean the world would change. You would be able to breathe, your family could live wherever it wanted. You could stop looking over your shoulder all the time."

"It's a hard prospect to believe, but I would like to," she said.

"We're here." Skye bustled inside along with Payson and Cooper.

"Is there any question in anyone's mind that we've just taken a hard right and left? What's next?" Cooper scratched his head.

"Well, I'll file a report of my break in with police and contact my insurance company. Keegan will do the same and get in touch with his insurance agent. Then we'll both rebuild." Ainsley shook her head.

Payson frowned. "Keegan, I'm sorry this happened. Dark Sides has been keeping us busy, what with attempting to kill Ainsley's family and breaking into her shop, and now this, I can't help but see big distraction in process. Something big may be about to go down."

Cooper ran his hands over his head. "I've felt a lot of anger. I've picked up temper flares around me."

"I haven't seen anything," Ainsley said, staring at Keegan.

He shared a glance with her. "I have something to share." Keegan shuffled his feet. "I'm sorry I don't have any chairs for you all to sit in. I can offer the floor." He laughed lightly. "Here's the thing. Diane suggested something that we need to discuss."

"Diane? What did she suggest?" Payson crossed her legs in front of her on the floor.

Keegan shared that he'd talked with Ainsley about Diane's thought and brought the rest of them up to speed.

"Is this the proof we asked for of her change?" Skye asked.

"Yes, that's what she said. I haven't had much opportunity to think about it, but you all should know she offered."

Benjamin grabbed his knees and pulled them close. "For what it's worth," he started, then swept his gazed around the group.

"Go ahead, Benjamin." Keegan nodded.

"I have a strong gut intuition that Diane is sincere." He closed his eyes for a full minute. "She mesmerized me and I know what that feels like. I'm not under her control anymore. I have my own mind. I believe her that she has had a shift in energy and wants to play an active role in saving Auralia from darkness."

Keegan felt into the proposition and eyed everyone in turn, bringing up their connection.

Cooper shrugged. "Maybe it's worth a try."

Silence sifted throughout the room, with only the backdrop of the sound of a breeze tossing the tree limbs outside.

Keegan felt Ainsley stiffen beside him on the floor. Her eyes distant, he held up his hand to the others to keep quiet.

THE VISION PLAYING before Ainsley's eyes took her over, and she stood outside Fancy This.

Someone brushed her shoulder on her left, then another on the right, as Ainsley passed through the crowd gathered at Old Town. It looked like more than one hundred people gathered in the parking lot in front of the various shops. She picked out the words they chanted and marched around her. "Old Town stays. Stop Stillwell Project now. Principle Industries pollutes."

Her heart swelled at the loud chant, and she glowed inside at the community support for Old Town and her shop. She loved it so, even though she'd questioned how long she would continue to keep it open. This display of appreciation gave her pause. Maybe it wasn't time to close down.

Commotion on the edge of the plaza grabbed her attention. The crowd shifted like a large wave on the ocean, and she heard the roar of heavy equipment. Someone on a megaphone shouted. "This property is condemned. You all must leave immediately."

The voice repeated, and the crowd started yelling back. "Old Town Stays. Stop Stillwell Project!"

Ainsley's eyes caught sight of approaching bulldozers and fear ran up and down her spine. Screams filled the air, and people ran, ran away from the heavy equipment threatening to inflict serious injuries.

Where were the other Aeons? They had to show up to stop this terrible attempt to thwart the protesters and destroy Old Town.

She climbed on top of a vehicle's trunk, trying to get a better look. Her hand flew to her mouth. She counted ten bulldozers coming closer and closer. How could she stop them? She screamed, and a hand grabbed her shoulder.

"Ainsley, it's okay. Snap out of it."

She turned to see Keegan and melted against his shoulder. "It was only a vision. It felt so real. Darkness was so strong, bearing down on us."

Love and light warmed her as she sensed all six Aeons stream it to her. Her body, heart, and soul soaked it up, rejuvenating her.

"Are you all right," Keegan asked. "What did you see?"

Ainsley relayed her vision, knowing they needed to learn about it but wishing it had not been so alarming.

"You know my visions, as I always remind you, are not predictions or set in a certain time. When I had this vision, it felt urgent. I wanted to stop what was happening." She bit her lower lip, processing their reactions, the despair on their faces, and the determination.

"Take it easy, Ainsley. Your aura around your heart is pale red, which indicates stress, frustration, and fatigue." Skye smiled. "You'll be fine in a few minutes. I see our ancestors coming forward for us. We have their support. I don't often see them, but they've come now to reassure us."

Ainsley wrapped her arms around herself. "That's amazing. We must be facing something very important."

Braden pounded his fist on the floor. "We need to make a decision.

If Ainsley's vision is warning us of what's to come, I don't see how we can reject Diane's proposition. I say we believe in Benjamin's intuition and we tell her to proceed. With caution."

"I second that," Payson interjected, "with one stipulation. Keegan goes with her when she confronts Furey and the others."

Cooper raised his eyebrows. "Keegan? Just Keegan?"

Keegan nodded slowly.

"It's going to be dangerous." Ainsley's heart sunk. The thought of him going with Diane, alone, into the lion's dean thudded hard in her belly.

Keegan nodded again, holding her gaze.

"I am willing to go along," Braden said.

"Since Diane came to me with her suggestion I think I should go alone with her."

"I'm willing to go, too, but you have a point, Keegan. Let's take a vote. Who votes yes to accepting Diane's offer?" Cooper raised his hand.

Ainsley watched as one at a time, each one in the group raised their hand.

"Raise your hand if you think the best course of action is for Keegan to go with her alone?" Cooper raised his hand.

She couldn't. The thought of Keegan going alone with Diane into the lion's den thudded hard in her chest. "I don't like it. I want to go, too."

"I'll feel her out." He flexed his biceps, "But don't worry. I'm up for meeting with the bad guys."

CHAPTER 30

*I*n darkness of the evening, Ainsley walked inside her house, Keegan steps behind her. Her heart heavy as she closed the door behind her, she could think of nothing but the danger the group had voted to put Keegan in. She leaned against the door and stared at the floor, ignoring Keegan. He'd asked to follow her home, saying he needed to talk to her further.

He flipped on the light. "Don't despair. I'm not going to play hero. If I don't get satisfaction from Diane that she's being truthful, I won't move on her proposal." He tipped her chin up and forced her to look into his eyes. "I love you, Ainsley. I'm not going to throw away this relationship."

Her heart did flip flops. He'd told her he loved her. It was unexpected and touched her deeply. She knew his trust issues well, yet he was willing to bare his soul for her. She pressed a kiss to his lips and he received it with unmistakable greed.

He pulled her hard, close to his body, and she leaned into his muscled torso, her breaths coming fast.

Lifting her up in his arms, he carried her to the couch, but she shook her head and pointed to her bedroom upstairs. His strength surrounded her, cupped her in safety and exhilaration.

In her room, he set her on her feet and tore back the bedding with one toss. She reached for his belt, fumbling to unbuckle it and unzip his jeans, but he lifted her arms over her head and ripped off her T-shirt, tossing it to the floor. One strap at a time, he removed her bra and began kissing her breasts, slowly, deliciously.

He moaned, striking a chord in places of her body that hadn't been moved in such a way before.

She finished unzipping his jeans and he bent to remove them and step free of them and his boxers. He climbed into her bed as she got completely naked and slid in beside him, savoring the warmth of his bare skin against hers.

He ran his fingers through her hair, his eyes admiring, and she blushed. "What do you see?"

"Fire," he whispered in her ear. He kissed her hard, devouring her mouth, and she responded in kind. Urgently, he pressed for another as she caught her breath, and he took her deeper into passion.

Pulling away, he moved purposefully to kiss her shoulder, her breasts, down to her belly, her legs, and parting them to taste of her intimately.

Ainsley wriggled beneath him, pleasure filling her, coaxing her to release any remaining reticence. "Keegan," she moaned.

She pulled him up her body, and slid up willingly, slowly, enjoying himself, tempting her. Giggling, she scooted down beneath him to take his hardness in her mouth and teased him back. He pounded the bed with his fists and she continued. Finally, she pressed him to roll over on his back. He gripped her and pulled her on top of him, nestling into her breasts, kissing their tips, and she couldn't help but lean into him. Her hair fell in curtains around him, and his eyes hooded, sending her to the edge. For a brief moment, she slipped beside him as he paused for protection, then slid back under her.

He shoved her down to meet his mouth and they adored each other with a kiss. She gasped as he entered her and she welcomed him, hugging him.

He cupped her face and brushed his lips to her cheeks, then rolled her under him to thrust deeply inside her. She clung to him and rocked in synchrony with him as they reached a crescendo together, pulsing, clinging in the nicest most full-bodied way imaginable.

Her arms dropped to her sides and his head rested against her, still as one.

KEEGAN'S BODY HAD NEVER, ever been so content, so sated. This is what making love was all about, he thought, resting on Ainsley. He felt her chest rise and fall, listened to her inhale and exhale as she lay quietly under him, their legs entwined. He wanted nothing but to love her, through and through, as best he could, for ever and ever. He didn't need her to tell him she loved him. She'd shown him.

He lifted his head to look at her face, her hair curling and slightly damp around it. Her eyes still closed, he looked on, wanting this moment to stay in his memory forever.

"What are you looking at?"

"Beauty."

Her eyes crinkled with a warm smile that spread across her face. Glints sparkled in her green eyes. "I love you, Keegan."

She'd said it so softly he could barely hear her, but her words lodged in his heart. He understood what it took for her to say them, and he cherished her even more.

He held her gaze. "What do you see?"

"A future."

His pulse jumped. "Do you mean it?"

"I do."

He moved off her and pulled the sheet up around them, snuggling close. "Very interesting."

"I think so. Are you afraid we're moving too fast if we entertain that thought?"

The thought had caught him by surprise. The surprise swirled in his body as he sat quietly with it. "Hum, it's funny. With all my fears of being exposed and rejected, I've not thought about a future. I've gone through my days one at a time, staying the course without daring to imagine my future."

Ainsley sighed. "I understand that. I've been the same. I see it now that you describe it like that. But since you've come forward with what you've been hiding, I've sensed things about you that I trust."

He kissed her, one, beautiful short kiss. "I've addressed what has been holding me back. Things are changing for me. And now, when you said you see a future with me, it feels like freedom. Freedom to be myself, to occupy all my possibilities in life with a more open heart. I really like the way it feels."

Ainsley climbed on top of him, straddling him, and stared into his face directly engaging him. "We can take things slowly."

"Or not, if we like."

"Right," she beamed. "I still have my family to consider and the threat of the mob, but I feel free," she said, spreading her arms wide. "I'm so happy."

Her happiness lit him up. He pulled her down and kissed her hard, and then she rested against him. Peace flowed between him and her. He stroked her head, the soft feel of her hair melting him. "I see a future, too, Ainsley, with you in it."

She slid off him, pulled on her robe and walked out to the living room. He pulled on his boxers and jeans and strode to the couch, dropping beside her. He could read her expression, he didn't need to hear her thoughts. They sat together in silence. He ached to relieve her fears, but he simply sat with her, allowing them to be. He wouldn't make hollow promises.

Looking directly ahead, Ainsley remained still for what felt like an eternity to him. Sounds from outside filtered in; birds chirping, leaves rustling, car horns honking in the street. Life was going on all around, while Ainsley wrestled with her emotions and he simply waited.

Finally, she dropped her head onto his shoulder. "I don't want you to confront Furey. I don't trust Diane. Anything could happen." She sat up and he faced her. "I'm going with you."

"I don't think it's a good idea."

She hit her fist on his thigh. "Argh! You said you'd talk to her about it."

"Ow."

She jumped to her feet. "You know I'm right and you're wrong."

He rose to face her. "Not true. I know I could use you."

"Then it's settled." Her face was stone.

"Only one of us can accompany Diane. You know that. If anyone, anyone, goes with me or you, it weakens the other." He watched her expression soften and knew she recognized he was right. "And since Diane told me her plan, it has to be me. Otherwise it makes me look weak. The Aeons can't afford to look weak." He took hold of her shoulders. "I can do this."

Ainsley nodded. "I know you can. I hate the idea, but I know you're right." She gave him a weak smile. "Do you want anything? Something to eat, drink, TV?"

"Just you."

She took his hand. "Come back to bed with me?"

"Of course."

CHAPTER 31

Quietly opening drawers and cupboards in Ainsley's kitchen, Keegan went about his search for coffee filters for the ground coffee beans while she continued to sleep.

"Ah. Found it." He prepared the coffee pot and started it running, then leaned against the countertop, savoring the aroma. He'd already found her cereal and set it on the kitchen island with bowls and spoons. Eagerness ruffled his nerves, while he let her sleep.

The world outside her kitchen window was still waking up, with only a few pedestrians walking dogs and a school bus passing by. Contentment softened his body, a nice contrast to the angst he'd been carrying around for months, or was it years? Things were working out unimaginably well, and he was beyond grateful for all that had transpired in the last few days. He and the others had always believed they created their lives by their choices, but sometimes it had felt that nothing would go well. He'd learned a lot, including that hard things, bad things were survivable, and weren't always what they appeared.

The coffeepot beeped, letting him know the coffee was ready, so he tiptoed into Ainsley's bedroom and watched her sleeping. Peace on her face gave him joy. After all she'd been through, she deserved it.

Gently, he lifted a long lock of hair off her face, admiring its distinctive red. Her hair color was a part of who she was. He kissed her cheek and she stirred with a soft moan.

"Time to wake up, sweetheart," he said softly. "Coffee and breakfast are ready."

Ainsley lifted her eyelids and peered at him with sleepy eyes. "You're up?" She wrapped one arm around his neck and made to pull him back in bed with her, but he resisted.

"Let's go, sleepyhead. Your coffee awaits you."

"Aw, how lovely. I'll be right there."

"Okay, but if you're not in the kitchen in a couple minutes, I'm coming back to pull you out of bed."

"I'll be right there, pest." She threw off the covers and stuck out her tongue, then gave him a cheesy grin.

He struggled to keep himself from tackling her and making it worth her while to stay in bed, but he knew he had to follow up with Diane. He didn't want to continue to keep Ainsley's family and Old Town in danger any longer if he could end it. And he fully intended to if it was at all possible.

He poured himself a mug of coffee and sat on a tall stool at the island. He awoke earlier with plans forming in his head about how to approach Deglan Furey. He'd let Diane do all the talking, of course, and hang back ready to support and defend when and if necessary.

First, he had to convince her to let him accompany her.

Ainsley dashed into the kitchen, skidding in her slippers on the floor. "I completely forgot I was going to spend the night with my family. I told them I would." Her mouth dropped open. "I need to call them. Oh my God. They'll never forgive me."

"Yes, you should call them. Go ahead." He quickly poured her a mug of coffee and handed it to her. "Go. Do."

"Okay, thank you. You're the best." She waved her hand over the breakfast he'd laid out. "You can eat without me. Don't wait." She tossed him a kiss, and left for her bedroom.

His thoughts continued a hard push for solutions, but shifted while he crunched on cereal to the mess he'd left in his shop. He, too, had forgotten to make a call, so he punched in Ricki's number. Luckily, she wouldn't be in the office yet, but she answered her cell.

"Good morning, Ricki. Guess what. You might want to sit down."

A short time later, he'd gone through some of the details of what had happened to warn Ricki, and assure her she'd get paid for the days off they'd have to remain closed. She'd promised to begin cleanup of her stuff later that day and he made a mental note to check in with her again.

"I'll do what I can. What time will the insurance adjuster be there?"

"Her appointment is at one."

"Got it. Withstanding the clean-up, I can do some of my work from home, for the time being."

"Great. Thanks, Ricki."

Meanwhile, he called Braden about getting an officer to check on her at the office. Just as he was hanging up from Braden, Ainsley came into the kitchen. Her face, looking all rosy and happy, touched him. He shot a smile her way and she returned it as she jumped up on a stool next to him.

"How were things with your family?"

"Well, at first miffed. I don't blame them." She took a spoonful of cereal and chewed. "They got over it. I didn't make any promises to them, but I'm thinking I can get to them today."

"Should I apologize for distracting you last night?" He gave her mischievous grin.

She nuzzled up to him. "You should not."

"Did you sleep well last night?"

"Deliciously so. How about you?"

"Despite the worries and plans percolating in my head, I got a good rest, lying close to you."

"It was a nice surprise. I thought I'd be restless with plans, but I conked out. Did I snore?"

He chuckled. "No. Speaking of plans," he started. "What do you have planned for the damage to your shop? You've talked to your insurance agent. Is there a plan in the works for clean-up, rebuilding, moving?"

Ainsley warmed up both their coffees. "No plan has been started." She rolled her eyes. "Geez, what a mess to deal with, just like you."

"Before the break-in, you were questioning whether you'd continue with your shop? What about that?"

She pursed her lips. "What do you think? Should I give up the shop and do something more hands on for our work?"

Keegan stared at his fingertips for a minute. "I also questioned my work with the Aeons and measuring it beside my company. Could I do something that would exert more of an impact on the Aeon's mission, be more straightforward helpful to the community?" He ran his fingers through her hair, noting its glistening softness, even in—or especially—its disarray.

"What you do already does make a huge difference in the community. It offers hope and second chances and resolutions for victims. It manages crimes and penalties. Are you dissatisfied?"

"Those are the same things I would say to you, Ainsley. Your shop offers treasures to past that enrich the present. It's an anchor for individuals looking for deeper meaning in their lives, and stories that help them connect with history, helping them feel a part of the world. Those things are immeasurably good for individuals and the community." He searched her face for clues.

Her eyes misted.

"Are you happy in your work at Fancy This? That matters, too."

"You've made it seem like my shop is important, and that means a lot to me. It does make me happy, in a lot of ways. I love interacting with people and helping them find cherished objects to enhance their personal spaces. I guess I've been second-guessing myself because the rest of you directly serve people's needs. But maybe I can just enjoy my work, knowing I help people too, in my own way."

"Yup. You do." He sighed. "You know, for me, this B and E feels like a set-back, but I'm not giving up. That's what they were meant to do. Make us stop in our tracks, throw us off our games. Let's not go along with that."

Ainsley took him by the hand, and walked him into the living room with her. Laughing, she shoved him onto the couch and planted herself on his lap. "I agree with that philosophy. Things may be looking up for us. I want to grab hold of what's happening and keep going forward."

"We just have to take one day at a time, I think. What's up next is setting our businesses in order and at the same time, going after Furey, Farrod, Brody, and Russell."

"Yeah, that's all."

Keegan punctuated their resolve with a hard kiss to Ainsley's lips, eliciting a giggle. "You giggled into my lips," he said, laughing.

PARTING AT THE FRONT DOOR, Keegan loosely held Ainsley's hand, slowly releasing it. "Have a good day."

"You, too. Stay safe and keep me updated."

"And you, too." He backed out his vehicle far enough to allow her to leave the driveway first. He knew she'd be with her family. That was where she wanted to be and it would be good for her spirits and theirs. He wanted that for her. While their time together last night and in the morning had been glorious, serious situations had to be their focus now.

At this time of day in Auralia, traffic was heavy with people driving to work, to school, and to all the other things necessary for living, so it took him time enough to think before he arrived at the city building. He hadn't called ahead. He wanted to do an impromptu drop-in on Diane to catch her off guard, just in case she was up to something devious. He sat inside his vehicle, opening his psychic hearing to conversations she might be having that he should know about, but all he heard was mundane chatter.

He strode inside and took the elevator up, his senses picking up heavy fear and dark vibes that sent chills running through him. He wasn't afraid. It was helpful to gather the information that would prepare him for anything.

He stepped off the elevator and took a side trip to the city Planning Department. He walked down a hall, checking the nameplates on office doors as he went and stopped at one. Checking over his shoulders, he tapped on the open door.

A man's head popped up over a tall pile of papers and folders overwhelming a desk at the back of the office. "Can I help you?" he asked, rising.

"Hi Reid. Can I come in? I'm a friend of a friend."

The man walked toward Keegan, offering his hand and he shook it. A sharp shard of fear registered in his gut, and he sucked in his breath.

"It seems you know who I am, who are you? Who's the friend?"

Keegan focused a stream of light and peace toward the man. "Braden Powers. Detective Powers." He noticed the man's eyes softening. "I'm Keegan Barnes. I'd like to talk for a minute, if you have the time."

"I have a minute." The man set about stacking piles upon piles to free up a chair. "Have a seat. I am firmly planted in the age of technology, computer files, and all that, but I also keep one foot in hard copies, as you can surmise."

"I understand." Keegan's trust expanded as the man relaxed.

"What's on your mind?"

"I can see that you're busy, so I'll get right to what's on my mind." He took a beat, then proceeded. "From Detective Braden, I know a bit about some things that have gone on within the city that have not been quite kosher." The man squirmed in his seat. "I'm not here to pry into your affairs or threaten you in any way. I'm a small business owner. I run a bonds company, so I have had run-ins of my own with seedy situations. "

"What does that have to do with me?" Reid narrowed his eyes.

"You are not alone, Reid, in the shady activities going on around you. That's what I want you to know. Previously, Braden encouraged you to take care of your family first. I'm here to alert you that those shady dealings, of which you are well aware because you're an upstanding resident of Auralia, are intensifying. Braden and I and a few others are working under the radar to rectify the criminal situations you're bumping up against."

He stilled. "I see. I don't know how to respond to that, Keegan."

Keegan nodded. "Sure. You don't have to. But I would like to confirm that Principle Industries is attempting to ignore certain federal laws regarding its casino construction. Can you do that, Reid?"

That man's jaw muscles clenched. He stared at Keegan. "I guess if you already have suspicions, those are based on something concrete. Am I right?"

"You are."

He shook his head. "I told them they couldn't simply ignore the laws." He pulled up a file on his computer and printed a page. "Here," he said, handing Keegan a memo.

"This verifies that you've alerted officials of the discrepancies. It absolves you and is exactly what I need to prevent their illegal activities." Keegan held out his hand, and Reid shook it. "I'm trying to work through proper channels to alleviate any pressure or danger you might be going through. Do what you have to do, I mean, to protect yourself and your family. Now." He continued to send a gentle stream of peace and light to Reid, knowing it was the best thing he could do for him in the moment. "If you need help with that, feel free to call me or Braden. We're ready, willing, and able to help you."

He passed Reid a small piece of paper with his name and number on it and Reid immediately stuffed it in his shirt pocket, sighing heavily. "Thank you, thank you," he said.

"I apologize for sounding so cryptic, but I believe you understand why and what my intentions are." He touched Reid's shoulder. "I'll see myself out. Take care."

"Take care," Reid said.

Walking down the hall and back to the elevator, Keegan caught a phone call Reid made as soon as he was out of earshot, or so the man thought.

"I'm coming home early. Let's get ready, um, ready, for some fun. Right away."

"What kind of fun, sweetheart? This is sudden," a woman's voice said.

"Let's talk about it when I get home. Don't talk about it to anyone else until you and I talk."

Relieved to hear Reid taking his warning seriously, Keegan

watched the elevator doors open on Diane's floor and checked the list of names on the hallway wall for her office number. He kept his eyes down as he went to it and marched inside without knocking.

"Whoa, this is a surprise." Diane remained seated, motioning him inside. "Shut the door."

He walked directly in front of her desk. "Your proposal is accepted, with one demand."

Her expression remained sober. "What demand?"

"I go with you when you talk to Furey and the others."

Her hand went to one hip. "You don't trust me?"

"Do you blame me?" He hoped his glare conveyed his determination.

Her shoulders sunk. "No, I don't." She swept her gaze up and down him and around the room, then she dropped into her chair. "That would complicate things. I wouldn't be able to completely control the room. Is that a situation you could handle? I really don't want to die."

"Nor do I. I won't say anything in the meeting or do anything to weaken your stance. We have to approach them with strength and grit. Show them they can't oppose your offer."

"No one else, then, just you and I will go to the meeting. Is that understood," she asked, leaning forward on her desk.

"The other Aeons will be around for backup. Unseen until necessary."

"If necessary," she interjected.

"Right. We want the meeting at Principle Industries' headquarters for the casino and Stillwell project. Maybe in Russell's office." He held his breath. He'd added that last demand, but he wanted it that way. It would allow for more control in a confined space and keep the location of the Aeon's secretive.

"When do you want to do this?" Diane crossed her arms over her body.

"Why wait? This afternoon, two-thirty. I'll meet you there."

"I'll arrange it." She pursed her lips and stared at him.

"Okay, I'll see you then and there."

She continued to stare.

"Do you have a question?" he asked.

"Keegan, if you're setting me up, I promise—"

He held up his hand. "Diane," he interrupted. "We're Aeons, not DAs. We are truthful, forthright, and will follow through on what we say we'll do. We do not stab good people in the back."

"Am I good people?"

"I guess we'll find out today." He shot her grin and walked out of her office.

"Keegan," she called, and ran after him. "I want to be."

He closed his eyes momentarily and felt into Diane's energy field. It hummed with light and not the faintest hint of darkness. The beauty of it wasn't lost on him. He knew of her struggles and obstacles. "That is your choice, then, Diane."

Out in his vehicle, Keegan called his mom. He'd wanted to treat her to dinner but that would have to wait to another day. Instead, he hoped she could make time to drop over at his home before his meeting later.

By the time he arrived at his house, he had his mother's agreement and his brother's.

Inside, he straightened up and made fresh coffee. Nerves fired throughout his body, not knowing how things would go once they arrived. He felt into his heart and found love overflowing for them, then sent a stream of happiness, understanding, and harmony throughout his house. Peace settled over him, and he took a seat in anticipation.

Just as the coffee maker finished brewing, he heard a car drive up his driveway. He didn't wait for them to knock, he opened the door. "Well, well, that didn't take long." He hugged them both, and led them inside.

"Your invitation was sudden." Jayce perched on the edge of the couch next to his mom. "What's up?"

His mom gave Jayce a grin. "Yes, it was unexpected but why wait? It's good to see you both."

His mom's serenity registered with Keegan, further assuring him that what he was about to do was the right thing. "I'm glad you could both make it. Jayce, did you tell Mom about our plans?"

"Not yet," he muttered. "I'm going to start working for Keegan." He nodded. "Yup, and I might become a recovery agent."

Violet looked at Jayce and then Keegan. "Are you interested in that field of work?"

"You bet," Jayce assured her.

"Then I'm excited for you both. I think you'll make a great team." She looked down then up at Keegan. "Is that what you wanted to talk about?"

He pursed his lips, eyeing them both. But this had to be done. "Mom, Dad had an affair and I found out about it."

"What?" Jayce's eyes widened. "No one told me about it. I don't believe you. How long have you known?"

"I was a kid. I didn't say anything to you because you were way too young for something like that. Over the years, I believed I was being loyal and protecting my family. I hope you can understand that," he pleaded. "Mom, I'm so sorry." He gritted his teeth. "I hated what he did. I hate what he's done. Can you forgive me?"

His mom patted his hand and his brother's hand. "You did nothing wrong. The truth is, I knew all along. I thought I was protecting you two from your father's wrath. He could get so angry. And I thought the best thing for you was to keep the family together." Her face crumpled and tears flowed down her cheeks. "Did your father tell you to keep his secret?"

"I'm afraid so. He said if I told you about it, you would die."

"Oh my goodness. How awful for you." She sobbed, her shoulders shaking.

"Mom, mom," Keegan pulled her to her feet and grabbed Jayce in a three-way hug. "He hurt us all. But we have each other and always will."

"Yes, and that's the truth," she said.

"Sorry I jumped on you Keegan."

"Don't worry, Jayce. I know it was a shock."

"You're the best big brother a guy could have. It was you who taught me to play ball, how to pitch, how to hit. I'm sorry you had to suffer under Dad's lies. I'm glad you told me. I have another reason to walk away from him. Your advice was right on."

Keegan's heart swelled, the burden of a lifetime finally lifting. All it had taken was facing the truth with courage.

CHAPTER 32

*I*t wasn't always easy spending time with her family. So many memories, hard memories from her childhood, gurgled up around them. Resigned to it, Ainsley knew it was par for the course. She knew the memories signified trauma, trauma that needed to heal, so their surfacing was a gift. But it didn't feel like it.

"Spoons," Jane yelled, grabbing the spoon card from the middle of the table.

Her father quickly grabbed another, and so did her mother.

"Oh, I'm too slow." Ainsley faked disappointment. Her mind was off wondering about her shop and Iris and Keegan, and the games to occupy her family's time had been going on for a while. She checked her watch. "Hey, it's lunch time. Anyone hungry?"

"Are you?" Jane asked.

"I could use a sandwich." She shoved away from the table. "I'll make lunch. You all can continue playing."

Her mother stretched and yawned. "I've had enough for a while. I'll help you, Ainsley."

"That leaves you two and me," her father said, pointing to Jane and Benjamin. "Are you game for one more round?"

"Sure, I'll beat you again," Jane teased.

Benjamin chuckled. "You wish."

While they played games, Ainsley wanted to let them have a good time. But anxiety streamed through her body like blood in her blood vessels. Keegan's call earlier confirming a meeting with Diane and her bosses for the afternoon pressed her to have faith in him. Worse, did she trust Diane's abilities to secure a positive outcome for her family and Old Town. It reminded her of the pressure she'd endured as a kid, knowing at any minute she could lose her family to murder at the hands of the mob.

She loaded slices of bread with stacks of cheese, deli meat, and lettuce, without speaking to her mother. Her stomach knotted. She had little to no control over what would happen at the meeting. Everything in her wanted to be there with Keegan. Still, she had control over how she handled the danger, letting it get to her or allowing it to move through her like clouds floating overhead in the sky. Reminding herself that things were different now than when she was a kid helped calm her nerves, at least for now.

"You're quiet," her mother noted.

"Oh, sorry, Mom. I just have things on my mind."

"Care to share?"

She looked over her shoulder at the happy activity going on at the dining room table. "Just enjoying their smiles and laughter."

"Uh huh." Her mother shot her a disbelieving glance, but didn't say anything.

"Are you doing all right?" Ainsley eyed her mom.

"Sure."

"Is that the truth?"

Her mother chuckled. "Mostly. I'm grateful for all the support we've been given. I haven't asked a lot of questions, just appreciate that you and your friends have kept us safe. But hiding out is wearing." She kept her eyes on making lunch.

"I'm sorry all this is happening. I hope it ends soon."

Her mother glanced up at her. "Do you have reason to think it will?"

"I have hope, Mom." Ainsley hugged her mom. "I love you."

"And I love you, dear." She picked up some plates and carried them to the table.

Jane popped up. "I'll help, Mom."

Ainsley's phone rang, and she pulled it out of her pocket, walking to the living room away from the rest of them. "Hi, Payson."

"Ainsley, Keegan has let everyone know about his meeting this afternoon. I'm assuming he's told you already."

"Yes. He also mentioned there's a plan for the rest of us to give back-up on the Stillwell site. When and where do we meet?"

"I want to talk with you in person. Could you meet me downtown at the Sheppard Media building after lunch?"

"Uh, yeah. I can get away." She trusted Benjamin to watch her family and it seemed like he was fitting right in with them, the way they all were joking over lunch.

"Good. I'll see you there." She grabbed a sandwich and glass of water. "Mind if I join you for lunch, you silly people?"

They all stopped talking and looked at her expectantly. "What?"

"Don't you have an update for us?" her father asked.

"Oh, well, sort of." She took a sip of her water. "There is a plan about to be put in motion that may bring an end to the danger we've been under."

"What?" her mother asked.

"Why didn't you tell us this?" Jane frowned.

Her father just sat at the table quietly eating his food.

"I've been waiting for the okay. I didn't want to raise false hopes." She took a bite of her sandwich.

Jane rolled her eyes. "Tell us. What's the plan?"

"I'm not going to share the details. If it works out, just know you'll be free to go home. And I'll let you know as soon as I know."

Jane swallowed a bite and pounded the table. "When will that be? Give us some idea."

"She doesn't know," her father said. "Let's just hope for the best."

"That is the best thing you can do now," Ainsley assured them. "I'm going to have to leave. Meanwhile—"

"No, you're not leaving again," Jane spouted.

"I have to. I'm sorry." Ainsley grabbed her jacket.

Jane sighed. "Okay, I guess I understand. I'm just so tired of all of this. But I'm not blaming you."

Her sister's state of mind dragged on her. She wished for so much more than daily drudgery for her. "I'll be in touch as soon as there is something to report. Trust me."

IT WAS ALL she could do just to focus on what was ahead as Ainsley drove downtown to meet Payson. Automatically, she directed a steady stream of peace and strength to her family and Benjamin, taking satisfaction in her ability to ease their discomfort.

After parking her vehicle, she hurried inside the Sheppard Media building and found Payson waiting in the lobby.

Payson hooked her arm through Ainsley's. "Let's go."

They followed a hall to a private elevator, where Payson punched in a code to gain access. The elevator took them to the top of Sheppard Media Tower, fifteen stories up.

Payson strode out of the elevator toward the edge of the deck, lined by a short wall of blocks. Ainsley stepped onto the deck and just looked around. She'd never been up here before, but she knew Payson came up here regularly to clear her head. The CEO of the company, Carl Sheppard, had hired her to locate his daughter when she'd run away months ago and gotten involved with some bad dudes. After finding her, Payson freed her from the clutches of the bad elements and brought her home. Then she'd hooked up father and daughter with Claire Eve, getting them help with their relationship. As a result, she'd received Sheppard's never-ending gratitude, as well as permission to visit the tower any time she pleased.

Gusty breezes lifted strands of Ainsley's hair and flung it across her face. She laughed spontaneously, glee dancing in her arms and legs. "This is fantastic," she hollered to Payson.

"I know." Payson beckoned her close to the wall.

Looking out across the view of Auralia, Ainsley's skin dimpled in goose bumps. "What a grand view," she breathed. "It kind of puts a lot of things into a different perspective. All the people down there walking around are little." She took in a circumference of the view. "The city doesn't look so large from here, but it is."

Payson perched on the wall. "Come sit with me."

Ainsley shook her head. "No thanks. I'll stand here."

"I wanted to give you this perspective on your shop. Do you see it out there in Old Town?"

She peered across the miles and miles that laid out before her in every direction. "I see it. And there's the Wherryite River nearby." Her heart sank. "My shop is in close proximity to the casino."

"From up here, things look small and close together. They can look insignificant, or threatened by certain elements."

"My shop is too close to the casino. I feel like giving up. Is that what you want me to understand? That my shop is insignificant and I should let it go?"

Payson shook her head. "Do you recognize that Old Town sits near the river, but the casino is being built miles away. It's not the actual size of things or the proximity to each other that gives significance. It's us. What we put into things is what creates significance. Our values, our work ethic, our heart."

Ainsley weighed Payson's words, not knowing what to take away. Her shop had been intruded on, torn up, made insignificant to the community. She breathed in a deep breath of cool breeze, filling her lungs and letting it all out. Planting her feet on the concrete deck, she perceived the width, breadth, and substance of Old Town and what it stood for. Resilience in the face of time passing, and a sense of endurance. It was imbued with her values and ethics. It wasn't insignificant as long as she cared for it.

"I see that now. Objects, like buildings, carry our endeavors. They hold our purpose, parts of us, and the sum of what we put into them makes them good and healthy, or poor and ill." She looked at Payson, sitting solidly on her perch, so comfortable and at ease. "I see why you like to come up. It can lend a fresh approach. And who knows what could go up in the land between the casino and Old Town to buffer it from possible harm?"

Payson laughed. "I like the way you think."

"There's a lot of turbulence and drama going on this afternoon. Thoughts are flowing in my mind. A women came into my shop and purchased a tea set. It could seem inconsequential. But it wasn't for her. It reminded her of her aunt and tea parties that left an impression on her as a little girl. That purchase was a concrete connection to those moments in time that hold her feet to the earth."

Payson smiled widely. "That's a precious thing, Ainsley. It was a rarefied moment for you and her. No one can put a price on it, it's so valuable."

Ainsley's doubts about her path and the importance of her shop diminished in the face of a new outlook. How could she discount its sacred worth?

Still, she chewed on her lower lip, thinking of Keegan.

Payson walked closer and placed her hands on Ainsley's shoulder. "I know that Keegan has become important to you and you to him. We're going to be near Keegan, ready to jump into action if needed. We have what it takes and more to ensure his safety."

"You're right. I can't lose sight of that." She looked away, distress warring in her gut against reason.

"What's going on?"

"Keegan leaving me out of the meeting is prompting me to distance myself from him. I question whether he truly cares enough about me to stay."

Payson nodded. "Oh. That sounds like an old flight or fight mode to me. It's understandable, Ainsley. You've been through a lot of danger from a young age. That technique protected you. It's going to take time and inner work to learn you're safe now. Not because Keegan proves he'll stay, but because you take care of you so well. That's the secret. Believing in yourself."

"I know that in my head." Ainsley patted her chest above her heart. "Not completely in here. You're right, I have to work on it, practice trusting him." Instantly terror bloomed in her body, and she gritted her teeth at the idea of it.

"Listen to me telling you what to do. Learning new ways isn't easy,

I know." Payson stepped back. "We're going to have a lot of positive vibes supporting us this afternoon. ACE has organized a protest at Old Town, remember?"

"That's today?" Alarms went off in her head. "My vision."

"I remember. We'll all have to keep our eyes open for interference during the protest if Diane's meeting doesn't go well. The protest is scheduled for three o'clock this afternoon. So members of the community will be gathering while Diane is conducting her meeting. And we'll be on site."

"I'm hopeful my vision proves faulty this time." Ainsley looked out over the city one more time, soaking in her awe of all that it was and all that it could be if she and the other Aeons could raise the level of light enough to create a healthy balance between light and dark.

If only, she wished. "Thank you so much for bringing me up here, Payson. I appreciate it more than you can know. This experience has been a real eye-opener."

"We can just sit here for a while, if you'd like. We don't have to leave just yet."

"I'd like that."

CHAPTER 33

Keegan checked the time on his watch and saw that he had enough time to park at the back of a dirt parking lot at the edge of the casino construction site and walk to Barry Russell's office on time for the meeting. He sat in his vehicle, surveying the progress of the casino. Regardless of the problems with drainage, the project was making steady headway. Mixed feelings churned in his belly. While he knew the mayor of Auralia had ulterior motives for the completion of the casino, he also suspected Economic Director Tim Brody could be right about it providing needed job to the area, even if he, too, leaned heavily into Dark Sides to get what he wanted: personal power and wealth. But if someone else, someone who valued right and wrong, were to operate it, could it be a positive thing for the city?

He opened his car door and heard his name.

"Keegan, over here." Diane was walking toward him across the parking area. "Wait for me."

He swallowed hard, preparing for going into battle. He could maintain optimism about the meeting while also being on guard.

Breathless, Diane walked up. "Are you ready?"

"I am. But I'm just along for the ride and to hold you to your word.

It's your negotiation." Waves of anxious energy came off her, surprising him. He'd never been aware that she had nerves or could be fearful.

He patted her shoulder. "You got this."

"I can always mesmerize these guys to get their cooperation." She gave him a half-smile.

"No. We're doing this right. No funny business. Just lay out your facts and demand that they accept your terms. The only alternative is that you turn over your documents, and we'll still get the best of them. They'll go to jail."

"Or kill me."

"The other Aeons have our backs, Diane. We have the upper hand all the way around. Furey and the others just don't know that yet."

She sighed and nodded vigorously. "I'll make that perfectly clear."

"Good. Let's go."

Inside, Keegan fell behind Diane walking up a flight of stairs. The sound of their shoes against the hard floor echoed down the hallway. Instinctively, his muscles flexed as they walked in to the office.

"We have an appointment with Barry," Diane told the secretary.

"Yes, Diane, Mr. Russell is expecting you." The secretary eyed him. "Who are you?"

"I'm with her." Keegan gave her a warm smile. "I'm her bodyguard."

The young woman chuckled. "I'll let him know you're here." She left for his office and returned quickly. "He's ready for you," she said, giving Keegan a small smile.

Again, Keegan let Diane lead the way inside the office, assessing the room and its occupants. The men were lined up along the wall, and he nodded to them. Each one—Furey, Farrod, Russel, and Brody —ignored him. While she shook hands with her bosses, he took note of the dark vibes all around him. He grounded himself to the earth and made a point of filling with peace and understanding, then sending it out to Diane and the DAs in the room. He watched their reactions to his energy, but these guys were sophisticated con men. They maintained their cool.

Furey lifted one brow as it registered with him who Keegan was.

Keegan continued to stare at him until Furey looked away, taking a seat behind the desk.

Diane sat down in a chair on the opposite side and Keegan chose to remain standing behind her.

"What's this meeting about, Diane?" Russell smiled, but his tight expression belied his casual opening.

Her shoulders back and her head held high, Diane appeared the epitome of professional. "I'll get right to it. I am here to make a deal, one that has your best interests in mind."

The men exchanged glances and chuckled among themselves.

"Really?" Again, Russell appeared collected, but little lines along his lips deepened. "I have to admit, I'm curious what kind of deal you could possibly make that would interest us."

Keegan crossed his arms over his body. He opened his psychic hearing to the room. He had all he could do to keep himself from putting his hands to his ears. What he heard was like chalk screeching on a chalkboard, or a small animal screaming. Worse than loud static, it drowned out any thoughts he would normally be able to pick up.

Well, this was different. No matter. He eyed Furey. Could he somehow be jamming his psychic hearing? There had to be a reason why he'd been bombarded with noise, but for now, he closed his hearing down to the men, and just listened to their conversation with Diane. Maybe it was simply more important that he be present. He caught the middle of Diane's speech, and she was listing her accomplishments while working for the city and her previous connections as a lobbyist.

"So, I want you to know that I enjoy my job as Auralia's city manager. However, it has come to my attention that serious problems exist within management level of the city itself, and with the Stillwell project, as well as the casino, Deglan."

Deglan's attention snapped. "I beg your pardon."

"It's true. With all that has been going on, you all are vulnerable to legal action," Diane announced, then paused to let her words settle in.

His muscles taut, Keegan stood vigilant. The men, especially Deglan, were unpredictable and dangerous.

"What are you up to, Diane?" Deglan pinned her with his icy, steel gaze.

Keegan smirked. Diane had little patience. She wouldn't tolerate disrespect or attempts at intimidation.

A sweet smile and sultry eyes met Deglan's scowl. "Getting you what you deserve. A peaceful close to a chapter of your life that has been a thorn in your side for years. A way to move forward, not backward. A path to freedom, not imprisonment." She leaned across the desk, fairly daring Furey to turn her down.

Behind him, Russell swallowed hard. "After all we've done for you, this is how you repay us?"

"How dare you threaten me." Brody fisted his hands. "Who do you think you are? And why did you bring this guy with you? Afraid?"

Diane laughed. "Afraid of what, who? You four? You have no idea what I can do to you." She leaned back in her chair, visibly enraged.

"Tell them the deal, Diane." Keegan kept his eyes on the men. This was the Diane he knew. The take-no-prisoners-kind of person, but he was here for what was best for Auralia and Ainsley's family. Now was not the time for her to let the opportunity slip away because of her anger issues.

"It has come to my attention that there is proof of each one of you participating in fraud, conspiracy to distribute illicit drugs, conspiracy to launder money, and to defraud the government. Oh," she turned to Keegan and smiled. "I almost forgot." She turned back to face all four men. "And murder."

"We can't forget that one," he chimed in.

"Proof? What proof?" Brody asked, clenching his teeth.

Russell hit his fist against his desk. "It's not like you have been squeaky clean, Diane. You've been here with us all along."

She jumped to her feet and slammed her hand against the desk, too, staring Russell down "This meeting is about you," she pointed her finger at him, "and you, and you, and you" she said. "I have documents. Hard copies. But, I can make it all go away, if you'll agree to drop your vendetta against the Durham family, for good. Deglan, your brother is never getting out of prison. Killing the Durham family would not help him and it's time you moved on to other things."

Deglan's face hardened, but he remained silent.

"Is that all?" Farrod asked.

"No. In exchange for not facing charges, you all will agree to leave Old Town alone. You will drop your plans to build a new development of stores from which to launder money."

Deglan closed his eyes and sighed heavily. Keegan's energy stream faltered and darkness vibrated heavily inside the room. It dragged on him, and he struggled to breathe. He pulled in a full, deep breath and regrounded himself to the earth.

"You know, all I have to do is summon my boys from outside this room and you both would be dead people," Deglan said, his voice eerily course. "So much for your deal."

"Huh!" Diane smiled and stood. "Did I not mention that if something happens to me, the Aeons, or the Durhams, those documents I mentioned will be delivered to the District Attorney's office. Oh, and by the way, she's a friend of mine."

Deglan walked marched around the desk and close to Diane. "You don't have any friends."

Keegan flew to her side, poised for action.

Rapid fire, Diane's hand flew up to slap his face, but she just held it there, in front of his him, saying nothing, her nostrils flaring just slightly. A smile broke across her face, and she lightly tapped his cheek. "What's your answer, boys? Is it a deal or do I submit evidence to the DA this afternoon?"

Keegan closed his eyes and focused on letting his light stream with all his strength and courage. When he opened his eyes, Russell, Farrod, and Brody were watching Deglan, waiting for his response.

Diane slowly ran her tongue over her lips. The air in the room, heavy with emotions, crackled inside Keegan's head. Density lifted, and his breathing eased. He tuned his hearing to Deglan's thoughts, wanting assurances. This time they poured in without hesitation or noise.

I can't go to prison. My brother's in prison, and maybe I can't do anything about it. How did Diane get this leverage? I could kill her. Hmm. I might end up in prison like my brother. I could kill the DA. No, no, that's not a good idea. Maybe she would take a bribe. How to salvage my life from this?

Deglan's thoughts went silent, and Keegan could sense that a decision had settled inside of him.

"It appears you leave me no choice but to agree, Diane." Deglan's mouth twitched.

Diane lifted her chin. "Exactly what are you agreeing to?"

"Why, to your proposal."

"I gave you two choices. Drop your plans for the Durham family AND Old Town. If you refuse," she continued slowly, carefully pronouncing every word distinctly, as though the men were thick headed," you are choosing jail time. Got it?"

Keegan suppressed a chuckle.

Deglan narrowed his eyes and swept his gaze back and forth between him and Diane. "You don't have to talk to me as though I were stupid. I understand your offer, all of it."

She stomped her foot. "Quit stalling. Tell me your answer or I'll make an assumption and this will be the last you'll hear from me."

A scowl twisted Deglan's face, but he nodded at Russell, Farrod, and Brody. They nodded back. "You've got your deal."

"I'll be watching," she said, then marched out of the office, and Keegan followed.

Briskly, without a word they made their way outside. Keegan caught up with her as they walked to their vehicles parked out back.

Keegan's heart leapt when he saw Ainsley and the other Aeons waiting for them. He hadn't thought to take time to let them know their news as they walked out of the building. Angst colored their faces, but he fist-bumped the air and each one joined in his mini-celebration, circling Diane.

"Tell us all about it." Cooper touched her shoulder.

"Not here. Let's drive to Old Town and we can talk with privacy," she answered.

"It's not going to be private." Skye shook her head. "The protest has started. But I agree, let's move to a safer distance. How about Coffee Is?"

He raced to Ainsley, grabbing her and lifting her up against him. "The deal is done," he exclaimed. "Deglan agreed to let go of his vendetta against your family."

Ainsley kissed him. "I don't know how to feel. It's been so long since I've known what it feels like to be safe. I can't wait to tell my family."

He lowered her to the ground and took hold of her hand. "It will take time for it to sink in. I'm a little in shock myself." He noticed the others climbing in their vehicles. "Looks like we're leaving. Did you drive?"

"No, I rode with Cooper and Skye."

"Come with me. I'll follow their lead." The sound of her laughter was water to his soul. He wanted it to be true that her family would be out of danger for good. His heart thudded hard in his chest, though, with suspicious inklings remaining. Was it simply his usual lack of believing or was it too good to be true? Either way, he determined he would set things straight.

CHAPTER 34

The short drive from the casino construction site to Old Town gave Ainsley some time to begin processing what had been accomplished. Her whole world had been changed by Furey's agreement with Diane. Diane of all people had given her a new life, one without constant looking over her shoulder, as she had been since she was twelve. She didn't know how to break out of that pattern. Even an Aeon could be dubious of miracles, and she had been for years. Did she dare believe her family could be safe at last?

She turned to watch Keegan, who looked caught up in his thoughts. A simple thank you wasn't enough to convey the depth of her gratitude to him, or to Diane. Naturally, she questioned his feelings about her. She couldn't stop the fears, as hard as she tried. Stop it, she said to her thoughts. Be secure in yourself, she told herself, instead of constantly trying to read him to confirm her acceptance.

"Look at that," he said, beaming. "The protest is huge."

"How wonderful. So many supporters for Old Town." It did her heart good to see the crowds showing up to protest the Stillwell project.

Keegan took her hand and squeezed it. "You have lots of supporters." He held her gaze briefly before pulling his vehicle along the side of the road to park. "The parking lot is all filled up with supporters. Look at that," he exclaimed.

"It's jam packed." Glee bubbled up inside her. She pointed out the window. "There's Mickey. I'm glad to see her here."

"Of course she's here. ACE organized this protest."

TEARS MISTED AINSLEY'S EYES. "I'm going to go talk to her." She jumped out of the vehicle and strode into the crowd, weaving around people until she reached what appeared to be the headquarters for the protesters under a tent to check in.

"Mickey," she called over the noise. "I can't believe this turnout."

"I know. Isn't it great? Here, have a cup of lemonade. It's free to all vendors and participants in the protest against Principle Industries." She pointed to a cooler. "There are bottles of water in there, if you prefer."

"It's like a party." Amazement lit up Ainsley. "Thank you, Mickey. Thank you so much. It's thanks to you and ACE talking to the press and organizing it all that we have such strong support."

Mickey gave her a thumbs-up, and then returned to handing out beverages and attending to registrations.

Ainsley cast a glance all around, searching for the other Aeons and finally noticed Keegan entering Coffee Is.

Winding her way through the crowd, she bumped into Claire Eve.

"Ainsley, isn't this marvelous? I'm so pumped." She held a sign high.

"I like your sign. It's not the casino, it's the Principle, Group," she recited. "You're so right."

"It's good to talk with you. How are you doing?" Claire Eve eyed her.

Ainsley touched her arm, and felt her counselor's loving energy. It boosted her hope. "I'm a little unsettled. There's a lot going on." She pursed her lips, refraining from spilling her everything outside of a counseling session.

Claire Eve nodded. "I'll be thinking of you and crossing my fingers everything shakes out well."

"Thanks." She'd never forget how important Claire Eve was to her emotional well-being and that of the other Aeons. She meant the world to Ainsley.

Weaving her way around people, she saw a number of familiar faces, and greeted acquaintances: Carl Sheppard, Ricki, and even Reid Curtis and his family. She spotted Iris and waved before she finally reached the coffee shop. She walked inside, past the front counter, and spied the group at their usual gathering spot in the back room. Eagerly, she joined them, and took the seat Keegan motioned her to next to him. It did her heart good to see his whole-hearted welcome. She'd been wrong to second-guess him. Probably her perspective on many things would need reevaluating.

"Ainsley, welcome to the celebration. I'm sure Keegan told you everything." Diane's face glowed, something Ainsley had never seen on her before.

"He has, and I have you and Keegan to thank for the good news. I'm so grateful you got the deal with all four bad guys, but especially Furey." It was a strange but welcome feeling to be thanking Diane for something so good.

"Happy to do something good, Ainsley." Diane shot her a big smile. She dipped her gaze. "I'm so sorry for all the harm I've caused. I hope you can forgive me at some point, but I know it will take time."

"Thank you for that, too, Diane. It's a good start."

"Well, that's all I can ask." Diane shrugged.

Ainsley turned to Keegan.

He shook his head. "I did very little. It was all Diane. She came up with the plan and she laid out a convincing argument with Deglan. The others went along with his say-so." He winked at her. "I know. It feels strange that Diane would work out the deal for the Aeons."

"I don't know what to make of it, but I'm grateful," Ainsley said. "We didn't even have to use our special abilities, either."

"Me either," Braden said. "Anyone else use them?"

"Nope," Ainsley said.

"Me either," Payson added. "You, Skye, Cooper?"

Both shook their heads.

Diane shrugged. "I wanted to, but Keegan wouldn't let me," she joked.

Braden clanged his spoon against the table. "I streamed light, and I bet you all did too. That accounts for a lot. So, anything we need to discuss right now or can we join the crowd outside?"

Cooper nodded. "We can't let up on our efforts to build on light and love in the community. That hasn't changed. This is a good win, but DAs are still out there doing what they do."

Keegan punched him in the shoulder. "You're right, Cooper. But we can take a moment to relax, don't you think? Winning Diane back is a big win. It will have an effect on the DAs, bit by bit."

"Sure. I'm all for it. We need to get Benjamin and Claire Eve in on a celebration, too."

"My house, tonight?" Payson spread her arms wide and held them there. "What do you say?"

Agreement went up, and Keegan volunteered to get in touch with the others. "Anyone else hear that?" he asked.

He ran to the window at the front of the shop and looked out. "We better get out there fast."

"What's going on?" Braden peered outside. "Oh my God."

Keegan opened the door and let loose screaming and hollering. "Cooper, everyone, prepare yourself."

CHAPTER 35

*S*hock and anger swept through Keegan like a tidal wave as he stepped outside Coffee Is. The peaceful protest had turned into an onslaught of heavy equipment advancing toward them.

He exchanged a rueful glance with Ainsley.

"What happened to the deal?" Ainsley asked him. "Is this the reckoning we've been fearing?"

"This can't be happening." He scanned the line of heavy equipment slowly making their way across open fields, slowly gaining ground closer to Old Town. Bulldozers, end loaders, graders, and a crane with a breaking ball dangling. All roaring with power aimed at destroying Old Town, regardless of the protestors blocking the path.

"We've got to do something," she yelled. "Diane, what's happening?"

Diane shook her head, her phone to her ear. "Deglan, our deal. What are you doing?"

Keegan waited for her to give them an answer to the question in all their minds. Noise all around blocked out her voice. Urgency pressed and he couldn't wait for an explanation, he opened his hearing to capture the conversation.

Deglan laughed. "I changed my mind, Diane. Did you really believe you could force me into an agreement? I'm more powerful than you can imagine and you're going to regret trying to overthrow me. You've done things people would criticize, too, Diane. You're not safe from the law, either."

"Stupid," Diane uttered. "I have been promised immunity."

"I've got great lawyers."

"You can't proceed with tearing down Old Town while people are there."

"Protestors." Disgust dripped from his voice. "What do I care about them?"

Diane hung up, her mouth gaping. "Deglan has backed out of the deal." She pursed her lips. "I did not plan this, this, betrayal. Please believe me," she begged.

"I'm calling APD," Braden said. "They'll help."

"But they won't get here in time to protect the crowd. These people are under assault right now," Ainsley cried. "We need to spread our energy outward, filling this whole space. Including you, Diane. Don't worry about whether we don't have faith in your integrity. We can feel it in you."

Keegan swallowed hard. He couldn't believe his eyes. "I think that's my dad in one of the bulldozers. Oh my god!"

Ainsley took his hand in hers, and her warmth and love spread through him. But it couldn't block out the pain from his father's choices, from his lifetime of his father's rejection, or his own fears for his brother and mother. It all tore up his gut, and he fell to his knees. "How could he be so evil?"

Ainsley knelt beside him. "It's his right to choose something you don't believe in. But it's hard to watch, when we believe in light and love, not darkness and negativity."

"I thought I'd let go of any expectations of him." Keegan stood, transfixed. "I still love him, though."

"Of course. Let's go."

Keegan shook his head, opening his senses to the chaos around him, beyond his father, to realize the other Aeons were standing firm in their light and love, emanating it out and around. Neither the protestors nor the DAs approaching would be aware of their efforts, but the energy would affect them, the protestors, and the situation. Joining them, he knew the use of their ability wasn't meant to control, but to strengthen an outcome that would align with what was right and perfect for all. Obstruct the darkness with the power of light.

Diane stepped forward, at the front line and raised her hands to her shoulders. Sensing her ability to deconstruct, he wanted to intersect her, tell her to let the positive negate the darkness. He ran toward her, but her telekinesis held him back. Fierce wind and debris thrashed against his body. He sent his gaze around and saw that no one was noticing that Diane was raising the winds, too occupied with their trauma from Furey's attack.

"Diane, Diane, stop. You don't have to do this alone." He bent into the wind, stepping firmly, one foot at a time. The torrent pushed him back, and he watched as the heavy equipment stopped in place, some of the engines sputtering into stalling, and some drivers revving the engines but going nowhere. The drivers clambered out of the machines. And Diane continued, threatening to tear apart the drivers with her powers if she didn't stop.

Keegan didn't want her to kill anyone. He tried again, striding deliberately to her side, finally reaching her and grabbing her body. "Diane, you did it. You've stopped the machines," he yelled.

She looked at him, her eyes glazed. "You don't understand. They deserve to die."

"That's not up to us." He had to get through to her. "Justice will prevail. It's the better outcome."

"No! I have to stop it. For once in my life, I'm on the side of good. I'm not going to let the bad win."

"If you persist, Deglan wins, not you."

Again she faced him, tears on her cheeks. She dropped her hands, and the rush of wind subsided. The cloud of debris settled to the ground like drifting like feathers. Diane collapsed, and he caught her.

"Keegan, let's get her to my shop. There's a cot in the backroom where we can lie her down. Hopefully she'll come around soon. Her aura looks bleak. She's exerted so much energy." Skye led the way through the crowd. Now quieted down, they parted to allow them to walk freely to Coffee Is.

The other Aeons accompanied them inside, sheltering Diane from curious onlookers. Inside, Keegan laid her down and Skye covered her with a blanket. He checked her pulse and breathing, confirming she was okay.

"She's just spent," he suggested.

"I'll stay with her," Payson said.

Skye nodded. "Thanks, Payson. I should check on my employees. We're handling a lot of orders today, what with the protest and all."

Braden and Cooper exchanged a look with Keegan, and he nodded.

"We should go," Braden said.

Skye's eyes widened. "Go where?"

"Russell's office at the casino. With any luck, Deglan will still be there, along with his accomplices."

Keegan pulled out his car keys and strode toward the door. "We need to be there right now. Let's go."

They sprinted along the edge of the parking lot, trying to avoid the crowd.

"Wait, wait for me."

Keegan psychic hearing detected Ainsley's voice over the noise around them, and he stopped. She ran to his side.

"I'm going with you." Her face shown with determination, bringing a smile to his face.

"Of course you are."

Keegan floored the accelerator and sped toward the casino site while they discussed their plan of approach. In no time, they stormed inside and found Russell gathering his things inside his office.

"Hold it right there," Braden ordered.

"You can't stop me," Russell spouted.

"Oh yes I can. You're under arrest." Braden brandished his badge, then cuffed Russell. Sirens screaming outside grabbed Russell's attention, but he firmed his lips.

"One down, three to go." Ainsley slapped her hands together. "Where will we find your cohorts?"

"I'm not saying," Russell proclaimed.

"You're in pretty big trouble, Barry," Braden pointed out. "If you cooperate, you may receive leniency. It's worth a try. Prison is not a pleasant place."

Russell sighed heavily. "Deglan is in the security office. Brody and Farrodd are in the weapons room."

"You're coming with us. You can show us the way."

"I'm not doing that." Russell set his jaw.

"You misunderstand us," Keegan said. "You don't have a choice."

"They'll have me killed."

Cooper grabbed Russell's arm and pulled. "C'mon."

Russell struggled, trying to tear away.

Keegan quickly punched him in the stomach. "Stop it. Resistance is pointless."

Doubled over, Russell moaned, but Cooper ignored him, yanking him along. "You're wasting time, Barry. Keep quiet and lead on."

With Russell's forced cooperation, they hunted down first Farrod and Brody in the weapons room in the lowest level of the casino. Three against two, they took them on too easily. The men weren't up to fighting, they were soft. Keegan and Ainsley secured them with zipties and Cooper stayed with them to guard.

By the time Keegan and Braden reached the security office, sirens were silent, assuring Keegan that the crowds were being helped.

They quietly opened the door and peeked inside the office. Deglan wasn't in sight. Braden gestured to Keegan and Ainsley to check the room, while he crept to the adjoining office.

The hairs on Keegan's arms stood erect. Something was up. He went in first, shielding Ainsley. She gave him a dirty look, the same one she'd given him earlier when she'd insisted she could take of herself. He didn't care.

As they searched the security room for Furey, Keegan motioned her to be quiet as he leaned his ear against a door to the next room. Sounds of papers shuffling and zippers came through. He opened his senses, trying to ascertain who was inside, in particular, if it was Furey. He closed his eyes to gather every bit of information he could. Instantly, he knew it wasn't someone he didn't know, it was Furey. He nodded, but held her still.

He waited, not moving. He wanted to give Braden, the detective, the chance to make the first move.

CHAPTER 36

"*D*on't move, Furey," Braden ordered.

Ainsley remained frozen behind Keegan, listening to Braden on the other side of the door. She could imagine, in his role as detective, Braden was holding a gun on Furey. It frightened her to think of the danger he was caught up in.

"Put down the gun," she heard him say. Tension knotted her body. Anything could happen.

"You don't scare me," Furey yelled. "My gun is bigger than yours." He recited sing-song, as though playing with Braden.

"You're under arrest. Put down the gun and get on your knees."

Suddenly a shot was fired, and fighting sounds came through the door. A thud resounded through the door.

"We've got to go in," she whispered to Keegan, and he nodded.

She stepped out of the way as he pulled on the door and they rushed inside.

Quickly, Ainsley streamed strength and support to Braden, who was wrestling on the floor with Furey on the other side of the room. Blood trickled down Braden's arm and his face contorted as he tried to hold on to Furey.

Ainsley seized her moment, tackling Furey's back and striking his head over and over. "Get off me, you bitch!" Furey hollered, trying to throw off Ainsley.

Keegan wrestled with Furey's hold on his gun, while Braden stepped back to catch his breath.

Finally, Keegan ripped the gun out of his hand, and Braden lunged, bashing him in the gut, sending him to his knees.

Ainsley jumped off, but wrenched his arm backward. "Stay down, you fool," she commanded. "I'm done with you and your whole lot. This is your last look at freedom."

Furey continued to resist her hold, and he yelled obscenities right and left. His words meant nothing to her and determination tightened her grip.

The sounds of feet running in their direction got her attention, but she stayed on the floor holding Furey in place. She took a moment to exchange a glance with Keegan and he grinned at her, like a Cheshire cat who just got a mouse himself.

"Miss, we got him. You can hand him over." Zane Yates strode in, registering surprise at Braden, but quickly leaned down and cuffed Furey. Two other officers took his arms and pulled him to his feet.

"You have no right," he yelled at Ainsley. "She's no one. Take her into custody. She assaulted me."

"Keep quiet," Braden ordered. "I'm in charge of this arrest. Get him out of here."

Zane surveyed the scene. "Looks like once again I've arrived late, Braden. You seem to have things handled."

"Sort of. Good to see you, though." Braden grimaced.

"I've notified emergency services, so let's get you checked out." another officer said.

"I don't need that," Braden objected.

"Detective, you've been shot, you're going to get looked at. The ambulance is right outside already. It was called immediately after we arrived at Old Town for the disturbance. No more arguments."

"Don't make me force you, Detective," Zane teased.

Ainsley followed the officers as they retrieved the other men

Cooper was watching, and they all walked out. Exhausted, she was filled with peace, a peace she couldn't recall having before.

Outside, the police had arrested the drivers and loaded them in APD vehicles lined up in the parking lot. But watching the officers stuff Furey, Russell, Farrod, and Brody into squad cars gave Ainsley a particular satisfaction. They'd be held accountable for the harm they were responsible for creating in the community and against her family. She wanted to stay in the knowledge that the individuals involved, including the drivers, would see the natural consequences of their choices, not move past it into the rush of daily living. She needed that awareness to last.

As the last of the drivers were packed into vehicles, she suspected things looked bad now for them, especially in their eyes, but for her, it meant they—the mob head, the mayor, economic director, project head, and the complicit DAs and drivers—had opportunities to learn and perhaps do differently. That went for Keegan's father, too.

Ainsley scanned her mind for a glance of Sully being arrested. She walked toward the line of machinery, trying to figure out where he'd gone, when he'd been arrested. She had no memory of seeing it.

She twisted her neck around to find Keegan. Across the way, she spotted him running toward her. Taking steps in that direction, urgency sped through her and she began running to him.

They met, standing a foot apart, and he searched her face. Her mind raced, emotion flaring in her body. "Where's your father?" she asked.

"I don't know. I checked every vehicle. He wasn't picked up." He slammed his fist together. "I can't believe he was involved, first of all. But to top it off, he's gotten away? I have to find him." He paced in front of her, and she sensed his agony.

"I know. I'll help you."

Keegan's face contorted. "No," he shouted. "I don't want him near you. He's poison."

"I can handle him. I'm going to help you." Were they really going to argue about this again?

Ainsley noticed Payson standing at the edge of the remaining crowd in the parking lot, waving to them.

"Payson wants something. We should see what's up." She took Keegan's face in her hands. "I understand you have to find your father. Right now, though, we probably should check on Diane and touch base with the others."

His shoulders crumpled, and all she could do was be there for him. She could point out that they already had a big win, that they had each other, that Old Town had been saved. But no, she simply tried to allow space for his indignation and sorrow.

"You're right." He draped his arm over her shoulders and together they walked to where Payson stood waiting.

"Are you two all right?" she asked.

"Yup." Keegan nodded toward Braden standing near the remaining officers, talking. "Is he okay?"

"He is. And Diane is up and walking around. Skye gave her something to eat and drink and a dose of healing touch."

Ainsley pointed toward the coffee shop. "She surprised us, didn't she?"

"I'll say." Payson shook her head. "I never would have guessed she would come through for us. It's very encouraging to witness her transformation, after all that's happened."

"I guess we need to have stronger belief in what we subscribe to, that there is always hope." Keegan stared into the setting sun.

Payson chuckled. "Good point, Keegan."

"It never hurts to remember that we're only human." Ainsley kicked at a small dirt pile at the perimeter of Old Town.

Keegan eyed her with soft eyes. "That too." He kissed her, sending little sparks flying inside her.

"Okay you two lovebirds. How about we follow up with Mickey regarding the protest. It turned out to be a good one, though it almost turned deadly. I want to pat her on the back."

"I'm going to make sure to talk to Iris, if I can find her."

"And I'm going to thank Reid and Carl for showing their support. It meant a lot." Keegan pointed a finger at Ainsley. "Shall we get to it?"

"Don't forget, the party is at my house tomorrow," Payson said, then headed to the registration tent.

Keegan pulled Ainsley into an embrace, one she knew he also needed. He pressed against her, not leaning, but she felt him all up and down her body. It renewed her, and she hung on to him tightly, for as long as he needed her.

CHAPTER 37

*L*ying on his side in the muted light of early morning, Keegan listened to Ainsley's soft breathing. Bliss awoke him. It filled his body and he didn't want to miss a moment of the breaking day. It took all of his self-discipline to refrain from caressing her soft cheek.

The rest of him yearned for more than that of her. But just being close and watching her sleep was enough, for now. They'd left the scene at Old Town yesterday and gone their separate ways to deal with their own situations, hers, delivery of good news to her family, his, looking for clues to his father's whereabouts.

But then they'd met here, at his house, and last night had been perfect. Intimacy. Sharing thoughts. Falling into sleep together.

His brain kicked in, assessing this new "them." For so long he'd blocked his feelings for the Aeons, not wanting them close enough to expose his secrets. Now those blocks still spoke to him: Don't let them close, don't let Ainsley in.

Could he have hope in a future with her? If he'd learned anything from the recent events it was that love followed believing. Persevering, following his heart, even into darkness, was simply the path out of fear and loathing. Love had won. At least for now, and that was enough for hope to thrive.

Ainsley stretched and yawned. She opened her eyes and rolled on her side to face him. She smiled, tickling his heart.

"Good morning." She planted a kiss on his lips and snuggled under his chin.

"Mm, this is nice. Good morning. Did you sleep well?"

"Like a baby. You?"

"I did, too. Tell me again what happened when you moved your family back home."

She wriggled closer, resting her head on his chest. "The best part was when I carried the last box of Jane's stuff into Dad and Mom's house. Jane ran out the kitchen to get it, all smiles and giggles. Then Dad and Mom came into the room. We twirled, all four of us, in a circle, chanting, 'We're home, we're home.'"

Keegan kissed the top of her head. "I love that part. I bet they wanted to pinch themselves, 'cause none of it felt real yet."

"Yeah, that's going to take a while. Jane was bummed about Mathias being a bad guy. I could have said, 'I told you so,' but I didn't." She laughed, but quickly sobered. "Do you think Furey and the others in custody will be put away for good?"

The trepidation in her voice registered inside him, and wished he could make promises. "The FBI is doing a thorough investigation of the Irish mob and those involved in Auralia. When their cases go to court, all the evidence will stack up against them."

"I hear you, and I hear what you're not saying." She blew out a breath. "I'm hopeful."

He hugged her tighter. "So am I. About everything. I hope that detrimental entanglements with my father are over. I don't know."

Ainsley sat cross-legged beside him, looking down at him with his head on the pillow. "So much has changed for me. I'm excited to rebuild my shop and, um, um," she stuttered.

He sat up beside her and gently swept his finger down her nose. "For me too. There is a lot I don't know, like, where is my father, will I do right by my mother and brother now, and," he paused to look squarely into her eyes. "I don't know the right way to say this, Ainsley. I meant it when I told you I don't want to lose our relationship. I don't see the capture of Furey and the others as an end to what we have going. It's a new beginning."

She lowered her gaze, and Keegan's heart clenched. Was she having second thoughts?

"I want to tell you something. It's way too early to tell you, though." Her eyes met his. "Please know that it doesn't have to mean anything. I mean—"

"Just tell me," he interrupted.

She stared at her bare feet. "I had a vision, or maybe it was just a silly dream. I saw me and you at a ball park. I was up to bat. You were sitting in the bleachers. I hit the ball and ran and made it safe to first base. Someone yelled, "Yeah, yeah, Mommy.""

She stopped. Tears spilled down her cheeks. Keegan waited, wanting to hear more, dying to hear more.

"It was a little girl yelling at me. A little red-haired girl." Ainsley looked up into his eyes. "She was our little girl. I just knew it. When I told you I see a future with you in it, I truly do. I love you, Keegan. I'm not asking for a commitment, I'm just hoping we can see through this "us" as long as it lasts."

He grabbed her close, kissing her neck, her face, her lips. Shaking took him over, and she leaned into him, holding him in her arms. "For as long as we both shall live."

"Do you mean it?" She pulled back, pursing her lips. "It doesn't scare you? Make you want to run away?"

"Hell no. It will take a lifetime to show you how much I love you. Until we're both old and gray and all wrinkly." He pulled her down against the pillows and rolled on top of her. "I can see it now. You'll be playing softball in the senior's league and our children and I will cheer you on from the stands."

She put her hand on his heart. "As long as you have me here, you'll be here," she said, moving his hand to above her heart.

"I like that plan. I love you so much." He pulled the blankets over their heads, and Ainsley giggled.

"We have a lunch party to get ready for," she said under the covers.

He kissed her in places that made her moan. "It can wait."

The End

ALSO BY LYNN CRANDALL

The Dunes Bay Series
Then There Was You, Book 1
Meant To Be You, Book 2
Could It Be You, Book 3

Aegar Investigations Series
Dancing with Detective Danger, Book 1
Always and Forever Love, Book 2

Fierce Hearts Series,
Secrets, Book 1
Cravings, Book 2
Heartfelt, Book 3
Probabilities, Book 4
Unstoppable, Book 5
Finding Finn, novella

Two Days Until Midnight
Captured By Christmas
Nutcracker Sweet
Snowbound
At Midnight, (book bundle)
Dark Sides Series
Touch Me
Hear Me
See Me

Writing as Kelynn Storm:

Touch of Breeze

Love Between Universes, An Out of this World Christmas

Author Note

When I write a story, I want to tap into a character's living experience as the person they are, and who they can become, facing obstacles to peace, love, and a meaningful life. If there are inner struggles for characters, I want to expose them, make them so raw readers can't ignore them. When there are triumphs and joys, I want them to embed in readers and invite them to imagine possibilities in their lives. I want my stories to entertain, but in a way that ignites a drive in readers to embrace all the beauty in themselves and the world around them, including the struggles. Maybe that's an ambitious endeavor, but why not?

ABOUT THE AUTHOR

After cutting her writing teeth as a feature writer for commercial and trade magazines, a reporter for newspapers and radio, and an executive editor for a communications company, award-winning author Lynn Crandall tuned her voracious appetite for stories to writing contemporary and paranormal romance, women's fiction, romantic suspense, and sci-fi romance. In her books, she enjoys taking readers on emotional journeys with relatable characters who refuse to back down, and face challenges and tribulations with heart and soul. She believes every love has a story, and hers is with one handsome husband and a large, beautiful circle of family, including her cat Winter.

For more from Lynn Crandall, visit http://www.lynn-crandall.com . Stay up to date with releases, including upcoming book three in the Dark Sides series, See Me, by subscribe to her newsletter.

www.ingramcontent.com/pod-product-compliance
Lightning Source LLC
Chambersburg PA
CBHW022257190626
46812CB00014B/2201